THE LAST POPE

A NOVEL

BY DAVID OSBORN

SOURCEBOOKS LANDMARK™
AN IMPRINT OF SOURCEBOOKS, INC.®
NAPERVILLE, ILLINOIS

Published by Sourcebooks, Inc.
P.O. Box 4410, Naperville, Illinois 60567-4410
(630) 961-3900
FAX: (630) 961-2168
www.sourcebooks.com

Library of Congress Cataloging-in-Publication Data

Osborn, David, 1923-
  The last pope / by David Osborn.
      p. cm.
    ISBN 1-4022-0244-X (alk. paper)
  1. Catholic Church—Fiction. 2. Popes—Election—Fiction. I. Title.
PS3565.S37 L37 2004
813'.54—dc22
                                                    2004026315

Printed and bound in the United States of America
      QW 10 9 8 7 6 5 4 3 2 1

To Robin, and to Raphaella and Sebastian, with love.

ALSO BY DAVID OSBORN

ACKNOWLEDGMENTS

I am much indebted to the British Library in London for its help in providing rare books on the Vatican and the Papacy, as well as to the Library of Congress in Washington, which chased down—in of all places the cadet library of Annapolis—one of apparently only two existing library copies of the most definitive book on the papal conclave. My sincere thanks to the two inspiring former nuns, Barbara Ferraro and Patricia Hussey of Covenant House in Charleston, West Virginia for explaining their involvement in the famous *New York Times* advertisement that sought a dialogue with the Vatican; and of course to my editor Hillel Black, whose wonderful wisdom added much to the work, and to Bob Diforio, my superbly dogged agent. Laura Kuhn, thank you for having an eagle eye while copy editing. Finally, this book never would have been written without the extraordinary caring and moral support of my wife, Robin, whose patience continuously astonished me—nearly as much as her sincere and insistent conviction that the work would one day see print.

PROLOGUE

"Bless me, Father, for I have sinned."

"In the name of Jesus Christ our Lord, state your sin."

Early December, 1970. The cold in the great Basilica of St. Peter in Rome seemed even more unbearable in the still darkness of the dozen black confessional stalls in the transept where the sins of the faithful are heard in many languages.

The young priest, waiting for the man beyond the little latticed window in the stall's partition to speak, was gaunt in appearance. Staring into the darkness with disinterested eyes, he hugged his arms around his cassock, seeking warmth from his own body. He'd been hearing confession since matins, the first morning prayer, and was weary of the endless unburdening of sin by the British and American tourists whom his knowledge of English obliged him to confess. So many had come, one after another, that he had not even been able to vacate his post to relieve himself.

His thoughts flicked to His Holiness in the warm comfort of the opulent papal suite high in the sixteenth-century Apostolic Palace on the north side of the Basilica. He bit his thin upper lip, more determined than ever to escape the endless penury of ordinary priesthood and to scale the Vatican ladder as high as God and his abilities would permit.

"State your sin, my son," he repeated mechanically.

In the darkness, there was only the heavy sigh of a soul in torment.

The priest stirred impatiently. Let the man get on with it. He couldn't imagine what made him hesitate so, for since his ordination only two years previous, he was certain he had already heard every conceivable affront to God.

The confessor finally spoke, and in a voice choked with emotion. "I dream, Father. Nearly every night. Terrible things. And last night..." The voice fell to a whisper. "Oh, may God forgive me."

A dream? The priest's patience ebbed. "Speak," he commanded. "Reveal your heart."

The confessor hesitated, found courage, then poured forth words. "I dreamed—I dreamed I was in ancient Carthage. Yes, Carthage. But several hundred years after the death of our Lord, because people there were Christian and spoke of a bishop Cyprian, and he was beheaded by the proconsul, Maximum, in the year 257 A.D."

Surprised at the man's detailed knowledge of obscure history, the priest found himself bending close to the latticed window. Clearly, he was confessing someone who was highly educated.

The confessor's voice broke again. "I was a thief. I stole a golden cross from an altar. Soldiers pursued me. I took refuge in the home of an oil merchant. A wealthy old man I knew."

In the cold darkness, the priest pictured the ancient Mediterranean port of Carthage; the pink-tiled roofs of the oil merchant's home and warehouse, the sun-baked yard before them, the rows of giant olive jars filled with oil and waiting to be loaded on ships for Rome.

The confessor went on, each word a torture. "My friend had bought a new wife in the marketplace; she had only just become a woman and was his proudest possession—no man dared so much as look on her."

He broke off for a moment. When he continued, the priest heard an obscenity so vividly real as to make it seem an actual happening. He heard of the young woman's passionate infatuation with the confessor; he heard of the confessor's head turned with tales of her husband's hidden gold; he heard of deadly nightshade mixed into the old man's wine, then of two half-crazed people, exulting in freedom and wealth, who tore away each other's clothes to fornicate in frenzied, naked ecstasy in the very bed of their victim, who lay dying, helpless to stop them.

Sickened, he felt himself almost present as the couple bought passage on a ship bound for Sicily with the murdered man's gold. And felt present, too, as the confessor told how, fearful the woman might one day tire of him and bear witness to his murder, he drowned her in a stream they bathed in. And then, in a final descent into wickedness, had dragged her lifeless, naked corpse from the water to possess her one last time.

The priest's cold fingers clutched the crucifix at the breast of his cassock. When he spoke, he could barely hide his revulsion and contempt for the confessor enough to ask about his other dreams.

"The others?" From beyond the lattice, there was a harsh laugh. "My sleep is endless carnage, Father. Almost nightly I rape and murder and betray. And after every dream, this terrible voice condemns me to betray over and over—forever—as punishment for some even worse crime I have committed, I know not what."

In the dark, cold silence, the priest suddenly thought, *Perhaps the man has already murdered. Perhaps with his knowledge of history and by confessing a dream, he is masking an actual crime only recently committed.*

Suddenly frightened, he barely found his voice. "And your crimes by day? What are they?"

"By day? But there are none, Father. It's only my nights that are cursed."

"You must pray." It was the only thing the priest could think of to say. This man was mad. If he hadn't already killed, someday he would, and end his life on the gallows or incarcerated.

The harsh laugh again. Derisive. "Pray? I have prayed, Father, until my soul is empty."

"Pray, my son," the priest repeated. "Pray for God's holy forgiveness."

A moment's silence. Then, abruptly, the whole stall shuddered as the confessor stumbled away from it.

Quickly drawing open the narrow black curtain on his side of the cubicle, the priest saw the man he'd confessed. He stood an instant near the confessional, looking back, his face tortured, then stumbled blindly away past the papal altar toward the marble stairs that led down to the crypts and the tomb of the First Apostle Simon, who became St. Peter.

And the full horror of what he had heard in the cold darkness struck the priest. For he saw, from the cassock he wore and the rosary crucifix in his hand, that the madman he had just confessed was, like himself, a young priest.

CHAPTER

1

Forty years later, with Rome enjoying welcomed warmth at the end of April, Agosto Mancini, the gaunt young priest so shocked by the dreams of his colleague, had, through hard work and a coldly disdainful ruthlessness, risen to the rank of Cardinal Bishop of Porto, and had become Vatican secretary of state, a position second only to the pope himself in power.

Asleep in his opulently furnished suite directly beneath that of the Holy Father, he was awakened by insistent knocking at his door. He finally roused himself. "Yes?" He flicked on his bedside light.

The door opened. "Excellency?"

Mancini groped to find his thick, rimless glasses. Focusing his pale eyes, he first saw his valet, Brother Demetrius, a cadaverous, acetic Dominican monk in his late middle age. Behind Demetrius, he saw his new personal secretary, Father Julio Benetto, a softly fleshed and effeminate young priest, only recently ordained. Mancini had taken him on some months earlier as a favor to the priest's mother, a politically important contessa and the widow of a prince of the Church. To his surprise, Father Benetto, who also had a business degree, proved to be the height of efficiency.

The silver-framed alarm clock on the bedside table said ten minutes before two o'clock. To be roused in such fashion and at such an hour meant something serious had occurred. Mancini sat up. "Well, what is it?"

The monk and the young priest came into the room. Demetrius spoke first. "His Holiness, Excellency."

"Yes?"

The valet seemed incapable of continuing. His voice choked, and the face beneath his balding skull became a silent mask.

The young priest, in contrast, seemed unperturbed. "Father Tissot just telephoned, Excellency." Benetto's eyes in the soft, unlined downiness of his face were suitably downcast, but there was the faint trace of a smile in his voice. "God has taken His Holiness from us."

Absorbing the news, Mancini could not deny himself a silent moment of inner satisfaction before he swung his long white legs out of bed and stood up. He wore only a short nightshirt, and Brother Demetrius, quickly averting his eyes from such casual personal exposure, fetched the cardinal's brocaded robe from the foot of the bed and held it up for Mancini to shrug into.

Mancini ignored the proffered cover to his nakedness. He snapped an order at Father Benetto.

"Call Pasternelli. Tell him to join me in His Holiness's apartment at once. Use this phone." He pointed to one on his bedside table and went into his soft-carpeted, marble-walled bathroom. Leaving the door open, he urinated noisily. Returning, he grabbed the telephone away from Benetto.

"Guido. I want you in the papal apartment immediately. What? Yes, he's dead. Just now."

He hung up abruptly and, quickly shedding his nightshirt to briefly reveal the white, bony flesh of his upper body, dressed hurriedly in the clothes Brother Demetrius had already laid out for him: underwear, a light sweater, some heavy socks, and finally his cassock and shoes.

Five minutes later, on entering the reception room of the papal apartment with its ornately gilded furniture, he was met by graying Father Jean-Henri Tissot. The pope's quietly authoritative Jesuit secretary, hands ever laced before his chest as though in prayer, had faithfully served Antonio Petrucci not only as Gregory XVIII but for thirty previous years while the humble Sicilian rose from being an obscure bishop to the papal throne. Although nearly overcome by grief, he had managed to compose himself. Mancini wasted no time on sympathy. "Where is he?"

"He died in his bed, Excellency."

Striding ahead of the priest, Mancini proceeded through the opulent papal reception room and into the bedchamber, a place sparsely monastic in comparison. His cold eyes quickly took in the pope's personal valet, a portly old Franciscan, Brother Pietro Bertolino, who was still in his bathrobe and very pale, his monk's tonsure above a fringe of white hair shining in the lamplight. Just beyond him were the two nuns, responsible at night for papal housekeeping, who were kneeling in prayer near the deathbed, their black habits in stark contrast to their framed, parchment-white faces.

Ignoring all but the man who had so recently been titular head of the entire Catholic world, Mancini went directly to look down at him. One dead hand clutched a sheaf of letters.

Father Tissot came to his side. "He couldn't sleep and was reading correspondence," the Jesuit explained. In spite of his calm outward demeanor, his voice was close to breaking and his praying hands trembled. "I was in my office and I heard him cry out. I ran in. Brother Bertolino was already here. His Holiness was trying to reach his alarm. He collapsed, and I called the doctor at once—he was detained but should be here any moment—and we tried to resuscitate him." He broke off, head bowed.

Mancini glanced at the red alarm button on the papal bedside table, then at the expressionless, dead face with its big parrot nose. Without facial animation, the nose seemed larger than ever, the hollow cheeks to each side were dwarfed by it and exaggeratedly sunken from night-time removal of dentures. Something was missing, and Mancini realized he had never seen the man the Church regarded as the two hundredth and sixty-fifth successor to St. Peter, Prince of Apostles, without the horn-rimmed eyeglasses that always seemed too large for so frail a man. His eyes searched, saw them on the bedside table, then came back to the pope. The papal heart had finally surrendered, Mancini thought, to the long ordeal of cancer.

Vicar of Christ, Pontifex Maximus of the Universal Church, Patriarch of the West, Primate of Italy, Archbishop and Metropolitan of Rome, and State Sovereign of the domains of the Holy Church, Gregory XVIII had been a man who, for all his high offices, and as far as Mancini was concerned, had ever remained Antonio Petrucci. Born to a poor Neapolitan peasant family, he was seen by the hardened, Italian-dominated Vatican curia, or papal court, as a man far out of his depth in the Church's highest office.

But Petrucci was dead at last and would be buried with all the usual pomp accorded to a pope. That out of the way, a new pope had to be elected who could undo the mess that, in Mancini's view, Petrucci's weak and vacillating leadership had allowed the Church to drift into. God willing, that would be him. Meanwhile, until white smoke emerged from the Sistine Chapel, where the College of Cardinals would gather in secret conclave to announce God's choice to an awaiting world, he would be in sole charge of the Universal Church.

A muffled sob reminded Mancini of the nuns. He had no time now for such sniveling. There were a million things to do.

"Get them out of here," he said to Bertolino, "and open some windows. It's May, not winter any longer."

"Yes, Excellency."

Ignoring the valet's injured expression, Mancini turned back to the bed. When he had muttered a perfunctory blessing over the dead man, he snapped another order, this time to Tissot. "And you. Go immediately and prepare a death certificate for the doctor to sign."

"Yes, Excellency."

"Also, put in a call to the people who will prepare and dress His Holiness so he may lie in state."

"Yes, Excellency."

As he turned back to the body, Mancini felt, rather than saw, the great, corpulent bulk of Monsignor Pasternelli come to stand next to him. The Apostolic Chamberlain reeked of body sweat, garlic, and wine, and had clearly made a late night of it. Without looking at him, Mancini said, "Guido, I want the Italian representative to the Vatican and a couple of papal princes here. At once. Count Patrici and Prince Gambetta will do. Or anyone else, if they can't get out of bed."

Pasternelli wheezed an obedient, "Excellency..." and Mancini felt him move away. A new presence at once took his place. Galentieri, the papal doctor, had finally arrived. Mancini pointedly glanced at his watch. It was now twenty past two. "You were called more than half an hour ago, Doctor."

Galentieri didn't answer. When Mancini failed to budge from his position near the dead man's head, he went around with his small black bag to the other side of the bed, first to take out his stethoscope and apply it to the pope's chest, then, lifting each eyelid, to examine the pope's pupils.

"I had a delivery," he said finally. "A cesarean. I was operating when I got the call."

"Millions are born every day," Mancini observed dryly. "There is only one pope to die."

He left the bed. Many would be looking for new jobs in the next few days, a whole plague of weaklings who owed their present positions to Petrucci and who had subjected the temporal powers of the Church to the adulterating and destructive theological dissidence of the Left. Galentieri would be one of them. He was a brilliant doctor, but so were many others, and he had never learned his place.

Two graying prelates entered, now both second in power only to himself. One was Cardinal Berssi, the swarthy and inscrutable head of the Congregation for the Doctrine of the Faith, the Vatican department that oversaw the conduct of Church affairs by more than four thousand bishops in twenty-five hundred diocese. The other was Cardinal Pietro Saluzzo, the jeweled director of the IOR, the Vatican's Instituto Per Opere Religioso, or Institute for Religious Works, more commonly known as the Vatican Bank and one of the most powerful financial organizations in the world. Mancini greeted them with a silent nod. He could count on Saluzzo in the forthcoming election for a successor pope, but perhaps not Berssi, whom he suspected of having papal ambitions of his own.

The two cardinals approached the bedside to kneel in obligatory prayer. Mancini ordered the elderly valet, Brother Bertolino, to have coffee made, and went to the window. Slightly parting the curtains to look down at St. Peter's Square, empty and silent in the predawn, he allowed himself the luxury of thinking how close he finally was to standing at that same window as a daily practice. Close, but at the same time still perilously distant.

Presently, he came away and went into the papal study. Seating himself at the desk, he pushed papers belonging to the deceased to one side and began to write out a log of events since the death.

Shortly after three o'clock, there was a bustle of sound in the anteroom to the bedchamber. Roused from sleep in their palaces across the Tiber, the Italian representative and the two papal princes had arrived.

Mancini returned to the papal bed, regretting the march of time and modern medicine. Until recently, the papal death had been certified by the ancient ritual of striking the deceased pontiff on the forehead three times with a ceremonial silver hammer and after each blow calling out the pope's name, ending the procedure—barring an answer—by announcing, "The pope is truly dead."

After a terse greeting to the two princes, he asked for a medical appraisal of the pope's condition. When Galentiere pronounced the papal heartbeat to have ceased probably an hour earlier, and noted that there were no other vital signs present, Mancini formally asked the assembled witnesses to bear witness to the papal death. Next, he tugged at the papal fisherman ring Gregory had insisted on wearing, although it was a habit abandoned by several of his predecessors, from the fourth finger of the pope's now cold and rigor-stiffening hand. Then, accepting the papal seal proffered by Father Tissot, he ceremoniously announced both items destroyed and ordered them placed in the Holy Father's coffin.

Events moved swiftly after that. The death certificate was witnessed and signed; the demise of the pope was announced in a dozen languages to the world by Vatican Radio, and in English, German, Spanish, and French by four different editions of *L'Osservatore*, the official Church newspaper. The Vatican's undertakers, the Essotore brothers, arrived to take the papal remains to another room of the papal apartment. During the course of the day, the body was stripped naked, washed, eviscerated, and embalmed. Next, it was dressed in full ceremonial splendor, with a crucifix placed in its hands, clasped high on its stomach, so that it lay against the failed heart. It was then ready for display.

During the following two days, Father Tissot, assisted by clerks from Mancini's office, inventoried and transferred to the Secretariat all official papers, along with any correspondence and memoranda pertaining to the papacy. Meanwhile, Brother Bertolino, under the watchful eye of an officer of the Swiss Guards and aided by a Dominican friar, inventoried and packed the deceased pope's personal clothing and all his other private possessions, which were put under seal and sent into immediate storage until his will would be opened and read.

As soon as their work was done, both Father Tissot and Brother Pietro Bertolino departed, the former to retire to a family home in France, the latter to a monastery in Sicily.

By nightfall two days after Pope Gregory's death, there remained no trace of his ever having occupied the papal apartments.

CHAPTER

2

Surrounded by Rome, the Vatican is a state within a state, the world's smallest independent nation and sole absolute monarchy by election, although its sovereignty and international independence was only finally established through a treaty with Italy in 1928. Nor was it the official administrative center and residence of the popes until 1377, when Gregory XI abandoned the Lateran palace in Rome, the longtime papal residence. Prior to this time, the Vatican was largely considered a place of refuge from papal enemies because of the heavy fortress walls that surrounded the burgeoning Basilica and several smaller churches constructed in the ninth century.

Despite its miniscule size, only one hundred and four acres with its gardens, St. Peter's, and the Apostolic Palace each occupying about a third of the area, the Vatican totally rules the lives of some million and a half nuns and priests around the globe and controls, as well, the destinies of a billion of the world's population.

It has its own flag and an exclusive citizenry of several hundred, its own hospital and scientific research laboratories, its own police and security forces. It has its own bank, radio station, telephone system, and newspaper. It enjoys its own post office, supermarket, pharmacy, and railroad station, and, besides the great Basilica of Saint Peter, it is graced by several influential churches. All of this, along with administrative and residential buildings, museums, monuments, gardens, cemeteries, squares, and streets, is crammed within its ancient walls. And with the many other Vatican departments housed outside, the Vatican itself is administered by a Pontifical Commission composed of seven cardinals, one special delegate, and the governor of state housed in the Palazzo dei Governatori, a huge stone building in the center of the Vatican gardens.

Cardinal Mancini's gaunt figure was now seen everywhere, from the helicopter pad at the extreme northwest corner of the Vatican's walled gardens to the wide entrance steps of St. Peter's and throughout almost every room, hall, chapel, and courtyard in the jumbled maze of Medieval and Renaissance buildings that make up the Apostolic Palace itself.

He first made all the necessary arrangements for the forthcoming funeral. As Conclave Carmelengo, he affected, as well, whatever plans were necessary for the ensuing conclave that would elect, by will of God, the two hundred and sixty-sixth pope.

By long-established Church law, the conclave had to take place not less than ten and not more than twenty days after a pope's death. Mancini ordered members of the College of Cardinals, the Pope's electors and counselors, numbering one hundred and forty-three, to be summoned from the four corners of the earth. The papal corpse was taken to lie in state in the great Basilica of St. Peter.

There, the Holy Father was viewed from dawn to dusk by thousands upon thousands of the faithful. Their numbers stretched in a great serpentine queue, four abreast, beginning beyond the Ponte Vittorio, a bridge over the river Tiber, which divided Rome. Moving slowly up the wide reach of the Via della Conciliazione, the mourners crossed the vast expanse of St. Peter's Square and eventually entered the Basilica to pass reverently by the crimson-trimmed Holy Catafalque, watched over by select members of the Swiss Guard.

There were nine days of official mourning. During this period, the Vatican flag of yellow and white, adorned with the papal tiara and keys, flew at half-mast, while the giant bells of St. Peter's ceaselessly tolled a traditional and mournful cadence, hour after hour, day and night. On the last day of the obsequies, His Holiness was laid in a plain cypress coffin, along with his pontifical ring and seal and three bags of coins minted by the Vatican Treasury during his pontificate.

It was the second week of May now; spring was nearly over and the air was soft and warm. The coffin, without adornment, was placed on the paving stones of St. Peter's Square at the foot of the Basilica's wide steps. There, with a vast, silent crowd of laity filling the square beyond the central obelisk, a requiem mass was celebrated by the Cardinal Dean, the aged and senior Cardinal Carezza, and attended by the entire diplomatic corps, knights and princes of the Church, and more than one thousand bishops.

Dominating the scene were those cardinals who had so far arrived in Rome, some ninety-five in all. Wearing their tall white miters, their crimson robes ruffled by a slight breeze, they sat, as they had at every papal funeral for centuries past, in a silent observing line the full width of the top steps.

One of these was Cardinal Ignatius Heriot, a leading intellectual in American Catholicism. More and more spoken of as a candidate for the papacy, he was a man Mancini saw not just as a threat to his own ambitions, but one he disdained for a liberality that had won the praise of many of his Third World colleagues. Ironically, he was the same young priest Mancini had confessed so many years before on that cold December morning.

In appearance, Cardinal Heriot was a stark contrast to the opulence of the Vatican surroundings and the fleshy, bland expressions of many of the convening members of the College of Cardinals. He was a slender man of medium height. His soft voice, austere and quietly authoritative manner, along with his quick, determined gait, reflected the self-denial of an acetic, while his worn hands and slightly rigid shoulders testified to his early years in the Church as a lowly worker priest. His straight, very dark hair was only streaked here and there with gray, lending youth to his appearance in comparison to other prelates. A lock of it habitually fell down across his forehead before being impatiently swept away in a gesture remembered by anyone he was speaking to.

Although he offered an occasional gentle and caring smile, his weathered face with its sparse but firmly drawn lines, and a slightly crooked nose—broken in a childhood farming accident—was marked in its general gravity by religious intensity, while in spite of a determined mouth, a certain inner pain in his deep-set, dark eyes reflected the torment to which he had once confessed. For his nighttime terror had continued unabated throughout the many intervening years, though few, if any, could have ever guessed it lurked behind such an unrevealing exterior.

His beginnings in the Church had been as a humble priest to an impoverished parish of mostly migrant workers in the sugar cane and strawberry fields of the American South. From there, he had emerged through brilliance and determination with an international reputation as an historian of great insight and humanity. Among his writings were major and definitive works on the Church's role in the rise of western civilization.

Ever self-effacing, he'd eventually become archbishop of a diocese that he had raised from relative obscurity to national preeminence, and had received his cardinalate from the deceased pope. Gregory XVIII had profoundly admired him, not only for his achievements, but for the attitudes reminiscent of John XXIII that he himself shared, and for which, and for all his papal power, he was subjected to endless obstructionist opposition by the ultrareactionary clique of his curia, headed by Cardinal Mancini.

Raising his eyes from the coffin of the man he had so dearly revered, Cardinal Heriot was beset with the wave of memories that his coming to Rome and the Vatican had produced. Arriving at dawn two days after the pope's death and before His Holiness lay in state in the Basilica, he had left his things at Villa Stritch, the modern apartment haven for visiting Church dignitaries, and had gone at once to the Vatican.

His taxi brought him to the massive bronze door of the Portone di Bronzo. Getting out, it was impossible to ignore the thin stream of *bagarozzi*, or "black beetles," the name given to many of the Vatican's faceless minor clergy who uniformly wore black cassocks, black berets, and thick black shoes to work. More than anyone, they represented to Ignatius the hoard of minor bureaucrats, three thousand at the Vatican alone, who were the drone machinery of the vast corporate power that the nonreligious side of the Church had become.

It pained him to think of it, the dealing by Vatican powers around the globe in securities and real estate, in lucrative business ventures and even in governments—all in secrecy and accountable to no one—just as it pained him to think even briefly of the terrible gulf between the amassed treasures of the Vatican, a wealth that surpassed imagination, and the desperate, grinding poverty, the sheer misery in life allotted to the great majority of the faithful, whose labors provided most of that fortune.

Saluted and passed on when he had showed his identification to the towering, stone-faced Swiss Guard, resplendent in his Renaissance costume of red and yellow, he climbed the marble Royal Stair to the Sala Regia and from there went to the Secretariat to pay his respects to Cardinal Mancini. In an attempt to shake from his mind the coldness of the secretary of state during their brief meeting, he spent time at the Vatican Library, the repository of some of the world's most precious books. He then decided to visit the tomb of St. Peter, deep in the crypt of the Basilica. There, he thought that perhaps through prayer he might rid himself of the persistent memory of a particularly bad dream he'd had just prior to departing for Rome, and, as always, pray for relief from the strange unease that there had to be some divine purpose in so punishing him. He must have committed, at some time and somewhere, some unidentifiable and terrible sin, a crime against God so darkly foreboding, so cold in its terror, that his mind—searching for whatever it might be— could never focus long enough to identify it before recoiling in horror.

He had put on his spring coat, for he was certain the air in St. Peter's would still be gripped by the chill of winter, and, setting out, made his way through several courtyards and past the base of the ancient tower of Innocent IV, which had once been part of the outer fortifications of a far smaller Vatican.

From there, he passed through further ancient courtyards, and then beyond the medieval Pauline Chapel, through several vaulted halls, magnificent with frescoes, until a passageway brought him to the small and inconspicuous "Holy Door," by which a pope always enters the great Basilica.

Admitted by the Swiss Guards stationed there, he found himself in one of the Basilica's five main chapels, the Chapel of the Sacrament with the tomb of Pope Sixtus IV. Leaving it by the arch that led to the organs, he proceeded past the altar of the Madonna del Soccorso and then the altar of St. Jerome to enter the great Basilica's nave.

CHAPTER

3

To Cardinal Heriot, it was as though all the intervening years since he had come to the Basilica for the first time on that cold December day had never happened. Ordained only several years before that visit, his pilgrimage to the very heart of Roman Catholicism had been a gift, the money scraped together through endless sacrifice by the parishioners of his tiny Southern church. Calling him simply "Padre," or "Padre Ignatius," or Father, as did all who worked with him now in the archdiocese, they saw in him a trusted brother, the priest they could turn to day or night and in every moment of need, the humble man they so deeply loved, who worked side by side with them through long days in the fetid cane fields, or under the burning sun picking strawberries.

Alighting from the taxi that had brought him from an inexpensive *pensione* in a poorer quarter of Rome, he'd been almost overcome by the awesome size of St. Peter's Square. Embraced by the two hundred and eighty-four massive columns of Bernini's magnificent colonnade, the piazza could hold half a million people. But instead of reverence, he'd felt a certain surprise, even disillusionment. Save for its two fountains and, at its very center, the great, red granite obelisk which had once adorned Nero's circus but now held within it a fragment of the true Cross, the square seemed to him an empty, paved desert.

There had been few about on that cold, cheerless day: an elderly couple or two, a group of schoolchildren shepherded by nuns, occasional flocks of pigeons, a horse-drawn tourist's cab. For a minute, as young Father Ignatius, he'd stood marveling at the scores of statues of the saints capping the colonnade and, across the square, the great Basilica of St. Peter, its dome seeming to fill the heavens above, and next to it the sienna-colored medieval and Renaissance buildings of the Apostolic Palace.

Entering the Basilica itself, it was hard not to be awed by its interior immensity, by the fact that its first version was begun nearly seventeen hundred years ago, and that a Roman necropolis and a cemetery of Christian martyrs that included the tomb of St. Peter lay below his feet, deep under the crypts.

But although almost overwhelmed by all he saw, he'd been also badly taken aback by a completely different emotion. How different this place was from the dark cathedrals of France he had first visited, where the cold dampness of centuries mingled with the stale odor of incense, and where the shawled figures of praying old women could be seen

here and there in the shadows. There, he had experienced a
deep feeling of devotion; here, he'd felt complete alienation.
His impression had been of some monstrous and imper-
sonal public edifice, like a rail terminal; a gigantic material
and soulless monument, not to God but to the building of
all monuments everywhere.

Now, all these years later and no longer a young
worker priest but a cardinal, his impression was the same.
In the Basilica itself, he saw the same immense, cold desert
of stone, bathed in a blaze of white light that fell from
high windows onto the brightly-colored marble of its vast
floor and its endless columns; there was the same myriad
gilded ornamentation and painted statuary, the same self-
flattering tombs of popes, the same Rococo ornamentation and images, the same plethora of chapels, like islands
off the nave, some larger than an average church.

Fighting back the disillusionment he had experienced
on that day so long ago, he reached the transept and the
line of dark little confessionals where priests were solicit-
ing the sins of the faithful. Seeing them, it was hard not to
remember the confession he himself had once made
there, and the glacial tone of the priest.

Then, once again standing by Bernini's great bal-
dachin that canopied the main altar, he looked up at the
famous dome, hundreds of feet above, where Christ's
words to Peter were emblazoned in great gold letters
around the drum:

*Tu es Petrus et supra hanc petram aedificabo ecclesiam
meam et tibi claves Regni Coelorum—Thou art Peter and*

upon this rock I will build My Church and I will give thee the keys to Heaven.

Above it were the frescoed figures of Christ and the Virgin, of John the Baptist, of St. Paul, and of all the apostles and angels. And finally, higher still and just under the lantern, the column that capped the very top of the dome, the magnificent figure of God bestowed his benediction on all below.

Looking back down, Ignatius felt a wave of terror suddenly sweep over him, the awful sense of unknown darkness and evil that he could never identify. Closing his eyes, he waited until it passed and then descended, as he had years before, to St. Peter's sepulchre. There, in the half-dark silence of the crypt far beneath the Basilica's main floor, he prayed that God would reveal to him the offense that had caused the tormenting punishment for almost as long as he could remember.

But his prayers did not bring relief. He left the Basilica by its main façade, and, for a few moments, leaned weak from emotion against one of the great pillars. Slowly pulling himself together, he thought perhaps he was just overly tired. Perhaps a brisk walk through Rome would help; perhaps coffee at some little *trattoria*, renewed contact with ordinary people, with light and sound, laughter even, that such a walk might engender; perhaps for a short while he would no longer be a cardinal but a priest again.

The air had cooled, a chill wind had come in from the north. He turned up his collar, pocketed his crimson skull cap, so as to be anonymous, and started off.

Out on St. Peter's Square, he stopped to look up once again at the jumble of sienna buildings that was the Apostolic Palace, when he was startled by a quiet voice.

"You are troubled, my son."

Coming to his senses, Ignatius became aware of an elderly priest standing before him; a very old man, white-haired, his face seamed with age, and poor, too—the long black cloak he clutched to his shrunken breast nearly threadbare, the thin sandals on his gnarled feet worn through. But in his old face there was a look of peace.

"You are troubled, my son," he repeated. "Your soul is uneasy."

Ignatius realized the old man could not know he also was a priest, let alone his superior rank.

"I'm all right, Father," he said.

He started to turn away. He didn't want to talk to anyone, especially a stranger. He wanted only to be alone with his memories.

But the old man stayed with him, his brow suddenly furrowed. "Be warned, my son. God only bestows His blessing on those who follow our Lord in true faith. May He have mercy on you and light your way."

Making the sign of the cross, he stared penetratingly at Ignatius a moment, as though to emphasize every word he'd said, then turned and walked slowly off with the hesitant steps of age.

Ignatius, taken aback by his words, stood looking after him until the old man was just a small and inconspicuous figure against the vast bareness of the square and Bernini's great encircling colonnade; until his dark, bent figure finally disappeared behind a blur of tourists, and when the tourists moved on, was no longer to be seen at all.

That was a week ago. The present returned to Ignatius with a jolt. He was again seated with his fellow cardinals on the wide steps of the Basilica's façade. The lonely, dark coffin of the man he had so deeply revered was still at the foot of the Basilica steps. There was the cardinal dean, intoning the mass. There was the diplomatic corps, and there were the princes of the Church. Beyond them stood the great crowd of faithful.

The spring sun was softly warm, the slight breeze a whisper as it ruffled his cape. Pope Gregory had died; he, Ignatius Heriot, was a cardinal of the Church; there would be a conclave, and there he and his fellow cardinals would elect a new pope.

CHAPTER

4

Six months before Pope Gregory's death, and late one November morning in New York City, Francesca Berenson left the king-size bed in her penthouse apartment that she shared—whenever he was in town—with Dominic Garcia-Lopez, a wealthy international arms dealer, prominent among those who played their lives away at the exclusive European and Caribbean resorts that knew no guests save celebrities and the very wealthy.

Her head ached. They'd partied last night. She and Dominic and a Prince Giovanni somebody from Italy. She couldn't remember his whole name, was it Vinotti? Visconti?—just that he had a palace outside Florence, and another in Venice, and that he'd promised to fly her down to his villa on Martinique.

They had dined expensively and had drunk a lot of champagne. Then all three had gone back to her apartment for a long night that had started with lines of cocaine and shedding clothes before bed and every kind of sex imaginable between two men and a woman.

She went to the bathroom and, coming out, saw Dominic awake. He sat up. "Where's Giovanni?"

Francesca remembered the Italian getting dressed some time before and having a last snort of cocaine. And she remembered her dull anger at his almost dismissive air when she said good-bye—as though she were some hooker he'd picked up in a bar. He hadn't mentioned Martinique.

"He left. He said he'd call you."

Dominic groaned and fell back onto the bed, covering his head with a pillow. She stared at his nakedness, at his long, sprawled legs swirled with dark hair, at his thick, now-flaccid penis, and at his still-muscular torso, which had lost nearly all of its East Hampton summer tan. He was hardly young anymore, but still useful. And nights like last night kept him that way. Maybe the Italian would change his mind about her. She loved the Caribbean.

The maid was off for the day. Francesca went to the kitchen, not bothering with her robe and enjoying the warm air of the apartment on her bare skin. Her body ached all over from the night. She took coffee to the living room and sat curled up on the deep, modern couch facing the sliding doors leading onto the terrace with its shrubbery and roof trees. They had finally shed their summer mantle of green for the gray barrenness of winter. It looked as though it might rain, and the high buildings of Manhattan, under a heavy sky, seemed ugly and foreboding to her. The apartment had a dining room and guest room, which she almost never used. Her own bedroom was mirrored and had ceiling lighting that could be made to mimic the soft glow of moonlight or twinkling starlight. The Italian marble bathroom had a double shower and a sunken Jacuzzi with gold faucets. On one wall hung a half-dozen erotically graphic drawings of couples and threesomes in different acts of lovemaking; on another a half-dozen exotic photos of herself, several nude, others in various attire appropriate to the particular resort she'd been in.

She had bought and decorated the place with some of the sizeable settlement her lawyer had somehow gotten in her divorce from Charles, even though it was her third divorce and she'd been caught out with the guy in Paris as well. Christ, all that old North Carolina family respectability. What a mistake that had been. Never mind, it was over and she was free again. She could have her pick of trips to Paris and Rome, or London and Palm Beach. In *Vanity Fair* and *Hello!* she'd soon be seen once more dating somebody who counted. The Golden Girl. And she could again sleep with whomever made it worth her while without fear of getting caught.

Dominic came in. He'd showered, slicked back his graying hair, and put on a royal-blue track suit. He went to the mirrored bar to make himself a Bloody Mary. He didn't speak until he'd done so. Then he said, "I'm going to the racquet club. Work out and play some squash."

Without thinking, she'd covered her breasts and tucked her legs up under her. She was glad she'd gotten up first and hadn't needed to share the bathroom with him. He was like the Italian this morning, looking at her as though she were something and not somebody. She thought, *You asshole, Dominic, you're dead with me,* but knew dismally and even as she thought it that he wasn't. What the hell, he'd helped her get to where she was and didn't give a damn who she went with as long as she was there for him when he was in town and wanted to do his bi thing with another guy as well as her. Like last night.

He silently downed his drink and stared at her again a moment, taking in her nakedness, eyes moving slowly. "Giovanni left some money for you. You didn't see it? He said it was to get that watch at Tiffany you said you wanted. The one with the sapphires."

She didn't answer. He went out. She heard the front door thud shut and suddenly felt desperately depressed. She felt so more and more these days, especially in the morning, but today more than ever. Today, she felt dirty. Physically dirty. Like shit. But why, for Christ's sake? She shouldn't. "Last night was great," she said aloud. "Dominic and the goddamned Italian couldn't get enough of you. So snap out of it. You're on top of the world."

But she didn't feel on top of the world; she didn't feel anywhere but on the bottom. Oh, Jesus, fuck it. She'd tried to explain these depressions to Dr. Weiner and couldn't. Dr. Weiner kept telling her she was seeking revenge on her father. Her whole lifestyle was a revenge, she said. Well, so what? All her stupid father cared about with his tirades was what all his shitty, small-town friends at the Elks Club would think.

Besides, there was something else, something inside her she couldn't describe, not even to herself. Something like a death's head, it was so nearly physical in feeling. It had started a month ago, and she couldn't stand it much longer.

She went into the bathroom, took a long shower, and finally began to feel cleaner. Her body, anyway. She told herself she was just suffering from too much coke and that she was more beautiful at thirty than ever. Everyone said so. She could see herself in the mirrored walls through the steam of the shower, her rich titian hair like a bonfire in the mist, and her slender, high-breasted figure, her gorgeously long legs and the enticing darker-hair triangle of her pubis. Rubbing a circle in the steamy door with the palm of one hand, she could also see her strikingly beautiful face looking back at her: her wide, full-lipped, sensuous mouth, her high, sculpted cheekbones, almond-shaped eyes, her straight, delicate nose. No wonder no man could resist her. She waved at herself and laughed.

When Dominic didn't return at six or even close to seven, she thought, *To hell with him.* Sotheby's was giving a private reception for some important art to be auctioned next week; there might be someone there worth seeing.

She put an old Stan Goetz CD on the stereo and dressed quickly; an off-the-shoulder Yves St. Laurent dress she'd picked up in Paris last spring that showed her cleavage to its best advantage, and jewelry—a sapphire-and-diamond bracelet her second husband had given her, his mother's; a diamond choke collar and earrings that she'd wheedled from that Lord whatever his name was two summers ago on Majorca. She was quick with her makeup. She left Dominic a note saying where she'd be, grabbed her mink, and was off.

The crowd at Sotheby's was the usual *in* bunch of patrons with complacent status in the narrow world of international art. And there were walls solid with paintings by household names—Pissaro, Matisse, Courbet, and other Impressionists—all discreetly watched over by security guards in Brooks Brothers suits. Expressionless flunkies with silver trays of champagne-filled crystal glasses moved among the guests, many there just to be seen, and whose empty conversation was calculatedly reverent in the face of so many millions of dollars' worth of art.

Francesca put on feigned delight at the presence of those she knew, but the bad feeling she'd had in the morning came back. She felt choked with it. And with fear. The whole world seemed to be steamrolling over her.

She found herself talking to a dark, loose-fleshed man in his fifties whose eyes looked everywhere except at her. He was somebody big in films, and suddenly she realized she had once had sex with him and couldn't remember when or any part of it. She just knew she had and that he'd paid a lot. And she thought of all the countless other faceless, sweating, ejaculating men pinning her to beds, and the fear in her clamped colder and tighter and deeper.

She thought she was going to faint and went to the ladies room. In one of the cubicles, she got out a two-gram vial of cocaine and sniffed some up each nostril with the little spoon, tasting the tangy flavor of the coke high up in her throat. Coming out, she repaired her makeup and some of the fear went away. Her jewelry looked stunning on her, she thought, and her dress. Fuck this crowd. She'd leave and hook some jerk at the Polo Lounge and go to his apartment for the night so she wouldn't have to do Dominic and maybe the Italian again.

She went back out and began to make a slow way to the door until something about a small painting by Pissaro caught her eye and she stopped to look at it. The scene was a walled French farmyard in the spring. An old woman with boots and a long skirt and a scarf around her head was coming through the farm gates from green fields beyond, toward a tall apricot tree in full blossom. It seemed to Francesca so remote from her life. Yet the painting was so beautiful. It seemed to her to speak of the truth, and suggest that everything else a lie.

Filled now with a whole new emotion, a kind of inexpressible sadness, she became aware of someone next to her and a quiet voice saying, "How does one get oneself transported away from all of this and right into that?" She turned to find herself looking at a slender, almost fragile young man about her age. She had begun to reply when she realized that he wore a cassock and had to be a priest. That he was, and his presence in this crowd, struck her as so incongruous that she had to repress a crazy desire to laugh. Instead, she just stared at him silently until she finally realized what she was doing and said, "I'm sorry. I mean..." She gestured vaguely.

"Ah," he said. "What's a priest doing here?" His voice, like his manner, was gentle and without guile.

Embarrassed, she could only smile agreement and heard him say, "Could it be because I like art?" He laughed. "But I have to confess I am also here because of money. A friend wanted me to meet someone who might raise a little for me."

She had an odd feeling she'd met him before, or had seen him someplace. And she was struck by an ethereal quality about him, something that set him apart from anyone she knew or had ever met, an almost indefinable aura of peace, but at the same time a kind of strength that reached out to her magnetically so that everything around them stopped; the sound, the people, the room itself didn't exist. Nothing existed except him. She found she couldn't take her eyes off his. They were so gentle, so clear, and seemed to see right into her. And certainly, he didn't look like a priest, the clean, finely drawn lines of his face, the sculpted cheekbones and perfectly shaped mouth and jaw that made him resemble some of the Renaissance paintings of young Italian men way back then that she'd seen in an art book on someone's cocktail table, the rich mane of hair that tumbled almost to his collar. Masculinity without macho, she thought. The real thing. Sensitivity in every line of the face. Beauty, really.

It was then that she finally realized that she'd read about him in some magazine at the hairdresser, was it *Vanity Fair*? They'd said he represented a growing controversy between Catholics in America and the Vatican. And that she'd seen him on *60 Minutes* not long ago. "Oh," she exclaimed. "You're that man. I mean, Father…" She couldn't remember his name.

"Zacharias. John Zacharias."

"You were on television." She also remembered, then, his speaking out against practically everything people had begun to resent in the Church. A priest, yet! And how Dominic, sprawled naked on the couch and fingering the gold cross he always wore hanging from a chain around his neck, said he was nothing but a fucking anarchist. "They must just love that fuck in Rome. All over the place, all of a sudden, shooting his stupid mouth off. They don't shut him up pretty soon, he's going to be big trouble."

Why was he speaking to her, she wondered? Surely the way she was dressed, her reputation, the come-on she'd been giving some of the men there, he must have seen and suspected what sort of a woman she was. Or maybe had even heard. But in his eyes there was no disapproval or condemnation. "You want to get rid of the Vatican and the pope," she said.

"No, just put them into proper perspective. Give other voices a chance."

"David and Goliath," she said.

When he smiled at the metaphor, she remembered more of the program. There'd been film clips of him addressing small assemblages; a gentle figure who urged his listeners not to abandon the Church through disillusionment or fatigue or even resentment, but to renew their faith in God's charity through the Eucharist, to experience God's love through the presence of His son during communion.

Watching him speak, even so briefly, she'd thought him so different from any other priest she'd ever known.

She couldn't imagine him fitting in with all the bishops and cardinals whom they'd also shown in some important ceremony at St. Peter's. Somehow, he'd made them look foolish, as though they didn't represent what you felt about God, that they were just grown men dressing up in fancy costumes.

He hadn't come across like a schoolteacher, either, like some priests she'd met who made you feel you hadn't behaved yourself without their saying a word. Made you wonder if the Church still had anything to do with Christ because it was hard to see much that was Christ-like about it with all the stuff you read about the Vatican. And all the orders about how you should lead your life that nobody paid any attention to. No contraception, or gays, or sex unless you were married, or anything like that. This priest was the first one she could ever remember who made her think of Jesus himself.

But the pope was okay, too. She had to give him that. He'd always seemed to her a wonderful old man. There'd been clips of him, also, with his big, thick glasses and big nose, as he blessed a sea of people in St. Peter's Square from a balcony. He didn't seem anything like all the Vatican prelates surrounding him. They had depicted him, too, as he walked in the Vatican gardens, a small, slender figure in white, alone except for an old monk in a brown robe upon whose arm he leaned, and with a lean, gray-haired priest on his other side.

There had also been scenes of Rome, with all its fountains and tiled rooftops, and they'd talked a lot about what the Church meant to people. She hadn't really watched that part. She was Catholic, but she hadn't received communion or been to mass or confession in years, and sometimes she felt guilty about being so fallen and wondered if she could ever renew her faith, although the Church probably wouldn't take her back even if she wanted to.

She'd turned away from the television because guilt had begun to creep in like an ugly, unwanted serpent.

"They interviewed someone besides you," she said. "A cardinal somebody." It had been a man, she remembered, who was quietly intense, and virile in a way that was attractive to women. He kept brushing back dark hair that fell across his forehead, and she noticed his hands. They were the strong, worn hands of a workman, of someone who had labored hard with them. He hadn't seemed like a cardinal. Or even a cleric. He was more like this priest. He didn't seem to fit with all the ceremony at the Vatican. He'd seemed real.

"They said he might become pope someday," she said.

The priest smiled. "Cardinal Heriot."

Her eyes went to the rosary and cross that hung from the waistband of the young priest's cassock. How distant it all was from her, she thought. Just like the Pissaro.

Memories of what she had once been rushed at her then like a dark, suffocating cloud and suddenly she had to get away from the gallery, from all the people there, the heat, the noise, the silent, liveried flunkies feeding the empty, meaningless chatter with drink. She felt she wouldn't live if she didn't. She realized she'd begun to cry and muttered quickly, "Excuse me, Father, please," and made it to the cloakroom and got her mink. There was a terrible weight on her chest. She had to fight to breathe and didn't care if her tears were ruining her eye makeup.

Out on the street, she had just spotted a taxi when he appeared beside her, shrugging into his coat. His quiet smile was one of concern. He said, "Maybe a coffee would help. Or something to eat." Just as casually as that. No scorn, or disapproval, or condemnation. Just caring.

He took her arm, and as though it were the most natural thing in the world, she found herself silently walking with him through the cold Manhattan night until they were seated in the warmth of an unpretentious little Italian restaurant on Third Avenue. He'd ordered dinner and the waiter had poured their wine before she realized they had not exchanged a word since they had started off. She saw women staring at her jewelry and dress and said, "I hope you're not embarrassed by the way I'm dressed. I mean, for in here."

He smiled. "What about me?" He held up his rosary and cross. "Oh, they'll have a wonderful time with us." He raised his glass. "To Pissaro."

They drank, and Francesca felt a compelling warmth toward him. Warmth and unexpected trust, as though she had known him for years. His eyes, a face that she could only think of as beautiful, his slender, expressive hands, his quiet strength, the magnetism that drew her to him, all of that seemed to have always been a part of her life. He seemed to be any goodness, or freedom from sadness and pain, she'd ever felt or experienced.

Quite surprisingly, she found herself beginning to talk. Almost compulsively. About herself, about her life, past and present. She felt absolutely safe and couldn't stop. She hid nothing. Not the affairs with big-money men, not even the kind of nights she had with Dominic and his bisexual friends. Not that she was born and raised a Catholic.

All the while, he sat listening, silently, without comment. When they'd had coffee, he walked her back to her apartment, and when they reached the door she said, "In your eyes, Father, I've offended God, haven't I?"

"Yourself, Francesca, perhaps," he answered gently. "But not God. God is love and forgiveness. You only need to ask."

The old doorman had awakened from sleep in a lobby chair and was coming to let her in. Impulsively, she seized one of the priest's hands and held it to her lips and cheek, and, when the door opened, hurried inside.

At the elevator, she looked back and saw the hand she'd kissed lifted in a good-bye that seemed, at the same time, a blessing.

Going up to her apartment, she knew she couldn't stay the night in it. The thought of seeing Dominic was suddenly unbearable. Or picking up some guy at the Polo Lounge.

Dominic wasn't there, and driven by fear he might return unexpectedly and catch her leaving, she hurried. Once, she'd gone somewhere without telling him when he'd planned an evening with her and a friend. When she'd returned, he'd punched and kicked her from one side of her bedroom to the other before he was satisfied. He left her with her mouth bloodied, barely able to stand, with pain everywhere.

She quickly took off her jewelry, put the vial of cocaine next to the money the Italian had placed on her dressing table, changed into a tailored daytime suit, and telephoned the Carlisle to book the room the concierge there always kept aside for her in case she ran into an unexpected date she didn't want to bring home. A toothbrush and makeup were all that she would need until she came back in the morning. She dumped them into a handbag. But going out to the elevator, she had an odd feeling that she might never see the apartment again.

CHAPTER

5

She couldn't sleep. She lay in the semi-dark of the hotel room and her life rolled before her eyes like a bad movie. The white frame house just off Main Street that had grown shabby with the years, her grandparents gray and silent in their chairs, speaking to each other only when required, their hostility to each other had grown so deep, like her mother and father; and waiting for her father to return from work, her mother hurriedly taking her upstairs and waiting while she knelt and said her prayers, "Our Father, who art in Heaven…" then muttering goodnight and turning out the light and rushing away before she climbed into bed.

School, the hated math teacher, what was her name? De Marcos? First communion in the white dress her mother had slowly put together with household savings, always blaming her for the sacrifice as though it had been her fault. But there was the excitement for days leading up to the actual celebration, the exultation she'd felt receiving the host for the first time, and knowing that Jesus was actually there with her. Later her confirmation, the visiting bishop tracing a cross on her forehead with chrism. Then high school. Cheering on the football team, Ken and Harry and Bert, the school-famous "Three Dragons" running backs; Mr. Hicks's pharmacy, where you didn't go unless you absolutely had to, like stocking up on tampons when you got older, because Mr. Hicks was such a creep and undressed girls slowly from head to toe, making them squirm; and the A&P supermarket where Dolly worked after school at a checkout counter and who was so fat no one ever wanted to be seen with her except she let you snitch Mars bars; and the Exxon station where everyone hung out on weekend nights and the guys got their cars ready for drag racing or just parading Main Street.

Where had it gone wrong? Randy saying he loved her when he didn't, but her believing him and getting caught in bed with him by her mother. Her father raging when her mother told him; the overwhelming relief of finding out she wasn't pregnant, even though Randy hadn't used a condom and their sex had been in the middle of her cycle. And her heartbreak because he had started dating another girl and denied ever having sex with her to everyone at school, except to say she was good for a blowjob if anyone wanted one.

And then the shock of Father O'Donovan's groping during the church picnic after she'd told him all about Randy in confession the day before, his hand sliding from her buttocks around to the front. Not daring to tell her parents because she was sure they would say she was making it up. No priest would even think of such a thing. Or, if he had—one chance in a million—then it had to her fault, she'd provoked it. After all, look at the clothes she wore to school. Jeans so tight you could hardly get into them, and even tighter when you soaked in them in the shower and let them dry on you, the crease up the back almost cutting you in half. And hot pants and miniskirts that left nothing to the imagination and gave all the guys an erection. And the jersey tops so plunging and so tight that nobody, but nobody, could take their eyes off your breasts. And her mother's mouth a perpetual thin line and hissing, *Who cares if the other girls dress like that, they aren't Catholic and brought up to know right from wrong.* Sex was for marriage and only if you had to. Then finally, high school was over and she was off to state college. On her own, her parents' nagging and anger behind her.

The freedom, the all-night talking. And partying, the binge drinking. The pot. The Ecstasy. Some other pill that sent you out of this world. And coke when one of the guys got hold of some. And the Church soon forgotten. Church and being Catholic seemed to belong to another life. It was out of touch. For little children, maybe. Not for a young woman who was free. It did nothing for her.

Freshman year, summer student exchange. Some poor French kid to her home, she to hers. The Cote d'Azur, Nice, motor scooters. Marc. A Catholic like her, but he hadn't been to mass for years. He laughed at the priests. All of his crowd did. You were baptized, confirmed, married, and buried by the Church. Period. The Church didn't care. Wine and pot and topless beaches; riding topless behind him on his motor scooter, hair flying, laughing and waving at their friends following; everyone screwing on the beaches at night. Sometimes swapping around.

Then not returning home. Going instead with Marc's father's friend to Paris. The lure of gray-haired maturity to a young woman. Disappearing. Not even bothering to write home. Then a friend of his. Balding, but fun, and paying for her rent and good times all over town. The fast-track, had-it-made crowd. The Italian tennis player who took her to Monte Carlo and gambling. The Brit and his country home. Barbados, Antigua. Aruba. The high life. Year after year. Higher and higher. Until Dominic.

Very early in the morning and quite suddenly, she thought of the little East Side church; she didn't know why. But she did. Was it St. Sebastian's? Three blocks from where she lived and two avenues toward the East River. She'd walked past it a score of times and was sure she remembered weekday masses and communion at six. Determination she hadn't felt for years swept through her, and with it a feeling of release from darkness. She knew exactly what she had to do, what she wanted to do more than anything else.

She got up, dressed quickly, and left the still-silent hotel lobby for early-morning, half-silent New York, where people were just beginning to get it together and come out onto the empty, lightening streets.

The church was a drab, narrow place. A dirty, New York–sandstone brown, whatever architecture it had

crushed to oblivion by nearness and a sidewalk choked
with garbage cans and by flanking buildings, the lighter-
colored stone over its arched doorway and windows
beginning to crumble. The age-dulled gold paint of its
sign sanded over with exhaust black. The door was open,
one or two people entering, nondescript New Yorkers,
their clothes matching the look of the church itself. She
followed them in, adjusting her eyes to the gloom, taking
in the rows of empty pews, their cushions threadbare, the
plaster statues of saints dwarfed by towering walls that disappeared into the darkness of the ceiling somewhere high
above. There was the stale smell of bodies and of city
damp and decay. Who would ever want to come there?

She didn't care. She felt only urgency and anticipa-
tion. She bent a knee, crossed herself without thinking.
The priest was elderly, slightly stooped; in the world of
priests, he was one who had never gotten far. Here and
there the hem of his surplice had come down. He celebrated mass in a high, quavering voice that sank almost to
a whisper of disinterest from years of repetition.

But for Francesca, the ugliness of the church disappeared, time rolled back, and during communion, when
she knelt before the steps to the altar and received the
host, she felt Christ truly with her for the first time since
her confirmation and, exalted by His presence, united in
faith with all around her.

Coming out and walking back to the Carlisle, the
world looked different to her—the streets, the sounds, the
lights, the people. A hostility she had always sensed in New
York was no longer there. There was belonging instead.

It was then that she knew something had happened to her. It was like a dream and totally unexpected. She couldn't explain it, and didn't care if she couldn't. There were things in life you could not express even to yourself. One moment, there was Dominic and the wild nights and all the years of faceless men; the next moment, all that had gone, and an overwhelming sense of freedom had taken its place. Freedom and safety, a release from every fear and anxiety, from all bad feelings. A sense of rightness and love.

There was no more death's head.

She felt overwhelming gratitude, as though her heart would nearly burst with it. She was not alone anymore. She had felt betrayed; when she was drowning, the Church failed to reach down and rescue her. Just as she had failed to reach up to it. But now she was with God again, Church or no Church, and because of Father John.

All during dinner with him, she had felt, for the first time in many years, the presence of Christ. And because of his gentle understanding and sympathy, because of his own deep faith that was evident in every word he spoke, in his every expression and in every gesture, he had gently led her back to grace, just as he must be leading countless others. And with the simple message of love that Christ had imparted to his apostles: "God is love and forgiveness." Nothing more. No pomp. No ceremony, no disapproval, no impossible orders. No betrayal anywhere. Just love and the truth that was God.

It took a dozen phone calls to find someone who knew somebody else who knew how to reach him. Frightened he'd say he couldn't see her, she went across town to the inexpensive West Side hotel where he was staying and waited for him in the lobby. That was shortly before lunch. It was late in the afternoon before he finally came in with three other priests, their hair and shoulders white from a light, powdery first snow that was falling.

Seeing him, she lost her nerve and remained frozen in the lobby chair. But the desk clerk pointed her out to him, and he came over and, without ceremony, pulled a chair up next to hers and took her hand.

"I'm glad you came, Francesca," he said.

All day, she'd rehearsed a speech and now couldn't remember a word of it. She blurted out, "I wanted to help." And then said, "However I can. I mean, with what you are doing."

"We welcome all the help we can get."

"I don't mean just money." She laughed awkwardly and forced herself to blunder on. "I meant help with work. Whatever."

He still had not spoken. His eyes fixed intently on hers, as though seeing into her mind. She found a last shred of courage. "Look, I told you what I am. Last night. Let's face it, I'm nothing more than a high-priced whore, and if you think I'd be a liability, say so and I'll leave."

He spoke suddenly, one hand firm on hers, the other lifted to silence her. "Enough, Francesca."

"But it's true, isn't it? For years I've abandoned Christ and..."

"Enough." He looked at his watch. "We're leaving shortly for Chicago. Could you come with us?"

He had to repeat it before it registered. When it did, it was as though a dazzling light had torn through a shadowy darkness. She found her voice and echoed disbelievingly, "Come with you?"

"Today. Yes. With me and those three over there." He smiled and pointed at the waiting priests. "My disciples. You can help keep us all organized." Then he said, "After Chicago and Des Moines, I think possibly Dallas and San Diego. It might be hard for you. We have to stay in inexpensive motels and eat on the road half the time." He took her hand again. "But come with us, Francesca."

Francesca stared at him, at his gentle, serious face, hardly daring to believe. Stared at him and felt tears beginning to well in her eyes and heard her own voice as though it was coming from a great distance, but with a strength and conviction she'd never before felt about anything.

"Yes," she said. "Yes, I will."

CHAPTER

◈6◈

Holding Francesca's hand, seeing tears of joy slowly descend her cheeks, Father John felt himself in the presence of a spiritual beauty he'd rarely seen in any other, and felt humbled by it.

The evening before, he'd planned to return to his hotel from Sotheby's and lay out his itinerary for the next several weeks; it was critical that he do so. Instead, he had grabbed his coat and followed her. *Why?* he wondered now.

He sensed it was not only because he felt he couldn't abandon the expensively beautiful but deeply troubled woman standing by the Pissaro, whom he'd thought was on the verge of some act of desperation, perhaps even taking her own life that evening.

Nor later, he knew, at the little Italian restaurant, did it have to do only with his deeply felt sympathy when she had poured out her soul and revealed herself to him. Nor just that he'd seen in her one who, frightened to seek love, as the unloved so often are for fear of betrayal, had drifted from the Church and, out of fear and desperation, had adopted a lifestyle that sought revenge.

Nor even entirely that she had been abandoned in turn by a Church that seemed increasingly to care more about ceremony, protocol, and doctrine than it did about protecting the lost and the lonely and the fallen.

There'd been something else. Something as compelling as all those reasons. Seeing her disappear into the elevator at her apartment building, realizing he might never see her again, he had experienced a totally unexpected and deeply painful feeling of loss. Trying to understand it, he realized that right from the beginning when he had seen her standing alone by the Pissaro, he had felt an almost mystical union with her. It was as though who she was, the devoutly pure inner woman hidden even from herself, had made him aware that a corner of his own spiritual life, until that moment empty, perhaps even lacking, had been filled by her very appearance.

All day, while out with his three accompanying priests, he had thought ceaselessly of her to the exclusion of almost everything else, and his heart had been heavy. Had he failed her? Thinking of her confession at dinner, he had worried over her torment, hoping he had, even in a small way, eased her pain, wondering what more he could do for her and whether she would even want him to help her at all.

When she had reappeared at the hotel, humbly offering her help instead, it was as though he had received the most wonderful gift from God. He hardly dared ask her to come with them. Would she misunderstand and think he had some devious reason that would betray her trust? That she had said yes had been for him a moment of rare beauty.

He introduced her to the other priests. There was Father Graham, a wizened little man with laughter in his eyes; Father Berthold, who was tall and portly and somber; and young Father Howell, a delicate soul who stammered except when celebrating mass, and who blushed like a girl if complimented.

Then, while she ran out to quickly buy some overnight things, Father John and his disciples went to their rooms to pack up their own belongings.

The fact that they were going to Chicago had brought back a flood of memories to Father John: the mill town he'd been raised in only a few hours' drive from the big city, his devout mother's shame and sorrow over his father's disgrace, the newspaper headlines about the falsified police evidence in a much-publicized case of bank fraud involving substantial paybacks.

And throughout all of it, suffering the taunts of schoolmates and the sideways glances of neighbors who went silent as he passed by their front yards, the endless questioning by a district attorney as to his father's friends and off-duty habits. Did he drink, did he womanize? Did he have substantial debts? Why did he do it? In his heart he knew his father had been on the take for years. That dishonesty, neglect of his mother and family, were chronic and were simply his character. That having abandoned his religion—and with it, God—he was a pathetically lost man.

It had been a bitter time. But he had found refuge and peace in the strength of Sister Agatha, his mother's old school friend. She had come evenings with Sister Marguerite, a nun from the same convent, to sit with his mother and help ease her pain through prayer. In the warmth of the nuns' love and in the purity of their devotion, he had rediscovered his own faith and had himself joyfully followed their lead in serving God by entering the priesthood.

Along with the happiness at his vocation, there'd been the excitement of his first church, the little stone building in which he had taken such pride. With it, there'd been the love he'd felt for his first parishioners, hardened mill workers and their families with all their problems and hopes, along with their sorrows.

He'd lived with them and for them, been a part of them. There had been weddings, funerals, baptisms and confirmations, confessions. Helping the dying face death and last rites. Reading to the elderly at night, visiting those injured and in the hospital, running errands for those who could not, easing the fears and burden of unwed motherhood, and of teenagers caught by pregnancy, or with a heart broken by a first failed romance. Helping other young ones caught by drugs or alcohol to break the habit. Settling family rows and easing the strain of rocky marriages. Gardening and household work for those who couldn't, along with painting and carpentry for them. There had even been baby-sitting.

There had been issues, too, that affected Catholics

everywhere, and that many in his flock questioned. And all the time, he had never stopped to wonder at the silence of his bishop. Or that he alone seemed the only contact his parishioners felt they had with the Church, the only one who would respond to them.

It was left to him to try to explain why the Church appeared to discriminate against women. Indeed, why not ordain women to fill the gap caused by the serious shortage of priests in the country? Disturbingly, much of the work involving the sacraments was being left to deacons or even lay workers, weakening the very catholicity of the Church itself, and thus, too, eventually putting at risk every Catholic individually. And why did the Church take such a hard line about contraception when millions of Catholic women used it, felt guilty about it, and were obliged to confess it?

And what about free choice? While abortion was anathema to most Catholics, a woman's right to determine the course of her own body was supported by an influential and vocal minority of Catholics whose devotion could not be questioned.

It was left to him, too, to explain and try to defend Church doctrine forbidding marriage in the priesthood. Couldn't priests, he was asked, better understand the problems of the married members of their congregation if they also were married?

As he dealt day and night with the hard realities that faced his Catholic congregation, there lurked in his heart a growing rebellion against attitudes in Rome that he felt did not mirror the love and forgiveness of Jesus Christ as he had experienced it through Sister Marguerite and Sister Agatha. There were attitudes that only caused confusion and a feeling of betrayal for many among his flock.

Finally, there were attitudes in Rome, too, he regretted, that weren't just neglect. They were attitudes that caused terrible physical suffering as well as spiritual pain to many. It was as though Rome had even abandoned the Eucharist, and thus Jesus himself, and it needed only a spark to light the fire of revolution in him.

That spark struck like a thunderbolt and without warning. It came in the form of a full-page advertisement in an important national newspaper. One hundred leading feminist Catholics, including a score of priests, an equal number of nuns, and many prominent Catholic theologians, had signed a petition asking the Pope for a dialogue on issues that were burning in the hearts of many American Catholics and causing great divisiveness among them. These were contraception, freedom of choice, and equal rights for women.

Action by Rome was swift and merciless. To the Vatican, it was not a matter of theology, doctrine, or even faith. It was a question of obedience. By threats and intimidation that ranged from job loss or forced resignation to actual excommunication, Rome managed to bypass the failing Pope Gregory and slowly dismember the petition. Hardest hit were those members of canonical colonies, the nuns who had added their signatures. Facing expulsion or severe discipline by their orders, the nuns fell away one by one, either by recanting or through abandoning their vocation.

All except Sister Agatha and Sister Marguerite. They

bravely refused. Trying to avoid the public embarrassment their stubbornness might engender through the
media, Rome sent over Monsignor Pasternelli to negotiate. He failed with behavior that emphasized precisely
what the advertisement's call for pluralism was all about.
He treated the two sisters with appalling chauvinism,
condescendingly patting the knee of one, pinching the
cheek of the other, and asking both the elderly religious
if they had told their "mommies" and "daddies" what
they were doing.

But where Rome failed, the badly frightened and
coerced canonical order of the two nuns did not. There
was bitterness and anger at their stance. Faced with eviction from an organization that was their vocation, their
whole lives, they resigned.

Sister Agatha prevailed. But Sister Marguerite did not.
Her spirit broken and in ill health, she went into a deep
depression and, a few short weeks after her eviction, took
her life.

In his closeness to both nuns, Father John suffered
their agony and fully shared Sister Agatha's grief over
Sister Marguerite's passing. For hadn't it been Sister
Marguerite who so often had held him in her comforting
arms when he was little, protecting him from all the blows
he'd had to suffer, and later furiously defending him
against the neighborhood ostracism his father's scandal
caused? And when it came to college, it was Sister
Marguerite who had counseled him on where to apply
and helped him through his first undergraduate years with
what little money she could scrape together through end-

less small personal sacrifices.

The Sunday after she died, and after he had celebrated mass, he made an announcement from the pulpit of his little stone church. He had not slept the night before, his mind in a turmoil with emotions and a sense of mission he had not felt since the ceremony of his ordination. What good did it do to resent and do nothing to rectify?

"To all of us," he said, "comes a time when we must give up something we love dearly, something close to our hearts, for a path in life we feel transcends all personal consideration. It is not without a terrible sadness that I must tell you, and you, and you," his eyes swept the silent congregation with each word, "all of you whose lives have become such a part of me, that I am today informing the bishop of my resignation as priest of this parish."

There was a shocked murmur of protest. "No," came from several. Many rose in disbelief. He saw sudden tears in the eyes of others.

He raised a hand for silence. "I don't want to leave you, but I must and I ask your forgiveness. In my conscience I can no longer remain in isolated silence about so many things that so many of you, as do I, as do so many Catholics everywhere, feel of such importance to our faith.

"I feel that our Church has lost the meaning of Christ, and I intend to go out across the country and preach His message to whomever will listen and to ask Rome to heed it. We Catholics need the Church, but many of us feel we do not want it the way it is.

"Let me be clear: I speak not of the thousands and

thousands of my devoutly hard-working fellow priests and nuns throughout the world with whom the Church as been blessed. I am not speaking, either, of many fine higher prelates, nor of many devoutly brilliant theologians and administrators even at the Vatican itself. I speak of our need for a leadership that comes not from a mafia of celibate old men of the papal court, many of whom don't speak English and have never been out of Italy, and whose reactionary intransigence is often too much for even the strongest of popes. I am speaking, too, of those Cardinals, in many different countries, whose ambitions and politics have taken over their hearts. Their attitudes are far from all the realities we live with and face every day, even farther from the millions who live in grinding poverty.

"Our blessed Lord, we all know, was for centuries too often used as an excuse for every sin imaginable. Is he perhaps not still being often used? The Eucharist is the center of our faith, its very essence, the very soul of each and every one of us. In our prayers and in the psalms of the liturgy of Eucharist, we honor the Father, Son, and the Holy Spirit. In its communion, we feel the mystery and the mystical presence of Christ, who died for us. He is there, with each of us, come to us to lead us and bind us in community in our mutual adoration and faith. I ask if the Eucharist is truly the soul of the Church, also. If not, I intend to ask the Vatican to restore it, just as I intend to ask American Catholics everywhere to renew their faith through it and to pray for Rome."

That had been three months ago. He had made a slow beginning, although much had happened just the same.

Three priests had left their churches to join him; his outraged bishop had summoned him to the diocese immediately after the television program and handed him a
written order to desist at once and to return to his parish.
And although he had received some financial support
from friends as a result of the program, as well as from his
fellow priests, and had dug deep into his own meager savings, he was rapidly running out of money.

That Francesca might help financially had never for
one instant crossed his mind. To him, the help he had
received was of another kind. By her mere presence, he
felt his spirits uplifted and his determination renewed.
When they stopped in Buffalo for a short night in a cheap
motel, he thanked God once more for her existence and
asked the Lord to bring her true happiness in her new life.

CHAPTER

7

Only a day or two after Francesca changed direction in her life and joined Father John Zacharias, a glittering White House reception marked the president's honoring of four leading citizens with the nation's highest civilian award, the Medal of Freedom. Among the four was Ignatius, rewarded for his tireless effort in bringing to public and legislative attention the ruthless exploitation of migrant workers across the nation, as well as their vital contribution to the nation's economy.

The evening over, he accompanied the president away from the tide of guests leaving the Gold Room, where there had been entertainment, and went up to the private presidential residence for a late-evening coffee with the First Lady and one of the six presidential daughters, who was home on vacation from her senior year in college.

Ignatius had known the presidential family for some time. They were from his diocese and he had officiated at the wedding of their eldest daughter. When in private, he was simply Father Ignatius, as he was with his staff.

The relative quiet of the president's library, where he was given coffee and made comfortable, was a welcome relief to Ignatius. The award, which he could hardly have refused, disturbed him. He couldn't see why one should be singled out and rewarded for helping others. It made help, which should have been universal, seem isolated and unique. Somehow, he thought, the well-intentioned award was, instead, a sad commentary on the cult of self that excluded others, and was everywhere among all levels of humanity. Besides, he'd always hated being the center of attention, and the whole evening, especially the president's effusive praise that he thought he hardly deserved, had added to his discomfort.

For half an hour, time flew as he caught up on all the family news. Suddenly, the first lady turned the conversation.

"Father, that young priest—what's his name, Father Zacharias? The television program you and he were on the other night. Why is he allowed to say what he does? Going around the country and openly challenging the Church, calling for women in the priesthood and getting rid of the papacy, and everything else?"

Ignatius at once felt a slight unease. Discussing controversy in the Church was something he tried always to avoid. And these days, he particularly did not want to get involved in conversation about Father Zacharias, who, in defiance of orders from his bishop, was beginning to attract considerable attention. More and more where the young priest was concerned, he felt a growing inner conflict. The part of him that wanted to agree with much of what Zacharias demanded was at odds with his deep-felt adherence to the structure and dogma of the Church that had become his life. The priest was demanding far more from the Vatican than a change of heart on public issues such as contraception and women in the priesthood. He was seeking reform in the very structure and composition of the Church itself, demanding change in a hierarchy that had had survived for hundreds of years without it, while giving the Church the necessary secular power with which to meet the demands of its widespread religiosity.

While defending the Vatican had never been a problem before, his recent television role as an apologist had left him feeling vaguely troubled at his possibly having been hypocritical on some matters.

He had been equally uncomfortable in condemning Father Zacharias when replying to a request by Cardinal Mancini for a report on the television program as well as on other public appearances by the priest where he was disturbing in his outspokenness.

Meanwhile, the president's daughter leapt on her mother's remark. "You mean challenges like pro-choice, Mom? And contraception? Some Catholic women I know even keep condoms in their handbags, just in case. And plenty of Catholic women in America have had abortions. Or, while we're at it, isn't celibacy one of the reasons behind all the pedophile priests? And the reason, too, that priests are leaving the Church in droves?" Her smile as she spoke was touched with youthful superiority over a parent's datedness.

The first lady flushed. "Well, yes. All of that too, I suppose."

She was a warm, motherly woman whose life was a model of a woman's traditional acceptance of all Church doctrine. "I simply don't understand it," she continued to Ignatius. "I took the trouble to check up on him. He comes from a working-class background. His father was a police officer who was involved in some sort of scandal, I can't remember just what, but they were strict Catholics. He worked his way through State University, where he graduated summa cum laude and Phi Beta Kappa, mind you, and then went to seminary at Holy Cross. And ever since, he has had a very good position in a mill town between Chicago and Gary, Indiana. He's obviously not stupid and you'd really think he'd know better. I was so glad they allowed you time to speak, also."

Ignatius glanced at the president's daughter, curled up in a chair opposite him like a warm and sensuous kitten in her décolleté evening gown, her evening slippers kicked off and her long, slender legs tucked underneath her. He felt sure that the condom remark, at least, pertained to herself as well as others. She clearly was one of the growing army of young people who were turning to the maverick priest in protest against the restrictive prohibitions by Rome that had little to do with many of her generation.

Before he could speak, she turned to him. "Father Ignatius, be honest, what do you think about Father Zacharias?"

She ignored a warning glance from the president, who saw potential friction between mother and daughter. "Not the Vatican feelings you argued on television, Father," she insisted. "Yours."

That was too much for her mother. The First Lady bridled. "I should hardly think Father Ignatius has any opinion other than what he expressed the other night."

"You mean the Vatican 'line,' Mom?"

Ignatius raised both hands in a gentle request to the two women to desist and smiled faintly at the president. But he felt trapped.

"What are my personal feelings? About Father John?" He unconsciously ran a work-worn hand through his hair, pushing strands away from his forehead, and toyed with his coffee a moment, trying to collect his thoughts. Unwittingly, the young woman was forcing him to face his disturbing inner conflict.

Waiting for him to speak, the president's daughter felt a little guilty about going at him the way she had. He was one of her very favorite people, a cardinal someone could admire because he was not the complacent and patronizing half eunuch that so many bishops and cardinals became. She could really talk to him.

At school, she had two photos of him she'd cut from a magazine and framed. One showed him years ago in a sugar cane field with a group of migrant workers. He was dirty and unshaven and wearing old trousers and boots and a tattered undershirt. There was a smiling young migrant couple beside him, and he cradled a naked baby in one arm while in his free hand he carried a machete. The other showed him in Vietnam with a group of exhausted young Marines who had just come out of a fire fight to a waiting evacuation helicopter. There was an M1 slung over his shoulder, and he had one trouser leg cut off and a blood-soaked bandage around his thigh. He'd been a chaplain who had not been afraid of staying with his charges when they went into battle.

He didn't look any different today, she thought, even conducting mass in all his ceremonial robes that never quite seemed to suit him and which she suspected he felt uncomfortable wearing. There was the same strong, quick body, the same expression in his eyes that was both gentle and intense. Except now he looked older and a little world-weary, and there seemed to be a touch of sadness in his expression sometimes. Not for himself, she thought, but for the world. And tonight, whenever she glanced his way, she'd thought him troubled, too. She wondered why. She didn't think it was just Father Zacharias. She'd thought him that way even during the awards ceremony. So it had to be something else.

She heard him repeat, "Father John." And then say, "Okay. It's really not his beliefs that are the problem. It's how he expresses them."

Aware of the fine line he was walking within himself, Ignatius went on to explain that the Church had well-established channels by which those who disagree could make their voices heard. Slowly, he admitted. But certain.

By going public in defiance of his bishop, Father Zacharias, he said, could bring about a backlash within the Church that might well see the Church taken over by a wave of reactionary fundamentalism that would set it back centuries.

"Think about a return to the sixteenth-century mentality that created the Inquisition, or the Church in the tenth century that underwrote the crusades. Or," he added bitingly, "centuries of persecution of the Jews culminating in the horror of the Holocaust that our Church cravenly did nothing to stop."

He paused a moment and, with a slight dismissive shrug, added, "It hardly compares to mega-evil, I suppose, but also what about a not-so-long-ago banking scandal that saw several high financiers murdered, possibly a pope; a hundred dead when a rail terminal was bombed; Italy close to bankruptcy; and the director of the Vatican Bank indicted for fraud with a warrant issued for his arrest by Interpol?"

Even as he spoke, he thought how glib and evasive his words sounded in his own ears—even if they were the truth. He hadn't answered her question. He hadn't said how he personally felt about Father Zacharias. Something in him had made him hold back. All he'd done was tirade against the Church's far-right Traditionalist party. He could see disappointment in her eyes and he prayerfully counted on her good manners to not pursue the matter and was rewarded. When her mother pointedly changed the subject to plans for the christening of their first grandchild, she became silent, toying with the hem of her dress.

Inwardly ashamed, Ignatius finally took his leave. The president went downstairs with him to the north entrance portico, where the official limousine waited to take Ignatius to his hotel.

"My apologies for my daughter's rather ungracious persistence, Father. She and my wife hardly see eye to eye on things."

Hearing himself answer, "Her question posed no problem," only made Ignatius feel even more craven.

The president laughed. "Just the same, I hope the question I have doesn't put me in her league." He waited while Ignatius put on his coat, held for him by a Marine usher. "The pope. Our ambassador to the Vatican says His Holiness won't last six months."

Ignatius thought of the frail old man he and the whole world revered and called "the humble pope"; a man worn down by endless opposition from the all-powerful and reactionary curia. "I fear the ambassador is right," he said.

"There are rumors about your possibly succeeding him."

Ignatius knew of the rumors. He knew, also, how badly many Americans would like to see one of their own become pope. "It's God's divine will as to whom is elected," he said. "And I can hardly imagine that He would extend such an honor to me."

The president, although obviously disappointed, accepted the evasion in good spirit, and Ignatius took his leave.

When the limousine reached Washington Circle, Ignatius told the driver to stop. He got out with the hope that walking the rest of the way would help him clarify his thoughts about Father Zacharias. Strive as he could, however, he got nowhere. His struggle was finally pushed aside by the intrusive and persistent memory of the nightmare that had shattered his predawn sleep.

In it, as in so many others, he'd been guilty not just of betraying one who trusted him, but of lust for the woman who had helped him in his deceit. The memory of possessing her had been so vivid upon rising that morning that he'd felt as though her naked warmth was still pressed against him.

Inwardly, he recoiled at the irony in his accepting the reverence of that evening's gathering while still faintly harboring such ghostly intimacy. Reverence, too, with no realization of how often such fantasized intimacy forced itself into his daily life, even sometimes with desire for a completely unknown woman passing by in the street. Or on an occasion such as this evening, when looking at the president's daughter curled up on her chair, he had for just an instant seen her, too, as sexually desirable. Or, as years before, he had often felt aroused by some young migrant laborer in the cane fields when sweat held her shirt to her body so that her breasts were clearly revealed. Perhaps, he thought, if he had never indulged in sex in college and then in medical school before he abruptly changed his course in life to become a priest, celibacy would not have been so painful. Memories persisted of the various young women with whom he had made love, their nakedness, their passion, their sharing, and the memories were painful and sharp with regret.

How little the laity understood how many thousands of priests suffered similarly, how many were tormented by celibacy, as he so often was? And how many left the priesthood because of it? The president's daughter had been right about that. In the modern world, with all its sensual temptations, celibacy was becoming an impossibility for many.

How many, too, he thought, barely avoided, through prayer, a loss of all reason in their desperation for relief?

Or, how many more somehow found that relief and were never discovered, or even confessed it, so that only their own consciences stood in judgement on them?

Or had any idea, either, of those priests, too numerous to imagine, who, possessed by the terrible sin of pedophilia, remained undiscovered and a threat to the innocent? Unlike so many others who had visited their victims with such awful and lasting trauma, and with their vileness had brought such shame and disgrace to the Church as well?

Dwelling on it became too much. He stepped up his walk and his thoughts turned instead to how much his receiving the Medal of Freedom would help in his lobbying efforts toward improving the lot of migrant workers.

Before long, he reached his hotel. There, in the comfortable suite reserved for him by his office, he took a moment getting ready for bed to reread the letter that he had received just before leaving for Washington. His old African friend and Nobel Laureate, William Ngordo, so honored for his tireless work in negotiating peace in explosive areas around the world, had written on behalf of ten other Third World cardinals to urge him to take control of the Church's centrist Conservative party, a move that would help them in enlisting future loyalties on his behalf in the ultimate event of a conclave.

The letter expressed a grave concern for the Church's future that matched his own. In it, Ngordo recalled the great reforms known as Vatican II that were initiated by John XXIII and implemented at the world gathering of bishops twenty-five years ago. He regretted their forced stagnation by reactionary elements within the hierarchy and in defiance of Pope Gregory, and he expressed anxiety at the Vatican leaving unaddressed all those popular issues that were of such major importance to many.

Perhaps even more dangerous, Ngordo said, were Mancini and the Traditionalists. They sought to increase the mostly unbridled power of the Vatican's eight administrative congregations, the name given the permanent committees, each composed of cardinals, that controlled nearly every aspect of Catholic life, from Vatican foreign policy and banking to the conduct of both secular and religious affairs in every diocese. Their reactionary attitudes were perpetuated by leadership invariably selected from their own ranks.

Heavy hearted, Ignatius put the letter away. How badly he wanted to tell Ngordo why he could not help him. But he could not. Only in the confessional or in the complete confidentiality of a doctor's office could he ever reveal the awful truth about himself. Such terrible sin as burdened his every sleeping hour, such a sense of dark and foreboding guilt he bore during the day, his surety of God's disapproval, would surely disqualify any man from wearing the papal crown. If God ever deemed that he should be offered it, he would have to refuse the offer.

He thought of the Sacred College of Cardinals meeting in secret conclave to elect a new pope. In his mind, he saw himself and his fellows seated on their thrones arranged around the walls of the revered Sistine Chapel. Their persons would be even more minimized by Michelangelo's monumental Renaissance work *The Last Judgment*, which covered the entire north wall above the altar, and by the artist's six great frescoes decorating the barrel-vaulted ceiling high overhead.

He thought of the several days of ceremonies shutting off the chapel from the world, of the rich pageantry of them, of the ancient and intricate procedure of the actual balloting itself.

And he felt a sense of awe, for he himself would be a participant in the two-thousand-year-old heritage of the Church as expressed in nearly every aspect of the conclave.

And yet at the same time, he felt keenly dishonest. For he knew, deep in his heart, that he felt sympathy for Father Zacharias's call for the abolition of that very conclave itself, along with its narrow, elitist ramifications, replacing it with a more democratic referendum of the Church's four thousand bishops, each of whom would then have complete governing power over his own diocese, rather than being governed by one of the Church's faraway administrative Congregations.

Sympathy, but only sympathy. His mind shied away from seriously contemplating the priest's demands and proposals as ever becoming actualities.

Finishing his preparations for bed, he humbly prayed to find some way to resolve the contradiction that he knew was in him. And he prayed, too, for some revelation of whatever dreadful sin he was guilty of that turned nearly every night into a tormenting hell.

"Show me, Lord, the truth. Reveal to me of what I am guilty. I ask not for your forgiveness, only to know my sin, so I may face it and pay whatever price your judgment calls for."

As he did almost every night, he closed his evening with a prayer in Latin.

"*Noctem quietam ad finem perfectum tribuat meum omnipotens et misericors Dominum*—Lord, almighty and merciful, grant me a quiet night and a perfect end."

CHAPTER

8

In Rome the following spring, the papal funeral of Gregory XVIII slowly came to an end. Mass and eulogy over, the cypress coffin was sealed with gilt nails planted by the Sampetrini, the ranking attendants at St. Peter's. That coffin in turn was enclosed first by one of cedar, then by yet another of bronze, with a final seal ritualistically applied by Cardinal Mancini. The mortal remains of Gregory XVIII were then taken down to the crypt beneath the Basilica and sealed up, the site to be regarded henceforth largely by tourists, and the man himself, his life and his work, eventually remembered only, and briefly, by history.

As conclave carmelengo, Cardinal Mancini was the ultimate authority in all matters pertaining to the forthcoming conclave and the vital business of electing a new pope. Tired but determined, he was at last able to concentrate on the myriad details involved. Most of the remaining cardinals under the age of eighty, and thus eligible to vote, had finally arrived in Rome. Of the one hundred and twenty in number, more than half were Italian and European; less than half came from Latin America, the United States, and Canada; some twenty-odd were African and Asian; a handful were from Oceania.

During the next nine days, and under Mancini's direction, the cardinals met in the huge, modern papal audience hall located within the Vatican walls to the south of the Basilica. Minor practical matters of the conclave were formalized and voted on; the cardinals were registered, their identities verified; the constitution of the Church was read; officials of both the Vatican State and of Rome were confirmed; priests, confessors, and doctors to the conclave were elected; a list of cooks, cleaners, maintenance people, fire officers, and others was approved.

During the conclave, the cardinals, to show true humility before God, were to live almost monastically in simple, prefabricated cells of rooms that were scattered in the halls and corridors around the Sistine Chapel, where the voting was to take place. The sole furniture in each would be beds, desks, dressers, and wardrobes for clothes, and usually a *prie-dieu*, a small individual altar with a step to kneel on when praying. Each cardinal would be allowed a staff of two, usually his secretary and a servant. Lots were now drawn for the location of the cells. The two most junior cardinals were appointed to check on all entering the conclave area. Three others were designated to watch over the official sealing of all exits and entrances around the Sistine Chapel. This would take place at the end of the first day of the conclave, which was entirely ceremonial and followed a strict ritual, as would the voting the second day, as laid down by Pope Gregory X in a papal bull in 1274.

In the morning, the cardinals attended mass in the Pauline Chapel at the opposite end of the great Sala Regia hall from the Sistine. Only those with an insider's knowledge were aware that many of these crimson-robed, graying senior members of the Church, theoretically united in reverent devotion, knelt to pray while harboring anger and hostility, sometimes positively venomous, against each other for their widely differing and hardened attitudes on how their faith should be governed and expressed.

In the afternoon, the cardinals installed themselves in their respective cells and then, preceded by the Vatican Choir, they gathered in the Sistine with the rest of the conclave personnel. The cardinal dean read the conclave rules, and each cardinal, his hand on the gospel, swore an oath of absolute secrecy forever as to everything that would take place in the conclave once it was isolated from the world. The cardinals were next joined by a huge congregation of glittering guests—heads of state, diplomats, princes of the Church, political lobbyists. Watched by the merciless eyes of television cameras, the entire assembly listened to a largely ignored but deeply moving exhortation given by the Nobel Laureate, Cardinal

William Ngordo, who urged love and unity within the college and greater sympathy for the less fortunate masses of the Third World.

After sundown, and when the Sacristan had intoned *Veni Creator Spiritus*—Come, Creator Spirit, and the *Oremus*—Let us pray, the master of ceremonies finally cried out, *Extra Omnes*—Everyone must leave.

The guests then departed, leaving the entire conclave area to the cardinals and essential personnel, the conclavists. All exits and entrances to the galleries and rooms around the Sistine were at once bricked up or firmly barred. Security guards checked everywhere for cameras, bugging devices, forbidden tape and video recorders, and for cell phones. Messages from the outside of true personal, national, or international emergency would be passed through a rota, or small revolving port in a door to the outside, guarded day and night by security officers.

Total seclusion had begun. It would not end until the election of a new pope was announced by a plume of white smoke, the famed *sfumata*, rising from the roof of the Sistine Chapel. This was caused by chemicals added to the ballots being burned in an ancient iron stove that had seen more than a score of conclaves, while black smoke during the days before had indicated no election.

Three sets of papal vestments had also been prepared by the Vatican tailor, depending on the size of whomever would be elected pontiff. Awaiting him, too, was the historic lambswool *pallia*, an ancient shawl with which the new pope would be adorned as soon as he was elected, as so many of his predecessors had been over centuries past. Wearing it, and in papal white, he would appear through a door to the balcony of the Basilica's façade. Preceding him, the conclave carmelengo would joyfully announce to the waiting crowd and world beyond, *Habemus Papem*—We have a pope. The newly elected Vicar of Christ would raise his hand to make the sign of the cross and intone the historic blessing of *Urbi et Orbi*, the Blessing of the City and the World, and a new era would then begin in the history of the Holy Roman Church.

During all this, however, the minds of most—especially Cardinal Mancini's—were not on ceremonial matters. God's divine will would determine the ultimate choice of pope, but meanwhile, and as an instrument of that will, it was up to each and every cardinal of the one hundred and twenty eligible to vote to consider how he should execute it. Responsibility for what lay ahead was felt by many as a heavy burden.

On the eve of first voting, lobbying among the various political factions of the college intensified. After dinner at a plain wooden table in one of the galleries, the College retired, each to his designated cell. Under Rule Fourteen governing conclave behavior and procedure, as laid down by Gregory X and established by a Council of the Church in 1274, "No one of the sacred electors shall speak to, make promise to, or entreat in any sort any one of the other cardinals with a view of inducing such cardinal to incline to their own wishes in the matter of the election, under pain of excommunication." The rule confirmed by Innocent VI in 1353 and by Julius II in 1505 had been consistently ignored ever since, and not one single cardinal had been excommunicated for breaching it.

Hence, as evening fell, the cardinals discreetly visited one another, or gathered in murmuring knots to espouse the various causes they believed vital to the election of a new pope.

Mancini headed the ultra-reactionary Traditionalist party. United with the entrenched bureaucracy of the curia, it arrogantly promulgated the Church's current position and willfully chose to ignore how dangerously the Church in America was hemorrhaging, with clergy leaving in alarming numbers and an ever-growing and silent defiance of Church doctrine among the laity by so many of those who remained Catholic by habit rather than devotion.

In slowly wresting virtual control of Vatican policy from the ailing Pope Gregory over the years, Mancini had seen himself as a contender with a relatively clear path to the papal throne, until one man had emerged to seriously threaten this dream.

This was Cardinal Heriot, who, in Mancini's opinion, had risen from total anonymity to prominence solely thanks to the beneficence of the deceased pontiff. With the bitter taste of irony in his heart, Mancini also knew Heriot to be the "madman" he had confessed so many years before on that bitterly cold December morning, the tortured expression on the confessor's face seared in his memory.

In most conclaves over the past two hundred years, the widely diverse political factions in the College of Cardinals had been able to unite to produce a compromise in theological attitude toward the forthcoming papacy before the actual voting began. This was to avoid the kind of voting deadlock which in 1670 had kept the college bricked up during four frigid winter months in candlelit, vermin-infested, and smoke-filled cells until released by the final election of Clement X. Heriot's presence threatened to throw the conclave into just such a stalemate. The American's steadfast Centrist adherence, with occasional evidence of a broader liberality, had attracted a considerable number of cardinals in the Third World, as well as in America, who refused to compromise. Their bloc of votes was not as large as Mancini's, but it was large enough to prevent Mancini and his Traditionalists from a readily attained eighty-one votes out of the one hundred and twenty that represented the two-thirds majority plus one that was required to win.

Equally stubborn were those forming a small bloc of independents unwilling to take a stand at present for any candidate for fear of being identified in retrospect with a loser, and who, in conclave, would probably cast votes for Berssi or some other until they saw who was going to be the winner and switch to him.

For although the voting was strictly secret, it became quite obvious at the end of each day from facial expressions, from avoidance of eye contact or even conversation, as well as from gossip and from the known attitudes of those gathered in little whispering groups here and there, just how most of the cardinals were voting.

Try as he could, the Secretary of State had not been able to produce even a drift toward compromise, and the Traditionalists and their allies were faced with the uncertainty that a stalemate could produce.

There was an even greater danger than stalemate, however. Oddly, it was an event that could, at the same time, break one. This was the extraordinary anti–Vatican movement started more than six months before in America by the maverick priest Father John Zacharias. His disruptive influence had spread like wildfire among discontented Catholics, both clergy and laity.

With some even calling him a "Second Coming," the priest, along with his woman companion, had opened a Pandora's box of demands for reform that would change the most basic structure of the Church. They would eliminate the infallibility of the papacy, reduce the holy office to the equivalent of the American presidency and the College of Cardinals to mere ceremonial figures, while elevating the bishops to an electorate in the form of a powerful voting parliament or congress.

Heriot had occasionally, through his writings as well as in public statements, indicated attitudes that were uncomfortably close to some held by Zacharias. For this, Mancini considered him equally dangerous.

He could trash the American priest, Zacharias, night and day, Mancini thought, for what the man was—a heretic consorting with a fallen woman. The reality was that the bloc of Third World cardinals along with what he suspected were a dangerous number of independents, didn't care about the man's character. They cared about the reforms he espoused. The possibility that his despised rival could come to think likewise didn't bear dwelling on. Heriot's character, considered by most as beyond reproach, would not be tainted by any endorsement of Zacharias's reform because of the heretic himself, and such an endorsement would more than likely win a critical commitment to him of the American bloc as well as that of the Third World. This, in turn, would almost certainly cause an equal commitment from the swing vote of independents. An irreversible rout to Heriot could follow.

Inexplicably, however, the American cardinal had so far not spoken out. In fact, at no time, even long before Pope Gregory's death, and in spite of all the rumors, had Heriot professed agreement with the maverick American priest, nor shown any interest in the papacy for himself whatsoever.

As though to emphasize withdrawal, he had spent much of the morning before the final closing ceremonies disassociating himself from his fellow cardinals to wander alone in the Vatican gardens, shut off from the world by high walls. Then, almost the moment *Extra Omnes* was pronounced, and the conclave area sealed off, he had closeted himself in his cell.

Indicating he did not wish to be disturbed, Heriot placed the traditional crossed rods before the cell's door, which was draped with violet, showing that he was made cardinal by Pope Gregory rather than by a predecessor, whence the draperies would have been green. He answered no calls and clearly had no intention whatsoever of declaring himself or joining the politicking that would be going on for most of the evening until the junior master of ceremonies rang his warning bell and called out, *In cellam, Domini*—To your cells, my lords.

Was Heriot going to remain just a threat, or become a threat realized? Mancini could only guess.

CHAPTER
❖9❖

When lots were drawn, Ignatius won a cell in a small antechamber adjoining the Stanza del Incendio, the Room of Fire, a great hall devoted to works by the Renaissance artist Raphael. He had immediately surrendered it, however, to Hungary's elderly Stepan Cardinal Stojadinovic, infirm from a recent prostate operation, only then to discover that the Pontifical Commission had somehow miscounted by one the number of cells necessary to house all one hundred and thirty seven of the cardinals able to come to Rome.

It being too late to bring in another prefabricated cell, Ignatius had been given a little room, long abandoned, in an attic high under the very roof of the Apostolic Palace and nestled between the ancient Borgia Tower, built five hundred years previous, and some administrative offices that had spilled upward from the Secretariat, a floor below the papal apartments.

The room was reached by the steepest of narrow wooden stairs, the door to which was so rarely opened that it had taken an embarrassed security chief some time to locate a key. Even the hedonistic chamberlain, Monsignor Pasternelli, escorting Ignatius to it, had felt obliged to apologize grudgingly.

"My most profound regrets, my lord," he had gasped with a touch of facetiousness in his heavy, wine-scented English. Cassock hiked to his massive white thighs, he'd labored his sweating bulk upward behind the towering Swiss Guard who led the way. "We will have to give some-one in the Pontifical Commission a lesson in counting."

But Ignatius liked the seclusion, the peaceful refuge from the halls and corridors below. He liked the history in the room, its closely spaced ceiling beams blackened with the centuries that had passed, the worn whitewash of its stone walls, flaked away here and there to reveal faded remnants of some long-forgotten and covered-over fresco.

The required conclave furnishings followed quickly: the plain wooden desk, the *prie-dieu*, a spindle-backed chair, a small dresser, an iron bedstead. Ignatius immedi-ately unpacked his few things and placed candlesticks on the *prie-dieu* to flank the little silver crucifixion statue he'd been given by his aged mentor at seminary when he was ordained. While he did, the young Franciscan friar assigned as his valet made up the bed, wondering at this self-effacing cardinal whose appearance seemed as spartan as the room, and who had come with neither secretary nor valet of his own.

When the friar had finished, Ignatius dismissed him, more than conscious of the difficulties he was causing the secretary of state, as well as the confusion about himself among his friends. He sat at the desk and placed on it, besides his breviary, a small, red-leather bound diary, one of the last in a line of them on a bookshelf in his study at home. In them, he had dutifully entered events of nearly every day, along with his thoughts since he had entered the priesthood.

The only other object on the desk was a silver-framed faded photograph of two young farm boys. They stood by a big tractor in the yard of a Wisconsin dairy farm. A look of sadness came into Ignatius's eyes when they rested on this photo. One of the boys was himself, the other his older brother Seth. Last night, after an especially bad dream and unable to return to sleep, his thoughts had strayed far from the Vatican and the conclave to his brother's death so long ago. He thought of that awful sun-drenched spring Sunday when he and Seth, ten and twelve, miserably hot from relieving their sick father of his farm chores, had stolen off with their air rifle, looking to shoot crows. Wandering through pastures filled with their father's Holstein dairy cows and then neighboring fields, he'd gotten the idea to swim in the usually sluggish muddy river that ran not far off.

"We're not allowed in the river this time of year, Ignatius. You know that."

Nagging and cajoling until a far wiser Seth relented, they went to find the river swollen into a rage from the spring rains.

"Forget it, Ignatius."

"There's no current right here by the bank."

"Ignatius, no."

Ignoring Seth, he raced out of his clothes, held onto a low branch, and dropped into the muddy water. Splashing, laughing, taunting. "Scaredy cat! Come on in."

He remembered the monstrous force of a half-submerged tree trunk battering into his body, pushing him away into the swirling current. And Seth suddenly there beside him, fighting the current, finally making the bank, heaving him up onto it, only to fall back exhausted into the river himself. And a last sight of Seth, his head above the swirling waters. Then nothing but angry river.

Nightmares had begun soon after that; Seth drowning over and over. Ceaseless, unrelenting. He had sought relief through psychiatry, which had helped only in reducing the frequency of the dreams, not their guilt-laden misery or their recurrence. But later, after he was ordained, his dreams of Seth were replaced by jumbled and confused scenes, strange surroundings of centuries past he recognized from history books he'd studied. Soon places and people became more and more clear until they were virtual reality, with himself participating by committing some terrible betrayal. And always that dark, echoing voice from somewhere condemning him to hell forever and the nagging guilt that followed during all his waking hours.

The psychiatrist had said these new nightmares were due to guilt he continued to feel about Seth, and perhaps even to guilt he'd felt about something else, although what that something else might be didn't know. Just that it was there—always—and lurking in him by day like some loathsome and cornered animal he could never identify, then reappearing in the torment of his nights.

When conferring on him his cardinalate, Pope Gregory had asked about his family, and he had spoken briefly of his mother's and father's struggle to hold onto their dairy farm after Seth was gone, which, due to his father's illness and the competition of giant agribusiness, slowly went under; the painful auction while he was in high school of all the livestock and equipment and their household furniture; the money from it soon gone on medical expenses; the move to the cramped apartment on the city's outskirts where there was never the smell of fresh-cut hay, or silage, or the lowing of dairy cattle, or the gentle sound of wind whispering through the wheat field and the branches of tall poplars that separated field from meadow; his proud father becoming a factory worker, a broken man, and the closed coffin at his funeral to hide the ghastly self-inflicted shotgun head wound; his mother, robbed of all spirit, becoming a pale and silent shadow of her former robust self, following his father to the grave only a month later.

"Were there brothers or sisters?"

"Just an older brother, Holiness. He died quite young."

He hadn't offered details, and the pope had gone on to ask about his life afterwards. Quickly, because he never liked talking about himself, especially about anything that was past, he'd run through his high school years when he'd captained the lacrosse team, then college when he had worked two jobs in order to pay the tuition. He spoke briefly of his dream of becoming a doctor, which had suddenly evaporated one day while attending medical school, to be replaced by an urgent and impulsive decision to devote himself to the Church as a priest, and finally his duties in his first parish.

He had described trucking to the strawberry fields two hours away in overcrowded, dangerously dilapidated trucks, the lines of workers picking from dawn to darkness; men, women, and young children, some of the women often heavily pregnant, or with an infant at breast while they worked; the backs of all endlessly bent to the blazing Southern sun; the cane cutting in the insect- and snake-infested cane fields farther south, the brutal bondage to the "coyote" who had got them across the border to "freedom;" the rat-infested, tin-shack quarters on the edge of a swamp; the less-than-minimum-wage pay; the lack of any medical help for even the little ones.

He had said very few words about his own life there in the back room of the tiny wooden parish church. It was a room so like the attic room he was in now that it almost seemed to Ignatius that his life had come full circle. He had skipped over the ten long years when, after each day spent in the fields aiding and consoling his parishioners, he sat by a kerosene lantern at night, immersing himself in library books on the long history of the Church and filling endless pages of yellow foolscap with his small script. Until one miraculous day when there was a letter from a publisher in response to a manuscript, wrapped in brown paper, that he had dared to send. When he achieved success with a second book, he received an order from his archbishop to leave the parish and come to assist him at the diocese.

After that, his rise in the Church was rapid. And perhaps in spite of himself, for it had only been at the endless urging of his archbishop that he consented to accept the honor of being a bishop, while the exalted position of archbishop had come only when his superior had unexpectedly died and there was an urgent need to fill his place with one who was familiar with the many problems the diocese faced.

Then finally cardinal, a sacred office bestowed on him by Pope Gregory that he never would have accepted, with all the sin and guilt he felt burdened with, if it had not been impossible to refuse such a gift from a man he so dearly revered. Throughout, he had never abandoned his old parishioners and had tirelessly used his influence and his voice toward seeing their lot improved. "A delegation came to me just the other day, Holiness," he'd explained. "A young woman was violated by the plantation foreman, and when her father dared to enter a complaint with the police, she was put in jail and threatened with deportation for making trouble. Can you imagine such a thing? Punishing the victim!"

Pope Gregory had smiled his gentle smile. "And you, of course, went to her aid."

"It was bitter, Holiness. So unjust. I took a lawyer with me, my own, and thanks be to God, we managed to rectify the wrong done to the poor girl."

He spared the pope the ugly scene when he had left the court with the girl. A deputy sheriff who was related to the rapist and bolstered by a crowd of leering men and women who shouted "two-bit whore" and "dirty greaser" and "fucking spic," had so threatened her with a gun that he had been obliged to stand in front of her, shielding her from their spit, until his lawyer could get her into the car and drive away.

The distant sound of a bell from one of the chapels in the Vatican gardens took Ignatius out of his reverie. Through the one little window of the attic he saw that the stars had appeared, and the huge dome of St. Peter's loomed over him, a vast dark silhouette. In the name of conclave secrecy, which was absolute, no window of any kind was allowed the cardinals, but Mancini, at dinner the night before with a dozen other prelates, had raised his glass in an ironic toast and said, "Apologies for the cell, your Excellency, but we will make the only amends possible. We promise not to brick it up."

In the ensuing laughter, Ignatius had refrained from pointing out that since the Borgia and Sentinella courtyards, as well as every other adjoining courtyard of Papilla, were sealed off for egress and access around the Sistine Chapel for the duration of the conclave, it made no difference whether he could look out the window or not. And it hardly merited thinking about signaling the results of the conclave voting to some imagined coconspirator on the roof of the great Basilica among the giant statues of the apostles there or up in the lantern above St. Peter's massive dome, which towered to his right.

He sat on the window sill and thought again of Pope Gregory, lying far removed from the lobbying cardinals and finally at peace.

He thought of him as Antonio Petrucci, born to the poorest of families. He thought of the mortal man, now sealed away in his tomb and soon to be forgotten; the saintliness of the man who, through the vagaries of Vatican politics, had reluctantly found himself seated on a papal throne he had never coveted. He thought of the man's loneliness at death, surrounded by anger and greed and corruption. His only companions in his last few moments had been his faithful secretary and his valet, two men as humble and undemanding as himself.

Ignatius left the window to the night outside, to the faraway stars, to the drifting scent of flowers from the gardens, and to the distant sound of a radio from someplace beyond the conclave. Kneeling at the *prie-dieu*, he prayed for Pope Gregory's soul. Profoundly touched by the death of one to whom he had felt closer than to his own father, something had happened within Ignatius; something in him had changed. Although he didn't know what it was, he instinctively felt that nothing in his own life would ever be the same again. It was as though the pope had left him a legacy, part of his own soul. What that legacy was, only time would tell.

CHAPTER

10

At the diocese. XXIX November. Anno Domine MMIX.
In nomine Patris et Filii et Spiritus Sancti: *Amen.*

    This day I returned home from Washington and being honored with the Medal of Freedom to a delightful celebration prepared by my staff. Their gift to me was infinitely more precious than the medal. By the miracle of modern technology, they had brought Pope Gregory into the room on a giant screen. His Holiness congratulated me, and he and I were able to converse a few minutes before he was ordered not to overdo it by his ever-faithful secretary, Father Jean-Henri Tissot.

    The gift was such a miraculous moment of grace that it wasn't until after it was over and some time had passed that I was revisited by all the pain of last night's dream, which I have had many times before.

Six months before the death of Pope Gregory XVIII and the ensuing conclave, Ignatius sat back from writing in his leather-bound diary. Avoiding what he had to do, he stared out the window of the book-lined study of his monastic two-room apartment at the far end of the chancery where, other than a wall of books, his study held only a small couch, two easy chairs, an old oak desk, and an even older cuckoo clock—the latter two items were both his father's, salvaged from the sad auction of the farm. In the equally bare bedroom, there was only a narrow bedstead, a *prie-dieu* with candlesticks, and a plain pine dresser, on which stood a small framed photo of his parents. A wooden crucifix from early medieval times, which he'd found in a ruined abbey in Spain, hung on the wall above the bed.

From his desk, Ignatius could see the lawn beyond, its frosted surface glinting moonlight and broken here and there with the bare trees and ornamental bushes of winter. Farther still, there were the dark outlines of the old brick cathedral on the outskirts of the southern capital. He had inherited it nearly in ruins from his predecessor and, with infinite patience, had brought it back to life. Near it and barely visible were two smaller brick buildings, once slave quarters. One was a garage and workshop. The other housed the cadre of nuns, the Little Sisters of St. Agnes of Tours, sixteen in all, who were responsible for the medical, social welfare, and financial assistance offices of the archdiocese, as well as for much of the clerical work involved in its operations.

The haunting call of an owl jarred him back to reality. Pulling himself together, he hurriedly drew the curtains, shutting out the night, and forced himself to remember. Careful notes would help him locate the dream's basis on his next visit to the Library of Congress in Washington.

It had begun this way: He'd found himself in fifteenth-century Venice, at the time, the most powerful mercantile force in the Mediterranean. He was a wealthy merchant in his middle years, related by the marriage of his sister to the Prince D'Enzzino, the head of one of Venice's great families and a member of the Council of Ten that policed the exclusive patrician class, by whom the ruling doge was elected. He was at first a lone figure, hurrying across the vast and silent Piazza San Marco late on a summer night. Distant lightning flashes warned of an impending storm. Not a breath of wind relieved the rank and heavy air of the city's many small campos, or squares, or ruffled the dark surfaces of its myriad canals.

Passing the towering campanile as its giant clock struck the hour, he pulled his cloak tight around him and averted his eyes from the three priests there. Exposed to every element, they hung from the campanile in small iron cages, their naked bodies covered with excrement and filth thrown at them during the day by jeering passersby. They would stay that way, barely kept alive on occasional magotted meat, until merciful death finally took them. One, in terrible agony from the cramped confines of his prison in which he could neither stand nor lie, moaned incessantly; another, gone mad after two long months, screamed obscenities into the night. Venice was at odds with the pope and, as a deliberate affront to the pontiff, Prince Antonio Sicarnotti, who headed the dreaded secret police, had charged all three, although innocent, with being in the employ of the Inquisition. Summary Venetian justice had followed swiftly.

His mission lay across the city in the wealthy Rialto district and at the palace of that same dreaded prince. Although twice he heard the faint splash of gondola poles telling of water thieves as he crossed narrow canals, his passage over the damp paving blocks of twisted streets and alleys was interrupted only once by the dreaded night watch, an officer and four armed men. Shown his imposing credentials, they quickly retreated into the night mist with the dancing lights of their lanterns and the fading rattle of their swords and pikes.

There was a moment when he hesitated in the darkness outside the prince's small but handsome palace. An icy terror suddenly seized him, and a voice within him shouted, "Flee now, while you can."

He had written to the prince to arrange a meeting. But he knew it was too late now to flee. He was a prisoner of his own life, betrayal his only chance.

———— • ————

Ignatius, remembering, wrote slowly. In the dream, he had been admitted by a small side door. A footman had led him through richly carpeted corridors, then up the marble stairs of a great hall, lit by a score of candelabra.

He found himself in a study where tapestries warmed the walls, where dark-polished beams separated a flowery pattern of ceiling imagery. The study door closed behind him like the door of a prison cell, and with it fled a last hope of flight.

Beyond an ivory-inlaid writing table, the figure of a tall, dark-haired man in a scarlet robe was framed by heavy damask curtains, drawn to each side of the window from which he surveyed the night.

He waited. The figure turned and came into the flickering candlelight to reveal a face of unusual handsomeness: clear, deep-set eyes were dominated by prominent cheekbones; a wide, sensuous mouth was set in a broad, firm jaw. At the muscular throat, the scarlet robe was fastened with a brooch of diamonds in which, set in sapphires, were the initials *A.S.*

"Ah. Signor Vincenti." A warm welcoming smile. "Or, remembering your English heritage, should I greet you as Mr. Vincent? Please…" The security chief waved at an ornately gilded chair and from a drawer of his writing table took a folded sheet of paper embossed with a gold coat of arms. "You have come to explain this?"

He assented. Sicarnotti scanned the letter briefly before reading it aloud in a voice that was comfortingly reassuring.

Excellency, I have information of vital importance concerning an attempt to be made to seize the reins of government of the Republic. To avoid the risk of written words falling into wrong hands, I beg the favor of an interview.

His elbows on the table, his jeweled fingers interlaced, Sicarnotti smiled again, then looked concerned. "You came by way of the Piazza San Marco?"

"Yes."

"And had thus to endure those priests—a man of your sensitivity. I am indeed sorry. They tell me one screams all night." A shrug. "In a week's time, the three of them, poor fellows, are to be put all together in the same cage. So they may have the benefit of each other's company, you understand. And, with our nights soon growing cold, offer each other warmth. Considering that all three lied to us, one with words, two by their silence when questioned, you can see that we remain merciful." He paused and added, "When will the attempt take place?"

The deep-set eyes held his, looking for a reaction to the clear warning.

Now, noting in his diary that awful moment in the dream, Ignatius paused to remember how he had tried desperately to conceal his mounting terror; how, in the dream, his thoughts had briefly turned to a vial of deadly poison hidden in a chest at home. In minutes, he could have escaped this.

He had said, "The attempt will be made in several days' time."

In the candlelight, Sicarnotti folded the fatal letter and put it back in the drawer of his writing table. "Pray continue, Signor Vincenti."

He explained the plot. A naval force under Admiral Riccardo would first seize the arsenal, then arrest the entire Council of Ten, including Prince Sicarnotti himself. One member of the council would treacherously countermand any orders given the police.

A candle hissed faintly as wax swam in around the wick.

"The name of the plot's leader?"

In his ears, the relentless sound of his own heartbeat, in his mouth was sand. A vision swam behind his eyes— the warm and loving face of his sister, the laughter of her children, the happiness of her household. He thought of the long and intimate friendship between himself and Prince D'Enzzino, and of his own forthcoming marriage contract with the daughter of one of Venice's great families; of the talk everywhere that he himself would soon be elected to the Council of Ten.

He forced himself to speak. "Prince D'Enzzino."

The jewelled fingers laced together again as though in prayer. The security chief's voice was soft and matter of fact. "A friendly British Man of War visits us. Its captain, James Vincent, dies of the fever, leaving a Venetian woman's two children by him to grow up in our midst. One, a girl, becomes Prince D'Enzzino's honored wife. The other, using all the connections and privileges of such an illustrious name, as well as his father's good name in England, amasses wealth from foreign trade that is envied by all. Then he turns informer and betrays." Sicarnotti's brow knitted in puzzlement. "Why?"

"I am a Venetian citizen, Excellency."

"Ah." With a sudden touch of irony, "You seek to protect our sacred Republic."

"Its democratic principles are more important than any family ties."

"Its freedom, too?"

"Its freedom above all."

An almost conspiratorial smile. And then: "Of course. A freedom you might well lose as a relative and close friend of Prince D'Enzzino. For if, as rumored, D'Enzzino were to meet his downfall, you would risk being identified with the error of his ways before you had the chance to ensure against such injustice by bringing him down yourself."

He could no longer speak. The man had read his mind, had appraised his relentless anxiety over the debts that D'Enzzino had incurred, debts so enormous that perhaps the only way for D'Enzzino to save himself from disgrace and prison would be through a coup d'etat, with himself surely implicated by his close family ties. For weeks, his nights had been sleepless.

Sicarnotti unlaced his fingers and tapped their tips together meditatively. "I need evidence of what you say, of course, Signor. But before you give it to me, I expect you will want to express some wish, perhaps some guarantee against being identified with the Prince?"

He remained silent. Sicarnotti smiled, as if knowing. "Allow me to suggest one, Signor. Allow me to suggest that your knowledge of English commerce and your personal contacts in that country could be useful to friends of mine and provide such a guarantee."

A final door had closed. Without responding to Sicarnotti, he extracted from his silken doublet the forged and coded letter from D'Enzzino to Admiral Riccardo, the latter the unwitting but necessary pawn in this scheme. He had spent long hours to make it appear authentic and had been especially meticulous with D'Enzzino's signature.

He placed it on the ivory-inlaid writing table. "You will know how to unravel it, Excellency, I am sure."

Watching Sicarnotti, he saw the man's eyes darken for an instant. There was a cage waiting at the campanile if he guessed it a forgery.

But privileged access to important names in English commerce meant more to the Prince than the occasional upward glance of pleasure when he crossed the Piazza San Marco. Within an hour, Prince D'Enzzino was arrested and removed from his palace in chains. Before dawn, the accused member of the Council of Ten was also arrested, as was a bewildered Admiral Riccardo.

Punishment was swift. At noon, the Prince was taken to a public scaffold on the Piazza San Marco. There, before the eyes of his wife and children, and as the campanile bells tolled a slow, funereal beat, he was first stripped naked and emasculated, then dismembered limb by limb, his bleeding stopped by fiery pitch, and his still-living torso and head hoisted up to swing amongst the priests in their cages.

Vainly protesting their innocence and begging for mercy, Admiral Riccardo and the accused member of the Council were next. Chained to posts, their entrails were drawn out of them and rolled onto a drum, but slowly so as to keep them alive as long as possible. When merciful death finally stilled their screams, their eviscerated remains were hoisted on either side of D'Enzzino, and their offal fed to waiting street dogs.

———•———

Writing slowly, every word an agony, Ignatius summarized the dream in a few paragraphs and then wrote:

> *Every time I endure this dream, it ends the same way. The Prince's palace is confiscated, my sister and her children are turned out onto the street penniless, and every male member of their household is sent to the galleys.*
>
> *I am taken back to the Palace of Sicarnotti and there obliged to write letters of introduction to all my English contacts and to explain my business strategies and my records. When Sicarnotti is satisfied he can carry on my business with but my written hand, I am taken down to his dungeons, where my lips are cut away and my tongue torn out so I can never inform again.*

He looked back over what he had written. Last year he had done some intensive studies on the ancient city and had written a magazine article on the breech between Venice and the pope during the Renaissance. The dream had perhaps occurred in Venice because of that. Or its source could also be in something he might have once read when studying or researching Italian history, and he decided that as soon as feasible he would visit some major library, preferably the Library of Congress in Washington, and look, as he so often had with other dreams, for the specific source of this one.

The setting of the dream, however, could not explain the terrifying role he played in it. The absolute realism of every moment that was still with him. Exhausted with his remembering and reliving it, he wrote a last diary entry in Latin:

Domine, Deus salutis meae; in die clamavi, et nocte coram te. Intret in conspectu tuo oratio mea: inclina aurem tuam ad precem meam. Quia repleta est malis anima mea et vita mea inferno appropinquavit—*O, Lord, God of my salvation! I have cried day and night before Thee. O let my prayer enter into Thy presence,: incline Thy ear unto my calling. For my soul is full of trouble, and my life draweth nigh to the grave!*

When he prepared for bed, it was with less an understanding of the causes of his dreams than he'd ever had.

CHAPTER

11

At the Vatican, more than three months after Ignatius suffered his Venetian dream and on a snowy February morning, Cardinal Mancini, followed by Father Julio Benetto carrying his Moroccan leather dispatch case, mounted the broad papal stairway of the Apostolic Palace and, crossing the Clementine Hall, reached the papal apartments.

In the dispatch case was a report by his bishop on the American priest, Father Zacharias. There was also one from Ignatius. Mancini had no intention of showing the latter to the pope. He judged it indicative of the serious problem Zacharias had clearly become. He also wondered if the American cardinal was being deliberately evasive because of harboring a certain degree of empathy to what the priest espoused.

Admitted by silent Swiss guard, the gaunt secretary of state crossed the large outer papal audience chamber with its heavy gilded furniture, tapestries, and oriental rugs. He was then ushered by the brown-robed elderly Brother Bertolino into the pontiff's personal sitting room. This was a small, more comfortably furnished place. Framed photographs of the pope's Neapolitan family and friends graced a little spinet. The pope, who loved music and occasionally played, had brought it with him from Naples where, before his election, he had been patriarch.

Although there was still time until Pope Gregory would appear, Mancini, to his chagrin, was greeted by the Apostolic Chamberlain, Monsignor Pasternelli. Several nights before, he'd invited the chamberlain to dine with him at Il Cacciatore, a wine-cellar restaurant favored among the Vatican clergy. His purpose was to persuade Pasternelli to urge the pope to give Zacharias an ultimatum: cease all public appearances at once or face interdiction, a measure just short of actual excommunication. This would forbid the American priest any of the sacraments, including last rites.

For Pasternelli's help, which would remove possible onus from such a warning coming from himself, he had offered secretariat assistance in securing a prestigious job with the Italian government for a young man the chamberlain had said was a "nephew."

Attacking a heavily ladened plate of rich, cream-sauced taglioni that separated him from a bottle of vintage Sauvignon Collio wine, Pasternelli's little eyes narrowed and he'd asked, while chewing, "Wouldn't the normal procedure simply be to order the American priest's bishop to shelve him?"

Mancini had suppressed irritation at this ignorance. He'd stared at the food that dribbled from Pasternelli's fat lips down over his chin and onto his cassock, then answered, "That was done some time ago."

———•———

Waiting in the pontiff's personal sitting room, with the barest greeting, Mancini opened his dispatch case and extracted a letter on secretariat stationery. "Your nephew," he said to Pasternelli, "should take this with him to the interview with the person to whom it's addressed."

The chamberlain, with barely a glance at it, grunted his appreciation and slipped it into his cassock.

There was a knock, and Carezza, the cardinal dean, came in—a thin, bent old man whose mouth was the narrowest of disapproving lines in the pinched white face of a virtual eunuch. One claw-like hand clutched a video cassette, the other pressed against his body a bulging folder tied with scarlet ribbon. Without a word of greeting, and with a dry, barking cough, he held up the cassette. "I received this last night from the Congregation for the Doctrine of the Faith," he said. "A recent speech by the heretic."

Mancini frowned and took the tape. Protocol dictated it should have come to him first. But labeling Zacharias *heretic* pleased him. The cardinal dean might prove more useful than he'd hoped in persuading His Holiness. Sometimes one single word, if the right one, could speak volumes.

Carezza coughed dryly again. "If I understand correctly, his latest demand calls for the sacred office of the papacy to be limited to two terms of four years each, like the American presidency. He also demands an age limit of seventy."

Pasternelli wheezed a laugh. "A regular geopolitical rotation will come next. An Asian pope one time, a South American another. Perhaps he'd even have the Church presided over one day by an Eskimo."

His was the sole laughter at his attempted humor and he didn't say more. The slight, gray-haired figure of Father Tissot had appeared in a doorway. Hands clasped before him as though in prayer, he announced simply, "His Holiness..." and then stepped back from the door, giving way to the man the Church regarded as the two hundredth and sixty-fifth successor to St. Peter, Prince of Apostles.

Dressed in a plain white cassock and skull cap, a simple gold cross hanging against his breast, Pope Gregory XVIII came into the room to receive the homage of the two cardinals and Monsignor Pasternelli. One frail hand resting on the arm of Brother Bertolino, he moved as though breathed in by the slightest whisper of air, wearing his habitual self-effacing smile beneath his parrot-like nose that nearly eclipsed his thin little face. At best always frail, he seemed today one who would disappear into dust if a person so much as moved too quickly in his presence. In a few short years, the duties of his office had worn him to a wraith-like appearance and to a soul so burdened as to be nearly crushed.

When he greeted his visitors, his soft voice was reverent with respect for their rank, as though his own meant nothing in comparison, and before anyone could stop him, he had arranged a chair for the cardinal dean, a man less infirm than himself. Pleasantries were exchanged; royalty graciously asking servants after their wellbeing.

When the pope was himself seated, Mancini wasted no time in getting to the point. He briefly summarized the continuing demands for Church reform by Father Zacharias and touched on the growing media interest in the priest. He nodded at the scarlet-ribboned folder that the cardinal dean held in his lap. "You will see in this report brought to you by the revered cardinal dean, Holy Father, that we are confronted by subversive demagoguery of the most perverted sort, that apparently is catching fire with the media. The man's audiences have more than doubled in the last three weeks. If this continues, we could face a crisis with Catholic America as serious as the Great Schism."

The phrase referred to the dark days eight hundred years earlier, when the Church had been divided, with a pope at Avignon, France, as well as one in Rome. Mancini waited. It would not do, he knew, to speak more harshly. The pope was a man whose nature rebelled against force, even when force was clearly necessary.

For what seemed an interminable time, the pontiff's troubled eyes stared out the windows of the room, overlooking St. Peter's Square, now dusted with snow. Twice, holding a linen handkerchief to his lips, he coughed wrackingly, bringing alarm to the eyes of the silently waiting Father Tissot and Brother Bertolino.

Then, the gentle voice spoke out. "Although, my Lord Cardinals, Monsignor Pasternelli, we cannot find it in our hearts to say we disagree with all the reforms Father

Zacharias proposes, we do recognize that some, and certainly his insurrectionist manner, pose a serious threat to our own authority as well as possibly that of the Church we serve."

His eyes came back to the three seated prelates. "We look to your suggestions as to how we should minimize this threat."

Mancini shot a glance at Pasternelli. The obese chamberlain cleared his throat. "Short of excommunication, Holiness, although I personally..." He was stopped by the pope's frail hand, raised in immediate protest. "Close forever the doors of the Church to him? Deny him the ultimate salvation and love of our Lord? No, no. Our Lord seeks to administer and heal, not to punish."

Pasternelli barely concealed his contempt, "Then I would suggest, Holiness, at the very least, a serious warning of interdiction."

The pope again refrained from speaking a moment. Then, carefully choosing his words, he said, "Our impression of this man so far is that he is one who is resistant to reprimand or restriction while perhaps open to sympathy and conciliation. We think that sympathy would be far more the approach of our Master."

Cardinal Carezza said nothing. Only his thin mouth showed his disapproval. If possible, it grew even thinner. Mancini glanced again at Pasternelli. He'd been expecting passivity, but not this much.

The chamberlain took his cue to continue being the hatchet man. Spreading his great thighs, a fat hand on each, Pasternelli leaned his huge bulk forward in a gesture that seemed almost a bow of deference, but which, at the same time, was calculatedly threatening. "Holy Father, we would consider it a gift if you were to elaborate on your thinking."

It didn't work. For all his frailty, Pope Gregory was still a man of courage as well as one of principles. He glanced at all three of his visitors, seeing through their conspiracy. "On our choice of the word 'sympathy'?" A smile came into the pope's tired eyes. Ignoring Pasternelli, he fixed on Mancini as the leader. "We thought that someone Father Zacharias respects might be persuaded to approach him with some reasonable compromise. Perhaps His Eminence, Cardinal Heriot. He has always seemed to me an able negotiator."

At the mention of Ignatius, Mancini felt the meeting slipping away from him. The pope was far more resistant than he had anticipated. He tried a last shot. "Does Your Holiness not fear that compromise might leave the authority of your sacred office seriously weakened?"

This final attempt at bullying also failed. "Our authority, dear Cardinal Mancini, like authority anywhere, ultimately has no bearing if not respected."

There was a discreet cough from Father Tissot. The pope was restricted by his doctors to audiences of only twenty minutes, and the secretary was exacting in seeing the doctor's orders were followed.

Mancini rose. "I will write to Cardinal Heriot, Holiness."

"Thank you, Eminence. You are very kind to think of relieving me of that task, but I will indeed write him myself and shall see you get a copy of my letter."

Mancini bit back a retort. The pope's rejection of his offer was more than a reprimand. It was a clear indication that the pope didn't trust him to write objectively.

Carezza, who until now had not uttered a word, offered the ribboned folder. His thin voice was a serpent's hiss. "The report of the heretic by the Congregation for the Doctrine of the Faith, Holy Father. I am sure you will find it most alarming."

Father Tissot took the folder. Behind his glasses, the pope's eyes shone with sudden amusement. "We will certainly study it. Perhaps this evening after we have seen our weekly movie, an Agatha Christie mystery that Father Tissot informs us is excellent."

For Mancini, this levity was almost too much to bear. He had detected more behind the pope's words than his well-known addiction to Agatha Christie. He had the distinct feeling that the pontiff was laughing at him, and it was bitter.

The pope rose. The gentle smile again, the frail hand raised, the first two fingers erect, the murmured words of a blessing and, as silently as he had entered, Gregory XVIII departed with Brother Bertolino and was followed by Father Tissot, who closed the door firmly behind them.

The fool, Mancini thought. *The blind, stupid fool.* Petrucci was as dangerous in his own way as Zacharias. Another year, if he managed to live that long, and he would wreck the Church with his passivity and ill-placed sympathy.

Hiding his humiliation, he thanked Carezza and Pasternelli. "We have made a beginning. There is no question but that His Holiness will see things our way before too long."

Carezza spoke suddenly again. "The video I brought for His Holiness."

"I plan to view it myself before giving it to him."

Mancini departed without giving Carezza a chance to object. He had no intention of letting the pope see the video. Reporting his own version of it would be far more effective than whatever the pope would garner from it himself.

Back in his own suite, he sent Benetto off to his secretarial office with an order that he was not to be disturbed by anyone. When the young priest had fled, he put the tape into his VCR. Professionally made, it began with shots of technicians in an empty football stadium readying the stage with its speakers podium and microphone; next, there were shots of the considerable crowd that slowly filled more than half the stadium's seats; then it showed John Zacharias and Francesca Berenson, accompanied by several city dignitaries, as they arrived behind the screaming sirens and flashing lights of a police escort.

Finally, intercut with shots of rapt faces in the crowd, there was the priest's speech in which he reiterated his now well-known demands for reform in a quiet voice that was powerfully persuasive in its calm and matter-of-fact tone.

Before it had finished, Mancini turned the tape off, no longer able to bear what he saw and heard. Zacharias had clearly returned to the first-century, gnostic belief that the Holy Spirit communicated directly with each individual rather than through any apostle of Christ. Thus, surely, he was damned beyond redemption.

Even worse than the priest was the woman. Her presence was beyond understanding, for she'd been a prostitute, the papal nuncio, the Vatican's ambassador to Washington, had told him; a woman to whom the divine act of procreation as planned by God had been blasphemed in a cesspool of fornication for money.

Mancini rang his desk bell to summon Benetto and order coffee. It rankled deeply that the pope had suggested he ask the American, Heriot, to intervene. Gregory must have known that on the event of his death, Heriot might well be a candidate for the office God would take from him.

Before turning to the pile of official documents on the desk that required his attention, Mancini sat a long time in silence, staring at the gray sky over Rome, a victim of his own tormenting frustrations.

CHAPTER

◈12◈

There was no movie that night. The pope felt too ill. The next morning, however, he held a personal audience for Cardinal Ngordo, of whom he was deeply fond. The Nobel Laureate was ostensibly in Rome to head a delegation to a world conference on AIDS. His actual purpose, however, was to pay a last visit to the pope, whom he sadly knew to be slowly surrendering his life to cancer.

Pope Gregory had developed the additional burden of a fever during the night, and under orders from his doctor the meeting took place in the papal bedroom.

It was eleven o'clock in the morning. The sky had cleared, and there was a bright winter sun. While Father Tissot and Brother Bertolino stood at a respectful distance, Ngordo, in black cassock along with scarlet skull cap and waistband, sat by the pope's narrow bed. One of his short, dark hands, hardened in youth from the relentless physical labor of survival, held the pontiff's, whose feverish skin was parchment white in contrast.

The African was a small, solid man whose head—with its flattened nose, broad forehead, and widely spaced eyes—seemed disproportionately large for his body. In his childhood, he had daily herded his father's skeletal cattle from dawn until well past nightfall in the arid scrub land around his father's *kraal*. Today, when he moved, it was still with a certain restless energy that had become habit in such a task. Driven by fierce determination, missionary-educated in an outdoor schoolroom, he'd come to the priesthood through a Rhodes Scholarship and first honors at Oxford. Waiting for the pope to speak, his ebony face, normally so alight with humor, was filled with anxiety for the stricken pontiff.

It seemed an interminable silence before the pope finally spoke. "This terrible scourge of AIDS is only one tragic part of the great turmoil we live in. In our brief moment in history, our Church is challenged as much as it was during the Reformation. It's been thirty years since our beloved predecessor convened Vatican II. Now we must call the bishops once more to Rome for another great synod. It is time to rethink our role and debate the future."

He closed his eyes. Ngordo, feeling the feverishness of the pale hand he held, marveled at the pope's spirit, but with a sinking heart knew that such a massive undertaking would never occur during his lifetime. By intrigue, trickery, and endless opposition, and by taking advantage of the natural predilection of a gentle character to compromise, Mancini had managed to frustrate most of the pope's wished-for reforms even when His Holiness was well. He rose. "Your Holiness, you are tired and must rest now. With your permission, I will take my leave."

The pope held fast to his hand, and Ngordo sensed a kind of desperation in him.

"No, no, dear friend. We feel the years fall away in your presence." He waited to continue as Brother Bertolino came to adjust his pillows. Then he said, "His Eminence, Cardinal Mancini, came with Monsignor Pasternelli and Cardinal Carezza yesterday to urge us into rigid disciplinary action against the American. We are speaking of that young man, Father Zacharias, who seems to be causing such concern. But..." here, the pope smiled, his eyes brightening with sudden humor, "instead, we suggested a meeting between our dear friend Cardinal Heriot and Father Zacharias to see if there was not some more moderate path of conciliation. Our esteemed secretary of state was not happy with the idea. Cardinal Mancini sees Cardinal Heriot possibly credited with a success that could lessen his own relatively clear chance to walk away as pope from the forthcoming conclave."

Ngordo opened his mouth to protest, but the pope stayed him with a raised hand. "Don't upset yourself, my friend. We will die most certainly as everyone must in this life. And soon. That is God's will. And whomever God wills to succeed us shall have the responsibility for the future of the Church, if indeed not of all Christianity."

Ngordo was caught by surprise at the pope's candidly revealing his clear aversion to Mancini. Throughout his reign, he had consistently refused to take sides with any of the prevailing political factions among the cardinals, even though, as a bishop, he had been known for leanings toward some of the radical attitudes of Pope John XXIII and Pope John Paul.

Once pope, however, he had said, "We cannot risk impairing our true service to our Lord by affiliating ourselves with one faction or another. We must always remain free of any ties that could unduly influence our ultimate and objective agreement."

"What is your reading of Ignatius Heriot?" the dying man went on to ask. "Is he, as we think, the man to follow us?"

Again surprised, Ngordo thought of Ignatius's visit two years before to Africa. Ngordo had taken him to the poor farm of his youth that his proud, elderly father refused to leave. They'd gone walking for miles together out over the thorny scrub land, and Ignatius, seemingly tireless, had helped two herdsmen round up their cattle in the evening. He had carried one injured calf into the *kraal* himself and then sat up half the night with his father by the cooking fire, drinking the bitter local beer and swapping stories about farming. None of the villagers had ever stopped speaking of him.

Ngordo had no trouble answering Pope Gregory. "He is indeed one to follow in your footsteps, Holiness."

The pope smiled. Ngordo waited until he spoke again.

"Lying here, we have been counting. Cardinal Mancini can muster sixty certain votes at present among the Traditionalists. He needs only another twenty-one for a two-thirds-plus-one majority. He can perhaps pick those votes up from the many who, convinced he might win, would want to be on the right side of him if he does. Our friend Ignatius can only at present have a certain forty among the Conservatives. Where will the forty-one more he would need for a majority come from?" His eyes fixed questioningly on Ngordo.

For a moment, the Laureate could find nothing to say. At one point, while walking with Ignatius through the scrub land, he had brought up the subject of Pope Gregory's successor. Ignatius stopped him short and burst out, almost as though the mere thought of the papacy was agony to him, "I could never be pope, William, never! Even if drafted, I should have to refuse."

He had given no reason, but the pain and intensity in his voice when he spoke precluded any further discussion on the subject. Ngordo had to think that recruiting votes for him might thus be not only a near impossibility, but in the end a waste.

Then he rallied. Impossibility was something he had never let stand in his way. Pope Gregory was right. Ignatius was indeed the man to follow in his footsteps; he was perhaps the only man who could rescue the Church from its alarming downward slide; and perhaps the only man among all of them pure enough in heart to truly honor Christ and return the Church to His image, while at the same time the only man strong enough to silence the wolf pack that the curia had become. He silently vowed that he would raise heaven and earth to see Pope Gregory's wish come true.

He couched his reply carefully, however. The Holy Father was too intelligent to accept guarantees built on sand. "Holy Father," he said, "I have already mustered ten of those new voices that Cardinal Heriot can rely on. Others I am unsure of. But please know that when you leave us I shall do everything possible to see an affirmation in the conclave of all you believe in and wish for. You may go with peace in your heart, Holy Father, and with hope."

The pope stared at the earnest ebony face before him. He thought suddenly of the undernourished little boy herding cattle home through thorny African scrub land with all its dangers. He thought of the hope, even on his long struggle upward, that Ngordo had so selflessly given to so many others; the hope that Ngordo, just now, was giving to him.

Tears came to his eyes. Struggling to sit up, he drew the African close to embrace him and kiss his dark, weathered forehead before falling back on his pillows.

"Go now, old friend," he said and smiled at his valet and secretary, "before we are both chastised by my guardian angels. I shall specify in my will that the voting should be according to the ancient procedure as decreed by my predecessor Gregory X and practiced for so many centuries since. The slowness of it will give you more time in the conclave itself."

Ngordo helped Father Bertolino and Father Tissot make the dying man comfortable, knelt to kiss his ring, then quietly departed.

Finished with his report on the latest work of the world conference, he was preparing to return home the next day when he was surprised to receive an invitation to lunch from Monsignor Pasternelli. He thought it not polite to refuse, and arriving at Il Cacciatore, where the Chamberlain had reserved a table, he found, to his acute discomfort, that Cardinal Mancini was joining them.

Once dinner was ordered and wine glasses filled, the Vatican secretary of state wasted no time in revealing why he'd come. "Regretfully, if it is the Lord's will, we will soon be faced with searching for a successor to our beloved Holy Father. There is rumor that some might put forward the name of Cardinal Heriot. How closely, Eminence, do you feel the thinking of our American colleague has come to that of the heretic?"

Ngordo hid his anger at the question. Politely declining to have his wine glass refilled by Pasternelli, who sat, a grotesque presence, in unaccustomed silence, he pretended puzzlement. "The heretic? Dear me, who is that?"

The secretary of state smiled thinly. He knew Ngordo was quite aware of whom he meant. "Zacharias," he said.

Mancini's omission of the priest's title was not lost on the African, who had no trouble seeing through the transparent attempt to damn Heriot by linking him to the maverick priest.

"Ah," he said, "I understand." Then, offering Mancini his most forthright look, he added, "Cardinal Heriot, my lord, has not to date honored me with his opinion of Father Zacharias." It was with a certain relish that he deliberately dignified the priest with his proper title.

Mancini's eyes hardened behind his rimless glasses. "Forgive my error, dear colleague. I thought perhaps that he might have said something privately to you as a friend."

Pasternelli spoke for the first time. He wiped his mouth on the back of his hand. "I, too, would have thought that your mutual interest in farming would have caused you to develop a close and confiding relationship."

The contempt in his voice for farmers wasn't lost on Ngordo. The Laureate offered him a dazzling smile. "In my country, I have among my acquaintances, dear Monsignor, several eminent members of the government who still farm. Like all farmers, their sole conversation, when together, almost invariably has to do with the current market for cattle, the cost of artificial insemination, and always about the sale price per ton of ripened manure."

Back in his private study, Mancini fumed. He was certain that Ngordo planned to back the American with critical Third World votes. Well, let the infuriating little African have his moment of triumph. At some not-too-distant time in the future, Ngordo would have to face the reality that the Church, employing diplomatic and economic influence, could persuade the wealthier nations of the world to deny relief to his impoverished, backward country. Tight lipped, Mancini slammed a hand repeatedly onto the intercom buzzer to summon Father Benetto.

The young secretary came running. "Yes, my lord?"

"I want coffee and then I don't wish to be disturbed."

"Yes, Eminence."

Watching Benetto hurry off, Mancini reflected that Benetto was one born to be dominated.

In what seemed an instant, the young priest was back with a silver tray on which he'd arranged a coffee cup, a matching silver sugar bowl and cream pitcher, and an envelope bearing the papal seal.

He placed the tray on the smooth leather surface of Mancini's ornate desk, stirred in sugar and cream and backed away, eyes lowered. "Was there anything else, Eminence?"

Ignoring him, Mancini ripped open the envelope, but seeing him still standing there, sent him packing with an icy wave before extracting the single sheet of papal stationery inside.

It was a copy of Pope Gregory's hand-written personal request to Ignatius to meet with John Zacharias.

CHAPTER

13

Rome, three months later and enjoying the warmth of May, saw a marked increase in tourists. It was due in part to universal interest and excitement engendered by the papal conclave which, with Pope Gregory dead for two weeks, could now take place.

The first day of it opened, as it had for the previous eight hundred years, with all the ritual, pomp, and ceremony of the conclave itself and accompanied by intense public and media speculation as to who would be elected the new spiritual leader of nearly 20 percent of the world's population.

Each dressed in rochet, cape, waistband, and croccia, a long, plain mantle of serge tied close around the neck, and each wearing their scarlet cardinal's biretta, the one hundred and twenty cardinals eligible to vote assembled and marched solemnly into the Pauline Chapel. There, mass was celebrated by the arch-Traditionalist Cardinal Carezza, and each received communion.

The service over, the cardinals breakfasted, then, with their conclavists following, proceeded to the Sistine Chapel. At the door, each was given by his secretary or valet a closed box that contained the registers, or tally sheets, for the day's voting. On these, each cardinal would keep an accurate count of the votes. In the box were also printed voting ballots, or schedules, and for each cardinal his individual seal. When all were finally inside the chapel, the doors were locked firmly from the outside, and the last cardinal to enter placed a ceremonial chain across the inside of the door as well.

For the voting procedure, the papal throne directly under Michelangelo's *The Last Judgment* had been replaced by an altar. Two rows of small thrones were arranged around the walls of the entire presbyter half of the chapel, that half being separated from the other half by a high, ornate marble balustrade.

The rows began with the first thrones placed at the gospel, or left side of the altar when facing it, and ended at the epistle, or right side of the altar. Each throne was equipped with a small writing table. These, like the doors of the cardinals' cells, were draped in purple or green, depending on which pope was the particular cardinal's sponsor. Each supported, also, a token canopy of similar color which was to be brought down with a pull cord by the throne's occupant the instant the new pope was elected.

Carezza sat in the first gospel-side throne, and, starting from him, the cardinals took consecutive seats around the chapel in a descending order of their seniority until the most junior among them sat directly at the altar's epistle side.

At the express wish of Gregory XVIII in his will, the manner of voting would strictly follow the procedure established by Gregory X in 1274 at the Council of Lyons, reestablished in a papal bull in 1621 by Gregory XV, and respected for hundreds of years in one conclave after another. It was interminably slow and obviated any modern voting procedures, but Mancini, for all his power as conclave carmelengo, did not dare refute the wish for fear of alienating many cardinals who held the deceased in great affection.

A table covered with red serge stood before the altar, on which were six candles and a crucifix. There, the votes were to be registered and counted. Wooden balls, each inscribed with the name of an attending cardinal, had been lottery drawn from a purple bag by the junior cardinal deacon to determine the three who would act as registrars or scrutators. They would also determine the three cardinals who would take ballots to the cells of any who might become ill and unable to come to the chapel.

Also on the table were two large golden urns on which rested shallow patens, or dish-like covers. These were to be placed on the altar when the votes were scrutinized and counted.

Finally, behind the altar itself was the ancient iron stove with its long chimney pipe that snaked up out through the roof of the Sistine, and from which the black or white smoke of sfumata would issue to announce the result of that day's voting.

By conclave rule, there was one round of voting in the morning and one in the afternoon. Each round consisted of two ballot castings, the scrutiny and the accessit. The printed ballots themselves were divided horizontally into five sections. On the top section, each cardinal would write his name and surname. In the scrutiny, on the third section down, he would write after the printed words *Eligo in Summum Pontificem Rm. Dominum D.*—I Elect to the Supreme Pontificate the Most Reverend Lord, my Lord Cardinal—the name and surname of the cardinal he wanted to see as pope. A vote for oneself voided the ballot.

On the fifth section, the bottom one, he would write his motto and place his seal. The second and fourth sections were left blank.

Under Mancini's direction, Monsignor Spada, the senior master of ceremonies, read a traditional statement declaring the conclave in session and the bishop sacristan intoned the *Veni Creator Spiritus* and the *Oremus*. The scrutators were selected and the voting then began at once.

When the ballots were duly marked, each cardinal, one by one and beginning with Carezza, approached the altar, bent a knee to it, and holding out his ballot, swore:

Testor Christum Dominum, qui me judicaturus est, me eligere quem secundum Deum judicio elegi debere, et quod in accessu prestabo—I attest before Christ our Lord, Who shall be my judge, that I elect him whom before God I think ought to be elected, and the same as to the vote, which I shall give at the accessit.

Each then placed his ballot on the paten, and, after tipping the ballot from it into the urn, returned to his chair. Ignatius, who had marked his ballot for William Ngordo, was among the more junior cardinals, and thus among the last to approach the altar.

All ballots submitted, the senior cardinal scrutator mixed them together by shaking the urn, and the urn was brought to the scrutators' table. There, the junior scrutator removed them from the urn and counted them. Each ballot was then unfolded by the second scrutator, so as to only reveal the name of the cardinal the voter wished to see elected, and each was passed on to the third scrutator, who read the name aloud.

Like all his fellow cardinals, Ignatius kept a record of the vote on his specially printed tally sheet. A two-thirds-plus-one majority was necessary for the election of a pope. On this first round, no one had come close to it. He himself had received thirty-four votes, Mancini thirty-six, Berssi twenty-seven, and Ngordo twenty-three.

The junior scrutator then took a needle and, piercing it precisely through the word *Eligo*—I elect—threaded all the ballots together so that none would be mistakenly mixed up with subsequent procedures. He placed the bundle of them before the altar.

There was now the immediate second casting of ballots, which were delivered and counted in exactly the same manner as the first, except that instead of *Eligo*, the printed word on the ballot was *accedo ad*—I accede to.

The voter was not allowed to repeat the name of the man he had previously voted for, as this would amount to a vote cast twice. He could only indicate that he yielded, or acceded, to one who had received votes on the first round; he also could write *Nemini*—to no one—in the place of a name, indicating that he had not changed his mind over the first round; or, finally, he could vote for someone completely new.

In this second casting, known as the accessit, the seals on the ballots were then broken after the ballots had been counted and the ballots unfolded all the way so that the name of each voter was revealed. This was to ascertain that the first and second votes were by the same person. The votes were then added up, and the total of each candidate announced.

Many stayed with their initial vote by writing *Nemini*. Some had changed their preference. No new candidate appeared, and Mancini now received fifty votes, Ignatius thirty-eight, Berssi twenty-two, and Ngordo ten.

The morning session was over. The ballots were burned. To the disappointment of the ever-growing crowd waiting expectantly in St. Peter's Square, black smoke rose above the roof of the Sistine Chapel.

Cardinal Carezza rang a bell. The cardinals all rose. The first to reach the door unchained it and rang a second bell to order the chapel doors unlocked. The cardinals filed out for lunch.

It was becoming clear that if Ignatius now finally declared himself, he would pick up Ngordo's votes and most of Berssi's, in all an additional thirty-eight. This would give him at least seventy-two, only nine short of the necessary majority, and the desertion from Mancini would begin by those who saw Mancini as a potential loser.

Once again, the corridors and cells around the Sistine buzzed with lobbying, with a desperate Ngordo trying to collar more votes for Ignatius, who once again took no part in it. He retreated to his little garret room, wrote up a page of his diary, and knelt in prayer at his *prie-dieu*. His heart was filled with the pain of knowing that all the Laureate's ceaseless efforts to raise votes for him, if successful, would have to be rejected. Worse was the additional knowledge that his silence would almost certainly give the papacy to Mancini with all the ruin that would spell for the Church.

Thinking suddenly of Pope Gregory and his struggle to the very last for reform, he felt profound disloyalty to the deceased pontiff's memory, for Mancini was diametrically opposed to everything Pope Gregory stood for. Yet, he could find within himself no possible solution to the dilemma. He could never be pope.

CHAPTER

•14•

Ave Maria, gratia plena: Dominus tecum benedicta tu in mulierbus et benedictus fructus ventis tui, Jesus, Sancta Maria, Mater Dei, ora pro nobis percatoribus nunc et in ora mortis nostrae.—Hail Mary, full of grace; the Lord is with thee; blessed art thou among women; and blessed is the fruit of thy womb, Jesus. Holy Mary, Mother of God, pray for us sinners now; and at the hour of our death.

In a chilly dawn the previous February, when Pope Gregory was still able to conduct the affairs of his office, the voices of priests and nuns reciting this ancient prayer to the Virgin Mary resonated throughout the chapel in the cathedral at the southern archdiocese.

Almost from the first day he'd taken over the reins of the then relatively obscure diocese, Ignatius made it a habit to officiate at the 4:30 A.M. matins, the first prayers of the day. He found peace in the ancient service, especially if he'd had a tormented night. And in more recent years, he knew how much his young administrative assistant, Sister Jessica, appreciated his doing so. Barely in her twenties, she had become not just an invaluable part of his clerical life, but to him personally, almost the much-loved daughter his vocation had denied him.

She came from a miner's home in a West Virginia coal town, where, with her mother chronically ill with a bad heart and her father an abusive and embittered man, she'd had the responsibility during all her adolescent years for housekeeping and raising six younger siblings.

Given such a background, Ignatius never ceased to wonder how she could always be so ebulliently cheerful and so keenly positive. No matter what the office crisis, the weather, or any personal problem, she would appear by his desk each morning, a burst of youthful sunshine that would jar him out of any fatigue or depressed thoughts about a bad night. Dressed in the simple tailored skirt and plain cotton blouse that was the new mode for many younger American nuns that still seemed too formal for her, her hazel eyes would be sparkling, a mischievous smile usually decorated her clean-scrubbed Slavic face, and her short, copper-colored hair would be tousled as always.

From tales she had told him of her childhood, as well as seeing it still in all aspects of her character, he knew that she'd been her town's most incorrigible tomboy. She had held her own, as she'd often been obliged to do, against most of the boys, as well as the town drunks, a fact often born out by her joking and slightly irreverent remarks about Sister Andrea, the little colony's Mother Superior and the Mother General, the head of the order in Rome. And if the former complained that there was restiveness among some of the younger nuns at necessary regulations in their house, it was a safe bet that Sister Jessica was one of them.

Ignatius loved her for all of it, as well as for the many moments when the grown-up, efficient young woman, along with her earnest seriousness, warmed his heart beyond measure. She brought the best of irrepressible youth into his life.

At the same time, he would often wonder at the strength of faith that had led Sister Jessica to a nun's vocation. Her personal life in the spartan quarters of the nuns of her order had to be nearly as hard as the one she had escaped. She rose at three thirty every morning in the barren little room that was her cell, where there was only a bed, dresser, a desk, and a wash basin, and where the only decorations were the posters she'd bought and framed at her own expense and the photographs of her family on the desk.

Each week she allowed herself only a half day for shopping or a movie in town—"I have too many duties for more, Father," she'd say. And her devotion had to be further severely tested by Sister Andrea's strictness. The older woman's rules, as well as many of her attitudes, were more often than not completely contradictory to the relatively modern and liberal style with which most orders

in America were run. This was true, also, as to the educational level of the colony of which she was in charge, for
most of the sisters were college graduates and filled
responsible administrative positions in the archdiocese.

Sister Andrea was a large, prematurely gray woman
whose otherwise handsome appearance was slightly
marred by a mouth a little too small for her face and by a
large and distinctive mole just at the hairline of her right
temple. Barely in her forties, she seemed to enjoy strictly
enforcing any new rule from the order's highly orthodox
Mother General in Rome. The latter deeply resented the
liberality of American nuns and firmly believed in turning back the clock to a time when, for women, God was
not to be found in the world, but only out of it in clois-
tered silence.

Her latest edict was cold showers only, and every morning before matins. Sister Jessica, standing under the icy
water, trying to find courage to soap and then rinse when
only a few minutes before she'd been sound asleep, thought
herself punished in a manner far worse than the flagellation
she'd heard was still practiced by nuns of some orders.

"What am I supposed to do?" was Sister Andrea's
smiling answer to an outraged chorus from her charges,
frustrated that the order had come from Rome, leaving
them with no one to appeal to except the Mother
General herself, who invariably turned a deaf ear to any
complaint. "Surely you all understand that I can't report
an obedience to Mother General's wishes where obedience doesn't exist." And Sister Andrea's pursed mouth
would seem smaller than ever.

With that pronouncement, and leaving a numbed silence behind, she would exit whatever room in which she had so emphasized her authority, the little dining room with its four tables and sideboard, or the common room where there was a couch and chairs and a television set.

There were moments when Ignatius wondered, however, if Sister Andrea did not often welcome the enforcement of some of the old attitudes toward a nun's vocation as a way of compensating for failure to achieve the modern-life goals she had once set for herself. Often helpful to him in the early days of his administration, she was deeply disappointed, he knew, not to have been given the position of his personal assistant. He had felt, correctly, that she could not do the job justice with the additional responsibility of the group under her charge.

Sister Andrea had graciously agreed, but when Sister Jessica, just joining the order and at once enchanting him with her freshness, had been rewarded with the position instead, Ignatius thought he'd occasionally detected in the older woman's manner an undercurrent of vindictive jealousy. On two occasions, he had rescued Sister Jessica from being sent by Sister Andrea to another colony of the order under what he thought was a trumped-up need for her to embrace further the spirit of the Mother General, which the confines of her job with him made it difficult to do.

Matins over, Sister Jessica went directly back to the little brick building that housed the nuns. The sisters, in rotation, had daily duties, and this week it was her turn to wash the bathroom floor, wipe clean the mirrors over the four sinks, scrub the sinks themselves, remove soap scum from the walls of the three showers, and disinfect the toilets.

She donned a work smock that covered her skirt and blouse and got busy. There was no heat in the bathroom and the room was icy. Jessica, thoroughly used to work, did her job fast and hard, leaving the hated shower until last as though recoiling from what had caused her such stinging misery an hour earlier. Rising warm and sleepy from her bed, she had come into the bathroom, had bravely stripped off her bathrobe and pajamas, and, taking a deep breath, dove under the icy water, trying not to gasp and shriek as some of the other sisters did when it was their turn to be subjected to similar torture. When the water had been warm, it had been so lovely to stand under the hissing spray, to feel all her skin almost melt with pleasure, and trying to make the three minutes allotted to each sister to wash seem an eternity.

But sometimes, the hot shower also made her feel uncomfortable. It was hard not to be aware of the slim lines of her own naked body as she soaped herself down and then used her hands again to help the water rinse the soap away. And getting out, if she was not quick enough to wrap a towel around herself defensively, she would momentarily glimpse herself in the mirror above the sink directly opposite. Seeing her naked self, the way God had made her, her breasts and hips and pelvis, she would suffer twinges of regret that she had not been made a man, but almost at the same time would feel a certain pride in being what she was, and then a kind of sadness and upsetting doubt about her vocation because a woman was made to bring life into the world, and, although she loved kids, she never would.

Worse, sometimes there were moments when she was left with an almost desperate need for love from a man her age. She couldn't visualize it, only feel it. Sometimes at night she would find herself restlessly awake remembering boys in high school who had ardently pursued her, remembered their bodies against hers and their kisses when she had momentarily surrendered.

In those moments, her only refuge from an almost irresistible impulse to soothe a surge of forbidden sensations in her body lay in prayer. Regardless of how cold the room was, she would rise and kneel by her bedside and ask God's forgiveness for momentarily straying in her thoughts. Even then, her thoughts would often turn to mothers and their children she'd observed in the supermarket or in department stores, or in park playgrounds, and her sudden yearning to be like them would keep her at prayer and from returning to her bed until she was nearly shaking with cold.

Always, however, when awakening in the morning, she would chide herself for being so self-centered. Wasn't she the luckiest girl in the world to be able to give her whole life to God and to assist the most wonderful and kindest man imaginable, one who was far more a father to her than her own father had ever been? All the hot showers in the world, or the complete absence of all the Mother General's tedious and hated rules, or even the absence of feeling uncomfortable when fantasizing about love and motherhood, could never be greater than the really true blessings in life that she had.

Her cleaning duty over, she doffed her smock, shrugged into her coat, and hurried along the icy path that led to the chancery building, a once-great plantation mansion. Clerical offices, along with the kitchen and cafeteria, lay off the large main hall with its sweeping double staircase that led upward to the diocese library, some guest rooms, and one wing where half a dozen priests lived. Sister Jessica often imagined beautiful Southern belles in ball gowns descending those stairs to greet handsome young men.

It was only six o'clock, but already there were a few people at their desks in rooms that had once echoed with the voices of the family that had lived in them. Sister Jessica hurried to her own small office, which she suspected had once been the realm of the family seamstress, or the office of the powerful housekeeper, and where now her computer shared the surface of her neatly arranged desk with a filing tray and calendar and pictures of her mother and her siblings. There was a large pottery vase with dried flowers atop one of the filing cabinets, and she had hung three posters on the walls, one of Venice, another of Paris, and a third of Rome, to remind her of the summer vacation Father Ignatius had arranged for her the preceding year, along with a trip to the Vatican. To Sister Jessica, this room was far more *home* than her barren little cell.

Turning on lights, she had only just checked her calendar when Sister Margaret, in charge of the mail room and mail delivery every morning to each member of the staff, entered and dropped a small bundle of letters onto her desk.

"One from the Vatican today, Sister."

"Oh?"

"This one." Sister Margaret hooked a letter from the bundle, held it out, and when Jessica took it, left with a breezy, "Bye for now."

Jessica looked curiously at the letter. It was post-marked from the Vatican, but she didn't recognize the seal on the back. And it didn't seem at all like the usual official documents from the Vatican that often came, a dozen or so, in the same big envelope. It looked more like a personal letter, and she wondered who had written it.

Leaving the rest of the mail on her desk, she went with it into the adjoining office, which was Ignatius's. It was a room made to seem far smaller than its actual spaciousness by what Sister Jessica called the bane of her existence. This was the staggering amount of work in progress; the stacks of briefs, folders, and files that not only burdened Ignatius's desk and credenza, but littered half the floor space. The clutter at times seemed to eclipse the American Impressionist painting that shared one wall with a hand-carved wooden crucifix, a gift from some Bolivian Indians. On a table against another wall, papers and files threatened to smother the framed photos of the president and some prominent members of Congress, as well as world leaders, who shared space with photographs of migrant workers at his first parish.

Ignatius had come in immediately after matins and was hard at work. Sister Jessica went to stand by his desk.

"Father?" And when he looked up, "Someone has written you from the Vatican." She held out the letter.

Ignatius took it, surprised at the seal. Carefully opening the envelope, he extracted one thin sheet of note paper, on which were hand written only a few lines. Sister Jessica, watching him, wondered why he simply stared at the letter for what seemed minutes.

"Father, is something wrong? "

He silently held the letter out to her. She took it and read:

My very dear Ignatius. May we suggest that you meet, if possible, with Father Zacharias and perhaps his consort, also, to see if some sort of conciliation might not be worked out. If you succeed in seeing him, you may tell him that we send him our personal blessing.

It was signed simply, "Gregory."

Jessica could hardly believe it: a personal letter from His Holiness in his own handwriting, and so simply signed.

"Oh, golly! Father!"

"The seal on the back is one he used when patriarch of Venice." Ignatius smiled at the look on her face and waved at the letter. "Keep it," he said.

"Keep it? But, Father..."

He raised a hand as she started to protest. "And don't say no. One small present in advance for your birthday next month. And don't go thanking me either, dear child. You know how I hate that."

"Yes, Father."

Ignatius ignored her grateful smile and checked his desk calendar. "Now," he said, "while I run to an appointment downtown, perhaps you can try to contact Father Zacharias. See when it would be agreeable to him to meet. Perhaps suggest New Orleans when I am there next week meeting Bishop Andrews. We could eat at that restaurant run by my old college friend Rupert White."

When he had gone, Sister Jessica carefully folded the letter from Pope Gregory back in the envelope, kissed it, and crossed herself, then put it in the office safe.

That done, she got on the telephone. Within an hour, she had reached Father Zacharias's newly hired public relations person, who promised to call her back as soon as he had conferred with Father Zacharias himself.

She had hardly hung up when a call came in from Rome and the Vatican. The caller introduced himself as Father Julio Benetto. Ignatius kept a reference diary of leading Vatican personnel, and Jessica remembered Benetto as the new personal secretary to Cardinal Mancini. Ignatius had explained that he was from one of Venice's oldest and wealthiest families. His deceased father had been a lay prince of the Church of great influence, and unquestionably politics of some sort was behind his appointment. It was almost always the case, Ignatius said, when so young a priest was accepted into the inner *famiglia* of the pope. "In the Church," he had added wryly, "as with any other place, I'm afraid, it's often whom you know that counts."

"I'm sorry I missed His Reverence, Sister." Benetto's

English was slightly stilted and quite heavily accented. "But perhaps you could help. They said you were his administrative assistant."

Jessica was surprised by his pleasant tone and courtesy. So many priests at the Vatican displayed such arrogance that you were certain they saw themselves as having special dispensation from God himself to feel superior to everyone else.

"Actually, I confess I am calling not for His Eminence, Cardinal Mancini, but for myself. Unofficially, you understand. And for my family."

He went on to explain that his mother, the marquessa, had met Cardinal Heriot at a reception in New York a year ago. She wanted to send him a small Easter gift: two altar candles of Venetian glass with silver filigrees depicting the twelve apostles in attitudes of veneration.

"Just a small gift, Sister. They are copies of the ones in St. Mark's Basilica in Venice, which His Eminence happened to mention he admired so much. My mother asked me to call about it since her English is not very good and I wanted to make certain, before she sent them, that there would not be some reason why His Eminence might see the gift as inappropriate."

Jessica thought quickly. Would there be? A gift from anyone politically powerful at the Vatican usually had strings attached. On the other hand, Father Ignatius was not one to be coerced. People who tried to get around him with gifts usually found themselves frustrated. And, after all, this gift might be quite valuable.

She said, "Please tell the marquessa that I am certain

His Eminence would be most pleased and honored to accept her generous gift. I will see he writes her immediately on his return."

The priest was profuse in his thanks, and it was only after Jessica had written down the marquessa's address and she and the young priest had both hung up that she realized the old dowager probably was shrewdly lining up a favorable attitude by Ignatius toward her son just in case Ignatius should ever become pope. With the emotion of pride, if indeed that happened, conflicting with a wrenching in her heart at the realization that she would then be parted from him, perhaps forever, the young nun got back to work.

Sister Jessica was mostly right. In Rome, Benetto, who had made the call from his secretarial office adjacent to Cardinal Mancini's personal study, sat back in his chair with a smug sense of self-satisfaction and folded his soft white hands piously against the heavy gold cross that hung at his breast. It had not been easy to get a call in at the right hour to America, and when he was certain Mancini and Brother Demetrius would both be away from the suite for a safe interval. But his patience had been rewarded. In persuading his mother to send a gift to Cardinal Heriot, no matter how hard it had been, he had ensured he'd be known to the man who, if he ever declared himself, might conceivably dash to pieces all of Cardinal Mancini's ambitions for the papal throne. And in the unlikely event that Cardinal Heriot might someday reveal the gift to Mancini, no finger could ever be pointed at him. The gift wasn't from him.

Meanwhile, his own role continued to be exactly as he knew the disdainful secretary of state saw him, as nothing more than an eager-to-please secretary. He didn't mind. It was an easy job. Mancini had virtually no private life and, as his personal secretary, there was thus little to do other than put up with Mancini's bullying and continue to pretend obsequiousness.

He glanced at his watch. It was not yet three o'clock in Rome. He switched on the coffee machine that he kept on a table along with cups and saucers. Doubtless when he returned, his superior would immediately demand coffee. Mancini drank cup after cup all day, changing only to his ritual herbal tea at night. He insisted that Benetto make it in his office rather than having to wait for what he call an "interminable amount of time" for it to be brought by the nuns responsible for keeping house in his suite, which included a little kitchenette.

His thoughts returned to the phone conversation. What a silly little girl the American nun was, so easy to persuade! They were all the same, the Americans, as hopelessly naïve as they were undisciplined. The sister's ready acceptance that his mother couldn't speak English well had almost made him laugh. His mother spoke better English than she, and the candlesticks had been his idea, not hers. He looked down over the Cortille del Portico at St. Peter's Square. A considerable crowd was already gathering for the pope's weekly address and blessing at four o'clock. More were steadily joining the penitent. The day was clear. A strong, icy wind from the north swirled occasional clouds of city dirt across the great square, stinging faces and eyes and causing some to shield themselves behind umbrellas. The pope, at his own insistence, would not speak over the public address system from the warmth of the papal reception room or from his apartment. He had chosen to speak from the balcony in the Maderno façade of the Basilica above the huge fifteenth-century entrance doors.

Benetto thought of the frail old man, most of the time now bedridden, exposed to weather that could well kill him overnight. With the American Zacharias beginning to influence much of the Church's regrettable left wing with his persuasively heretical beliefs, who knew who might succeed him? The very devil was loose when prominent Church leaders like Ngordo had so far failed to condemn the maverick. His impeccable Eminence, Agosto Mancini, Benetto thought spitefully, was no longer as secure in his ambitions as he had always thought.

As the young priest sat relishing this realization, he noticed that the gathering crowd would soon fill all of St. Peter's Square. It added to his sense of well being. If born differently, he might have been one of those people, a nobody in the common herd standing out in the March cold. But he wasn't. His was the privilege, God's wish certainly, of belonging to the central authority that dominated their lives. And perhaps—who knew?—that with the further grace of God and his own acumen, he might one day himself be the ultimate power in that authority. Neither Mancini nor Heriot would live forever. There was time.

He picked up the phone and dialed a number that connected him to a small, luxurious apartment not far from the Vatican. It belonged to Luciano di Paolis, a young friend from a Florentine family as important as his own.

"Luciano. I'm coming over for lunch today. Order in something delicious."

Then he sensed, rather than heard, someone entering Cardinal Mancini's study. He quickly put down the receiver. It was either Brother Demetrius or Mancini himself returning early, and he hurried in to tell the Cardinal, if it were indeed he, that his coffee was ready, and to humbly ask if there was not some other service he might perform to make his Eminence more comfortable.

CHAPTER

15

Because of the notoriety he had achieved on television and in his several subsequent radio talks, the Chicago audience Father John Zacharias addressed on Francesca's first night with him that cold November, six months before the death of Gregory XVIII, was far too large for the church hall that the priest had booked. Scores of people had to be turned away when the Church became overcrowded. The next night in Des Moines, it was the same when in his self-effacing modesty, and with his heart entirely in what he felt and wanted others to hear and understand, he had arranged only for the auditorium of a suburban high school. It was as though he was unaware of the extraordinary impact he had had on people's hearts and minds, and of the major disturbance his insistence on living the message of Christ was causing in the hierarchy of the Church.

The three priests with Father John seemed equally inept at organization, and Francesca found herself anxious that people would be unable to experience John's actual presence and to feel the extraordinary closeness to God and the profound renewal of faith that personal contact with him brought. When she went to bed in the shabby Des Moines hotel with its stained wallpaper, stale odor, and scratched furniture, she vowed she'd change that. Although she had no experience at it, she would somehow organize things so that he had far larger places in which to celebrate mass and speak. First, however, she knew she had to organize herself. She used her credit cards to go shopping and raise cash. Then she called her lawyer to ask him to sell her apartment, along with all its furnishings and to also sell all her jewelry and to give her clothes to a thrift shop.

The lawyer was an old friend who had once been her companion in visits to a sex club in New York, where they would swing with other couples. When she told him what she wanted, where she was, and why she'd left New York, he was disbelieving. "Oh, for Christ's sake, Francesca, don't tell me you're now getting it off with a fucking priest?"

No longer amused at what once would have made her laugh, and to make him take her seriously, she threatened not to pay his bill. Even then, she knew he still couldn't quite believe her.

Father John stayed two days in Des Moines. Next were Denver and Albuquerque, with one night only in each city. There were times when Francesca felt that nothing that was happening was real. She feared she'd wake up suddenly from a dream and find herself back in her old life in New York.

Somehow, Dominic managed to run her down on the telephone. It was a bad moment. At first, laughing like her lawyer, then cajoling, he soon became viciously threatening. She finally found the courage to hang up on him, but for a long time she sat on the edge of the hotel bed, badly shaken and staring across the dreary room at nothing and struggling to erase memories of herself doing everything conceivable to him and his friends to satisfy their perverted sexual needs.

At the end of each day, before Father John was due to speak, she'd have dinner with him and Fathers Graham, Howell, and Berthold at McDonalds or some cheap diner. Then, after dinner, when Father John in his quiet, gentle voice addressed all those who packed into limited spaces to hear him, she would be almost as mesmerized as others were, and would feel all over again the sense of rebirth she had felt upon first meeting him, and all the darkness of the past would disappear.

The first week flew by, then December. Her personal affairs settled, Francesca devoted herself to booking far larger places to accommodate the ever-increasing number of people who wanted to hear Father John's message. With her own money, she hired a PR man and a manager to work out a schedule, to book stadiums or big concert halls well in advance, and to advertise and publicize every appearance well ahead of time in the local press and through television and radio. Since the priest had been threatened by people who saw him as dangerous, she also hired bodyguards.

The crusade, as the media called it, soon began to resemble one. Almost overnight, the crowds grew larger, media coverage became more intense, contributions poured in. Around Christmastime, support came from some prominent politicians. Shortly after New Year's Day, *Newsweek*, featuring Father John and the ever-larger following he was attracting, ran a lead article on Catholics in America and their disagreements with the Vatican.

Despite the outpouring of support, Francesca found it extraordinary that they continued to travel on buses and live in inexpensive hotels. "Unnecessary luxury tends to make one forget life's basic realities," Father John said. "That we live and then die, and in between we struggle in the harshness of life to find peace of some kind within ourselves and ways to live peacefully with our fellows."

He celebrated mass in a manner that made his devotion almost tangible. He spoke clearly and simply to audiences about the truth in Jesus, and they came from every walk of life, the young and the old, men and women, the wealthy and established as well as the poor and lost, each seeking peace and refuge from fear. They listened to him in rapt silence and, like Francesca herself, seemed to draw new hope from him as though elevated to some never-before-experienced spiritual realization.

It was April and they were in Oklahoma City when the call came from Cardinal Heriot's office. When Father John told her of his desire for a meeting, anxiety gripped like a vise around Francesca's heart. With practically everything Father John said a direct contradiction to every precept and law of the Church and its authority, Francesca knew he had to be regarded by the Holy See as a dangerous affront to Roman Catholicism itself. Father

John's bishop had already cited him for disobedience and denounced his public speaking. She was certain her worst fears of Vatican reaction were about to be realized, and that Father John surely faced interdiction. Worse, the Vatican might even excommunicate him, expelling him forever into eternal purgatory. And what was his sin? Urging the Church to follow Christ.

She tried to think of what she could do to ward off whatever was coming. She could think of nothing. She had never felt so helpless.

Father John was quick to see the anxiety shadow the serenity and peace that had replaced the lost look in her eyes when he first saw her at the reception.

"Francesca, you mustn't worry unduly."

"But surely this is a step to silence you?"

"I don't think so. Not yet, anyway."

"But why does he want to see you, then?"

"I'm not sure. I suspect he might have been asked, perhaps even by Pope Gregory himself, to find some sort of accommodation with us. It would be a gesture typical of His Holiness. Besides, if it were to silence me, he would not have suggested your being present."

"Me?"

"Of course. And why not? I think he understood that I wouldn't meet him without you."

Francesca quickly averted her face so he wouldn't see her emotion at such acceptance, and began to speculate on the number who would attend the mass that night in a local high school football stadium.

CHAPTER

◈16◈

A drizzling early spring rain threatened to cancel the mass. Rather than search at the last moment for an alternative location to the outdoor stadium, however, Father John chose to go ahead with it as planned.

To his chagrin, although he did his best to hide it, the mayor, a recent but ardent follower, had ordered a police escort that led them, sirens screaming, across the city through heavy traffic made worse by the rain. They were in two cars, Fathers Howell, Berthold, and Graham in one, Francesca and Father John in another. Before Francesca knew it, they arrived at the small stadium, which was full, and were engulfed by noise and the uproar of those outside whom the police in the name of safety could no longer let in.

The mood, the excitement that almost bordered on hysteria, made Francesca think of rock concerts. A mob of people, heedless of the weather, at once surrounded them, calling out to Father John. Some reached to touch him; others had autograph books ready; some, in tears, were crying out blessings. And more than on any previous night, there were the shoulder-held TV cameras and the insistent young men and women with microphones who accompanied them.

Inexplicably, as Father John headed into the stadium, the rain abruptly stopped. The crowd parted to make way for him like waves before the bow of a ship, and Francesca followed with the priests. By the time they reached the middle of the stadium and the speaker's platform, a hush had fallen over the crowd.

Father John mounted the platform, the stadium darkened except for the podium, which was bathed in a pool of white light and where a makeshift altar had been set up. There, helped by Father Howell, he celebrated mass, and when those who wished to had received the host, and mass and communion were over, there was an air of expectancy as all who had gathered waited for him to speak.

He remained silent for a moment before them, a slender, isolated figure, yet strangely strong and self-possessed. His head was bowed in silent prayer, as though asking for guidance, his hands clasped before his chest. In one, he held a small remote microphone. Then, when he spoke in a clear but soft voice, undistorted by the sound system, he seemed to be addressing not the whole stadium but each person there individually.

"I want you to know, all who are gathered here, whether you be man or woman, young or elderly, rich or poor, that I have not come to instruct, nor to lecture. I have come to pray and to ask you to pray with me.

"Looking out upon you, I feel uplifted as well as humbled by your presence, for I see each and every one of you as a guardian angel of that shining and holy cross that is our Church. I ask you to pray with me that it be not one of worldly thoughts and deeds, but instead a Church filled with the love that our Lord, Jesus Christ, has for even the least of us."

He paused, as if carefully considering what he wanted to say. "I ask you humbly to join me in silent prayer that our Church can share our lives, our hopes and dreams, as well as our problems.

"And let us pray—all of us—that as our Lord expelled the moneylenders from the temple, that those who govern our Church step down from their golden altars to alleviate suffering wherever it may be. Let our Church be governed, too, by men truly wise and representative of the world, and not by those whose lives have been largely confined to the narrow isolation of elitism."

He had thrown down a challenge and everyone there knew it. But rather than excitement, the mood was one of quiet trust and following. And of unity, as though each person there was holding the hand of his neighbor so that all in the stadium were joined in determination and devotion.

"Let us pray," Father John went on quietly. He moved slowly now about the podium so as to be sure to speak to everyone, not just those directly before him. "Let us pray that they, with our help, can guide our Church, given to us by Jesus Christ, so that it will dwell always and forever in His true image, just as His Spirit comes to us when we partake of His mystical Self during communion.

"Our Lord made no distinction on whom he bestowed His love. Let us pray that our Church looks also with love, as well as with understanding and tolerance, on those whose lifestyles, even in the way they see God, seem different from our own."

For the first time, his tone changed slightly. While he still spoke softly, he became more emphatic, stressing the importance of what he had to say. "Let us pray that our Church respects the wisdom and ability of women as equal to that of men in choosing their destinies, that our Church allows them into the priesthood to help minister to the needs of all of us.

"Let us pray that our Church permits the sanctity of marriage into the priesthood, so that those who help bring to us the love of our Savior can, through their own marriages, possess a greater understanding of the needs of each.

"Let us pray, too, that our Church reaches out to those in marriage, yes, even to the unmarried who are blessed by love, with sympathy and understanding. Let our Church allow a man and a woman in their natural, God-gifted passion for each other, the choice of creating life or not as they choose. Let no woman live in constant fear of unwanted or often endless childbearing, and no man suffer equal fear of having to support a family far beyond his capabilities. And, where God's love resides in their union, that they will not create an unwanted child who at the very instant of conception is condemned to perhaps inheriting a loveless lifetime of misery."

He paused again. Then, in a final word, he said, "Let us kneel now in silent prayer together, and pray in our own words and with all our hearts, for that Holy Cross that is our Church."

He knelt. There was the rustling of the entire stadium kneeling with him. Hundreds bowed their heads. There were tears in the eyes of many. Then a complete silence fell over the entire stadium. Even the distant sound of traffic beyond was stilled.

Suddenly a shout shattered the moment. A red-faced, balding man with a short, thick neck leapt to his feet near Father John and began to shout, "Judas!" and "Heretic!"

People tried to make him sit down, but he became even more abusive. "They used to burn bastards like you!"

Father John had firmly refused to allow the bodyguards Francesca had hired up on the platform with him. "Being flanked by them when I speak is not an image I want to project," he said.

But the man got up on the platform before they could stop him, whipped off his heavy leather belt, and lashed out. He was dragged away, shouting obscenities, but the belt buckle had caught Father John across the forehead. Blood welled.

Francesca rose to go to him, but Father Berthold held her back. "No, no, he wouldn't want you to."

Father John rose from kneeling and, ignoring the blood that trickled down to the corner of one eye, called out to his guards to stop. When they did, he came off the platform and approached his still-struggling attacker.

Seeing him, the man stilled, expecting to be verbally assaulted, if not struck. Instead, Father John smiled gently and held out his belt to him.

"You will want this, I am sure," he said. "It's a beautiful belt. Take it, remember me by it, and pray for me as I shall pray for you."

For a moment, the man stared at the priest in astonishment, then burst into tears. Father John took him into his arms and embraced him, and then, waving the guards away, walked with one arm around him through the silent, parting crowd to the stadium entrance. There, he spoke a few words with the man that nobody heard, and, when the man knelt to kiss his hand, blessed him and sent him on his way.

To Francesca, the rest of the evening at the stadium was like a dream. Microphone in hand, the priest walked up and down between the rising seats of the little stadium that were filled with people, and among all those standing on the turf of the football field and the cinders of the racetrack at the bottom. He spoke personally to one person after another, asking after them, counseling, putting an arm around one here, embracing and giving his blessing to another there.

It was as though, Francesca thought, he was in the little stone church he had so vividly described to her and was speaking to each and every family of his mill-worker congregation. She knew he felt a part of everyone there and they a part of him. He did not finish until nearly three in the morning, and even then had to be persuaded to retire. "There might still be some who need me," he protested.

When they got back to the hotel, the small but nasty gash on his forehead had stopped bleeding, but the flesh around it had swollen into an ugly discolored bruise. When he laughed and refused to see the hotel doctor, Francesca insisted on going with him to his room, where she ordered ice and, in spite of his protests, began applying it gently to his head.

He was seated on the bed, she beside him, the bowl of ice on the chair. Neither were speaking when their eyes met. For an instant, a sort of deeply intimate contact passed between them.

Tired, his head throbbing, Father John suddenly became aware of the physical Francesca, of the seductive woman— the soft halo of her hair, the gentle femininity of her hands as she held ice to the wound, the fine bones of her face, the tenderness in her eyes, the delicate perfume of her body.

And in him, Francesca saw the way a man looked just before he moved to possess a woman he wanted. There was a sudden smoldering depth in his expression, a dark intensity that, from long experience, she knew blocked out almost all other senses and turned the entire being of the male to raw desire.

Helpless, she felt the immediate, almost overpowering need in her own body to meet what she knew he felt. A second passed, two. An eternity. Then, quite abruptly, Francesca saw something happen to him. His features, for the briefest of moments so strained with passion, became gentle and acetic again.

He rose, something like terror in his heart at what had almost overcome him, and prayed she had not known. He said, almost with protective sharpness, "Enough ice, Francesca. You're freezing me."

The moment had passed. He had gotten control of himself, Francesca knew. There would never be another moment like it. She forced a light laugh, fetched a towel to dry his face, and made him promise to let the house doctor see him in the morning. They talked casually a few minutes about what would happen later that week in New Orleans. The crowd he would address there, the night before they dined with Cardinal Heriot, promised to be the biggest yet. Then she left him.

In bed in her own room, Francesca lay awake. John Zacharias, she realized, was the first man she had ever loved, the first she had ever wanted to give to, not to take from and then forget. But he had pulled away from her. She was certain she knew why, and the irony of it was bittersweet. He had done so not because of himself or his vow of celibacy, or for fear of falling from grace. Although perhaps if she had responded, he might have succumbed. She had never known any man who had been unable to resist her willingness. He had done so, she knew, for her. In the heat of his physical need, he had thought first of her, not of himself. He had thought first of the spiritual resurrection she had undergone her fragile trust that had been betrayed by men many times before.

Before she finally fell asleep, Francesca knew that there had been more for her—in that brief moment—a greater beauty, a greater love, than most women experience in a lifetime.

CHAPTER

◈17◈

It had taken more than a month for Sister Jessica to coordinate Ignatius's busy commitments around the country with those of Father John Zacharias so that a meeting could be held. A date, early in April in New Orleans, when Ignatius had to visit the city again to investigate a report of repeated sexual abuse by a prominent New Orleans bishop and when at that time the priest would be addressing a rally there, was finally decided upon.

After addressing an ecumenical conference in Boston, Ignatius had a day to spare before the meeting and he decided not to return home, but to go instead to New Orleans by way of Washington, where he could spend some time at the Library of Congress researching a particularly vicious nightmare. Like his search for the sources of so many other dreams, he'd so far had no success discovering what had inspired this one, but he suspected the answer might lie in a passage of obscure text on an aspect of the English Civil War that saw the forces of Cromwell pitted against those of King Charles I. In the dream, he betrayed a brother supporting Cromwell to a unit of King Charles's cavalry in order to possess the brother's estate.

Reaching the library, his whole being was immersed in the memory of seeing his imagined brother being hung, with his brother's wife forced to watch, then raped by cavaliers before enduring the same fate. Seating himself in the library's great central reading room before a pile of books, he methodically, hour after hour, leafed through one weighty volume after another. Time flew. It was late afternoon and he'd almost given up when he was struck by a particular passage that seemed vaguely familiar in a work by Thomas Wicks, a noted Scottish historian.

Especially among the great landowners in Gloucestershire and Warwickshire, personal betrayal of friend by friend, even of father by son and brother by brother, was rampant, and often for the most venal or vile reasons.

There was a reference number to an appendix of notes. Ignatius turned to the back of the book to find it, and read:

For a vivid literary description, see Tanworth Downs *by the English novelist William Burroughs, page 311, vol. 2. In this little-known work, the author describes a titled land owner in the northwest who betrays his parliamentarian*

brother to pursuing cavaliers in order to seize his extensive
property, and his wife as well.

Could that be it? He was now sure that he'd read the
passage and the appendix, but had he read *Tanworth*
Downs? He went at once to order up a copy and found it
unavailable. He decided that it didn't really matter. What
he'd already found surely would have been enough to
provide the dream's setting.

"Eminence?"

Ignatius turned to see the familiar, smiling face of a
female security guard he knew from previous visits.

"You asked me to let you know when it approached
seven o'clock."

Ignatius glanced at his watch, turned in his books, and
fled the library. He was expected for dinner in Bethesda,
the sprawling suburb north of the city, at the home of his
friends Allegra Shaw, a renowned novelist and poet, and
Amory Harper, a professor of genetics at the University of
Maryland with whom he shared life and a home.

He had met Allegra while still with his migrant-worker
parish. Ignatius had just then sold his first book. *The Hydra*,
named so for the mythological nine-headed monster, was a
history of the nine different popes when the papacy was
split between Rome and Avignon in the fourteenth century. Praised by nearly every critic as extraordinary and bril-
liantly written, *The Hydra* was snatched up by the public
and quickly made the *New York Times* bestseller list.

Ignatius had come to New York to see his publisher
about a second book he had in mind on the struggle

between the famed monk Savonarola and the corrupt pope Alexander VI. While there, he attended an Authors Guild meeting at which veteran members toasted newcomers.

Ignatius had long suffered isolation from his educational equals, in fact, from any cultivated society. He felt completely out of place in the presence of so much literary authority, and especially so in this catered gathering in which butlers served trays of canapes and glasses of champagne. He was standing awkwardly, a little apart from the crowd, so different from the world he was used to, and embarrassed by the worn, almost shabby appearance of his cassock and his unfashionable shoes. He had used up all the money he'd earned on *Hydra* establishing a modern health clinic for his parishioners, and had not thought to refurbish his own appearance. A gray-haired, large-bosomed woman loomed into view. She was the Guild's president and a writer of romance novels.

"Father Ignatius, there's someone here who is dying to meet you, and I'm sure you'll love meeting her. She's just over there."

He'd found himself propelled through the crowded gathering until he suddenly came face to face with a slightly stocky woman whose tawny hair was a disheveled tangle, while her amber eyes shone with ironic mirth. She wore little makeup, had taken no pains to dress for the occasion, and was wearing an old flannel skirt and a hooded sweatshirt emblazoned with the phrase, "Normal people frighten me."

"Allegra, darling. Here is Father Ignatius. And you're not to monopolize him all evening. Father, this is Allegra Shaw."

Ignatius was too awed to say much. Allegra Shaw, then barely in her thirties, was already internationally revered as a novelist who counted the Pulitzer among a score of other notable literary achievements.

"Ignatius Heriot? Oh, my God—you're that wonderful priest who wrote the book about all those nasty popes."

She held out her hand and laughed in delight at meeting him, and her laugh was a husky outburst that, like her voice, was filled with irreverence. "I'm so happy to meet you. The jacket blurb says you dwell in some Christ-awful swampy parish somewhere, but I want to know more. What brought you to write such an incredible book? And how did you ever manage to know so damn much? I mean, you're a historical encyclopedia. And to be able to tell it all so excitingly? And make it all so real? I was hooked on your first sentence, it was as though I was actually living back then."

Later, after he had tried to answer her barrage of questions, he found himself rushed off to dinner.

"I don't care if you have mass, or confession, or communion, or whatever you priests do this time of day, I won't take no, Ignatius, or excuse me, I should say Father Ignatius, shouldn't I? And I know you'll like Amory if you can understand what the hell he's talking about when he gets going on his genetic thing. I can't."

It was the beginning of a long and lasting friendship, one in which he endlessly argued theology with Allegra, faith against humanism, while both she and Amory avidly followed his career upward through the Church and his attendant literary successes.

She had a mind that was inquisitive, daring, rebellious, irreverent. She was filled with laughter at the ironies of life, but always deeply caring. She was an avowed atheist and sometimes biting critic of the Church. But Ignatius loved her, just as he loved Amory and all his extraordinary scientific knowledge. Over the years, he had come into certain official disapproval for his well-publicized friendship with such outspoken humanists. He didn't care. "We Catholics aren't the only ones in the world," he always said. "Nor the only belief. If we publicly express a need for ecumenical harmony, then we should be allowed to cultivate it privately."

Since that first meeting, little had changed in Allegra, Amory, or himself except for outward appearances. A big, shambling man, Amory's once-great mop of sandy hair had turned gray and he'd put on some weight. Ever good natured, he still could not understand why no one could understand him. *Time* magazine had recently put him on the cover of a special issue devoted to genetics.

Allegra's hair had grown partially gray, too, and her body heavier, her manner less abandoned. Gone were the defiant sweatshirts. Her success had continued, one great novel after another, and she had become a sort of senior statesman of the literary world. There were whispers, now, of the Nobel Prize. And yet her standard complaint was still, "Oh, Christ, if only I could write well."

As for himself, Ignatius knew he looked his age now and not ten years younger, the way he'd always used to look.

Outside the library, and in spite of it being rush hour,

he managed to find a cab and arrived at the colonial brick home on the quiet tree-lined street just in time for pre-dinner cocktails.

CHAPTER

❖18❖

Allegra entertained well and liked interesting people. Whenever Ignatius dined with her and Amory, she always invited others she felt would be fun for him. "Not like all those absolutely fascinating churchy folk you indulge yourself in every day, Ignatius darling, but confess, amusing just the same." And her amber eyes would light up and she'd tease with husky-voice laughter.

Tonight, she'd asked three people. There was the former film star, Merrill Christie, Washington's leading hostess and now married to her fifth husband, the Senate Majority Leader, who was currently away on a Mideast fact-finding junket. At forty-five, she was still an outstanding beauty, with creamy, pale skin, a stunning figure, the features that had made her famous, and a cascade of raven-black hair.

Then there was Aaron Feldstein, once an inmate of

Auschwitz, now a leading psychiatrist and amateur concert pianist. His elderly, crevassed face was filled with intelligence and, miraculously, a kind and humorous view on life. He had received the Medal of Freedom two years before Ignatius. With him was his wife, Helen. An outspoken feminist, she was charged with creating the new National Hebrew Museum, a job she'd come to after producing four Broadway musicals.

Amidst a flurry of small talk, Amory handed out strong cocktails, and, when called to dinner by Mathilda, the housekeeper of many years, all proceeded to the dining room with its eighteenth-century court cupboard and early-English primitive paintings. Seated at a worn Jacobean refectory table, Ignatius found himself next to Merrill Christie.

When told that the man who might possibly be the first American pope would be at dinner, she had not been able to resist the challenge of trying to make him forget, just for one evening, who and what he was. She'd never met Ignatius, but she'd seen enough photos of him to know he didn't look like a lot of other prelates she could think of, and she couldn't imagine what he was doing being a cleric. His acetic features, his dark-haired leanness, and intense eyes gave him enough sex appeal for several men. She had taken special care with her hair and had worn a particularly low-cut backless velvet dress that, in the soft, dinner-table candlelight, showed her beautiful shoulders and bosom to advantage. She'd worn her best jewelry and she'd been generous with her perfume.

For Ignatius, dinner was a delightful escape from all his anxieties. Here he was in a different world, one so far removed from the realities and strictness of his nearly monastic life at his diocese that it seemed a kind of magical *sortie* into delightful fantasy. Conversation, which was witty and filled with cheerful laughter, was mostly anecdotal about friends or Washington gossip, until Allegra brought up the *déja vu* she'd felt in an argument with her publisher.

"I swear to God it was like instant replay. Yet I can't remember the where or when of the first time."

"*Déja vu*," Merrill Christie said. "It happens to me all the time and always gives me a slight shock. Like, what on earth is going on here? Do you get that feeling, Eminence?" She exaggerated Ignatius's salutary title with a slightly teasing tone and rested one slender hand on his arm.

Helen Feldstein rescued him. "I think the phenomenon is perfectly explainable, myself," she said.

"Oh?" Amory's tone was skeptical.

"I do. Really. I think it's simply your brain circuitry making you feel something is being repeated because some of those billions of little wires we all have in our brains happen to be buzzing the same way they once did at some other time over something totally unrelated."

"Are you saying," Amory asked, "that a more or less similar action of our brain mechanism makes one *feel*, or should I say *think*, that the results or causes of that action are also similar, when actually they might be quite different?"

"Exactly."

"Oh, come on," Merrill cried. "It's far, far simpler, surely.

Ninety to one, *déja vu* is just a memory of a past life."

"Merrill," Aaron Feldstein exclaimed. "You really can't think that."

"Sorry, but I do."

"I do too," Allegra declared. "I think reincarnation is quite possibly the only answer. And don't 'Oh, come on now, Allegra' to me, Amory, about there being no evidence. Of course there isn't. It's just a very, very strong feeling that simply can't be explained. One that millions of people have. It's like Ignatius's faith. One just *knows*, that's all."

Amory winked at Ignatius. "Careful, Ignatius. You might once have been a pope."

"Ignore him, Ignatius," Allegra said. "Let me tell you of an experience I once had. Amory was lecturing at Cambridge, and we had a cottage in a little village with the most charming old Norman church. I used to sit in the churchyard and write. It was so peaceful, and the place smelled heavenly of boxwood. One day, a gardener was weeding around the old bench I used to sit on, so I went and sat instead on a flat tombstone, a very old and worn one, in a far part of the churchyard. Well, I'd been sitting there some time, when suddenly I began to have the strangest feeling. I really can't describe it. I felt I was sitting on my own grave. I mean, that the person below me in the earth was also me."

Helen said, "But how weird, Allegra."

Merrill shivered, "Brrr..." She leaned close to Ignatius in mock need for protection, and said to Allegra, "There was a ghost there. That's what you felt. You needed

Ignatius around to exorcise it. You do exorcise ghosts, don't you, Eminence?" Waiting for an answer, she found her own wine glass empty and drank from his.

Ignatius said no and explained that a priest could only exorcise evil spirits or the devil who had occupied a person. Merrill's eyes at once became mischievously flirtatious. "Which, of course," she said primly, "rules me out from ever needing it."

There were good-natured hoots and laughter.

"Could you see to whom the grave belonged?" Helen asked.

"No," Allegra replied. "The writing was too worn away. I could only make out the year she died—1782."

"You mean when *you* died," Merrill said.

"Presuming you were right and it *was* you down there, how did you know you were a she?" Aaron demanded.

"Well, of course I couldn't actually know," Allegra conceded. "But I *felt* who the me was. She was a young woman and she died in childbirth."

Amory scoffed. "Felt! Allegra, you felt whom you wanted yourself to be. Right, Aaron?"

"I would say most certainly."

"Sorry, Aaron. Most certainly not. Besides, dying in childbirth is not my thing."

"What I can't understand," Amory insisted, "is why, if neither of you can remember who you were in these past lives you so believe in, that you go right on thinking you ever had one."

He rose to refill glasses with a vintage Chianti. "The

trouble is, you can't face death—being thrust into uncon-
sciousness for all of eternity. The total annihilation of your
ego. Because if you can't remember a past life and have no
proof of a future one, dying does mean just that, doesn't
it? Being totally extinguished? And believing in reincarnation means you don't have to be, right? Gives the old
ego a break."

He stopped and smiled apologetically at Ignatius.
"Forgive me, Ignatius, for denying an afterlife in the
accepted sense."

Ignatius smiled back and raised his glass in silent
acceptance of the apology. He had long ago learned not
to dispute faith at any dinner table, especially one presided
over by Amory and Allegra. His two friends being so often
candidly critical of what he believed was proof of how
much they trusted him, and that, in turn, meant their love,
for which he was profoundly grateful.

Merrill leaned close to him again. "Eminence, what
do you think? Be honest. Wouldn't you love to find out
that you were actually a reincarnation of some famous
pope or even one of the saints?"

"The Church doesn't hold with reincarnation,
Merrill," Aaron interjected. He sensed a slight embarrassment in Ignatius.

"Doesn't it? Not at all?" she asked Ignatius.

"I'm afraid not," he replied.

"But you? Not even secretly?"

"I could hardly be at variance with the Church I
serve, could I?"

"Not even just a little?"

"Reincarnation," he said, "denies the miracle of resurrection. So I'm sorry, but you won't see me in your next life."

"I'm sorry, too," she said. She wanted to add, "You might not be a celibate priest then." But didn't. She felt frustrated by the clearly unassailable wall that isolated him from her. Her carefully planned flirtation had turned into plain desire that she knew she hadn't been able to hide completely. She found him magnetic, a man she could easily fall for, and wondered how many other women had felt the same way and had gotten nowhere.

Or perhaps had been successful. With everything you heard about priests these days, who would know? Either this was a man of iron self-control, or he felt nothing. Looking at him, at the strength of character in his face, and feeling the energy coiled silently someplace in his body, she found it quite impossible to believe he was always celibate.

Allegra, meanwhile, sensed that the conversation was not completely to Ignatius's liking. She skillfully moved on to another subject, and in a few minutes the table was once more a scene of levity, with conversation on a wide variety of less personally controversial subjects.

Ignatius was relieved. To him, belief that *déja vu* was memory of previous life was the sad and desperate yearning for immortality of those without faith. He didn't think less of them for it. Their weakness was God's deepest concern, and it was the duty of a priest to bring them God's love to help ease their fears.

The evening over and Merrill and the Feldsteins gone,

he helped Allegra and Amory take the after-dinner coffee
things out to the kitchen, which Mathilda had abandoned
some time earlier. He and Allegra were loading the dish-
washer when she said, "Ignatius, I'm sorry for the way
Merrill behaved. A senator's wife, my God. I don't know
what got into her."

Ignatius pretended innocence. "Behaved how?"

"Ignatius Heriot, come now. If you say you didn't
notice, you're a liar. Cardinal or no, you're not made of
stone. She flirted with you outrageously."

He smiled at her anxious expression. "That's just her
nature. It didn't bother me. Honestly. Not one bit."

Allegra didn't say more, but he knew she didn't quite
believe him. For, in spite of the almost farcical trans-
parency of her flirtation, Merrill Christie had, in fact,
made him feel acutely uncomfortable. In the soft candlelight, and with her so close at times he could feel her
breath on his face, he had found it difficult to keep his
eyes from her bare shoulders and nearly exposed breasts.
Her perfume got to him, too, and the extraordinary rich-
ness of her hair along with the warm huskiness of her
voice and the easy freedom with which she touched him.
At moments, he'd felt nearly giddy from her presence and
found himself drawn almost irresistibly into the aura of
her sexuality. He'd wondered if she knew how hard it was
for him to resist.

His occasional encounters with someone like Merrill,
the secret fantasies he often had about other women,
made him sometimes ask himself almost angrily if
celibacy was really necessary in order to follow Christ.

There were respected Christian scholars who thought that Christ was an ordained rabbi, and if so, under Jewish law, he would then have had to be married. There were some theologians who thought that Mary Magdalene, present always by his side, was his wife. Celibacy in the priesthood had only begun in the fourth century. Before that, priests, and popes as well, had often been married, and many years later, in the Renaissance, some popes had mistresses. One pope even ran a renowned brothel in Rome, reveled in its orgies, and waxed rich on its profits; another had a child by his mistress, a powerful woman who saw to it that her child by him in turn became pope. Even until modern times, there were popes getting away with occasionally consorting with a woman, the Church turning a blind eye as long as the liaison did not become public.

Always he would check himself. Celibacy was a fact of life now, and a profound responsibility he had both understood and accepted when he opted for the priesthood. It was his gift to God, perhaps the only gift he could give other than a life of helping others. Betraying it, he would betray his vow of personal sacrifice. The thought that he could be tempted by forces within him to fall from grace was unthinkable.

Called to board the plane for New Orleans the next day, he found in one pocket of his suit a folded sheet of Allegra's note paper on which Merrill Christie had written her private number. She had said to come and dine with her and her husband, but Ignatius knew the invitation would be for a time when her husband was again away.

He crumpled the paper with her phone number and, dropping it into a trash receptacle, hurried down the corridor to the waiting plane.

CHAPTER

❖ 19 ❖

New Orleans. VI April. Anno Domine MMX. In nomine Patris et Filii et Spiritus Sancti: Amen.

On the way down to New Orleans from Washington, where I dined with Allegra and Amory, I decided that I could best evaluate Father Zacharias by seeing him speak in person. It would help, too, in evaluating Miss Berenson's role. So last night I dressed anonymously and joined the crowd at the municipal stadium where he spoke. By the time he'd finished, I had the strong impression that things may have gone beyond the point where he can be silenced even by Pope Gregory. I suspect he has become answerable only unto himself and the multitudes who now rally to him.

Ignatius wrote in his diary in the guest room of an old town house facing a private church park that was the home of the Bishop Thomas of New Orleans. It was nearly seven in the evening; his elderly host had eaten early and retired to his study to prepare a sermon. He himself was due to meet Father Zacharias and Miss Berenson in an hour's time at Chez Rupert, the famed country inn of his old college friend, a few miles out of New Orleans.

Not quite certain how to continue his diary, Ignatius went to a balcony overlooking the silent park. Last daylight filtered through the branches of aged sycamore trees garlanded with Spanish moss. A rising full moon spread pale, fragmented light over a lawn that had just had its first spring mowing. The air was rich with the perfume of fresh-cut grass and newly planted flower beds, and with the heady odor of blooming honeysuckle.

With difficulty, he forced his mind back to his mission.

There had been twenty thousand people in the stadium, perhaps more, Ignatius reckoned. The crowd was quiet and orderly. Yet it felt electric. He'd seen any number of priests, both young and old, and nuns, too—hardworking, dedicated souls who, like untold thousands of other devout, were the unheralded backbone of the Church. In the eyes of each, there was the same fervor he saw in the eyes of the laity, the same look of hope and renewed faith.

Ignatius smiled to himself, remembering how he'd passed an evening without people calling him Eminence and without his having to wonder whether their attitude of respect was sycophancy or genuine. For a while he'd been simply, as of old, an anonymous priest; and for that while, heaviness lifted from his heart and he had felt a freedom nearly forgotten.

The years had rolled back to his priesthood in the cane fields and to Vietnam and the soldiers he'd chaplained and fought with; to when there had been no Church politics and no administrative duties, no ceremonial roles and no endless calls on his time to represent the Church in public matters. His only concern had been to be with God for his parishioners and to fulfill God's wish that he ease the harsh burden of their lives. In being a humble priest, there had been purity and honesty that had brought joy to his heart. Now that was mostly gone and there was no going back. It was too late.

His thoughts turned to Francesca Berenson. Seated behind Father Zacharias on the boxing ring podium with his three disciple priests, her presence was completely accepted by the crowd. There'd been an air about her that was at once almost chaste femininity and a kind of possessive reverence in the way her eyes never left the priest's face. He resumed his diary, writing down his impressions: the police escort bringing Father Zacharias to the stadium, the local politicians vying with each other to greet him, the wedge of bodyguards getting him to the podium, the silence when he spoke, the stadium in darkness save for the pool of white light in which he stood and which dramatized his pale, delicate face and his slender figure. Ignatius wrote:

> *Before a crowd, the man has a messianic quality; a sort of ethereal spirituality. Combined with a totally confident authority, it gives the impression that he holds the key to*

*all happiness, to all peace, and to the end of all misery. At
the same time, there is a kind of intimacy in the way he
reaches out to people that I've seen in no other priest. Each
and every person seems to reflect a feeling that he is there
for them alone. One has to wonder where all this will lead.*

Across the park, the church clock struck seven. Deep
in thought, Ignatius put away his diary and quickly
dressed. He'd decided it would not do to be too formal.
He would go as an ordinary priest, as he had last night,
and he donned a black rabat, fastened on a Roman collar,
and put on his dark suit.

Chez Rupert was in an old antebellum plantation
building, separated from the bayou that it overlooked by
green lawns shaded by ancient cypress trees, which at
night were hung with paper lanterns to light guests' way
up the worn brick pathway that led to the front door.

Ignatius's car was met by Rupert himself, a great
robust and bearded bear of a man in a chef's hat and
apron, who flung his arms around Ignatius and kissed him
soundly on both cheeks. "Ignatius, my darling, I am so
glad to see you."

"It's been years, Rupert. I'm glad, too." Ignatius had
always genuinely loved his old gay friend. He had no difficulty with reconciling Rupert's present lifestyle with
memories of him as the tough linebacker on their college
football team.

"Your guests have just arrived, Ignatius, and you shall
have a dinner fit for a pope, if I may be so bold, and which
I shall have the pleasure of serving myself."

Stepping inside Chez Rupert was to enter the past. Taking Ignatius by the arm, Rupert led him through the crowded main dining room with its early French provincial decor to a small private room where there were tall French windows complemented by Thai silk drapes, brocade-covered antique chairs, a mahogany huntsman's sideboard, and a table for four set with the inn's best china, silver, and crystal glassware.

Father Zacharias and Francesca, who had already been seated, rose politely when Ignatius entered. Although Francesca's guarded reserve betrayed anxiety, the priest seemed quietly at ease. So much so that even as they exchanged opening pleasantries, Ignatius began to have the uncomfortable feeling of one who finds that a guest in his house has virtually taken over the role of host. In the most courteous way, it was as though the priest, in coming to meet him, had authoritatively put himself in charge, thus ensuring that a compromise would not have to come from him.

Once seated and served an aperitif, and after John Zacharias had expressed his appreciation for the meeting, Ignatius saw no reason to make further polite conversation. He came straight to the point.

"I'm sure you know why we're here, Father John. His Holiness has specifically asked that we get together."

The priest smiled with a certain faint irony. "The request didn't come from Mancini?"

Ignatius laughed. "In fact, it did not. It came from Pope Gregory himself." He found it strange to actually be in the presence of the young priest of whom, until now, he had only had vague impressions. He was surprised to find in him, in spite of the lack of a crowd and near-theatrical lighting, a degree of the same mystical quality he'd seen on the podium the night before. And there was something else, too, a quality that he was unprepared for. In spite of his unpretentious appearance and a strangely serene quality in his speech and manner, Father John's was a presence that seemed to fill the room, to be everything, and with such magnetism that Ignatius, in spite of himself, felt drawn to him almost to the exclusion of everything around them.

Father John glanced at Francesca and was thoughtful. "First, Eminence, I know you have a good relationship with His Holiness. May I ask when you report on this meeting that you reassure him of my devotion? I have always found inspiration in him and my disagreement with him is not personal."

"Of course."

"That said," the young priest went on, "I have a second request." When Ignatius deferred with a nod, he said, "It would be helpful to me if I were to know what your personal feelings about me are."

Shades of the president's daughter, Ignatius thought. Should he answer the same way? He glanced at Francesca. Seeing her so close, he saw more in her face than beauty. She may once have been a dissolute, he thought, but she clearly was that woman no longer. Perhaps, even, she really never had been, not in her true soul, anyway. Who could cast the first stone when it came to motivation for acts for which we are condemned? For what he now saw was moral strength and true virtue, as though her sins had never existed.

He answered the priest. "I don't think I can give you the sort of unqualified answer I am sure you would like to hear, whether you'd agree with it or not. So much of what you are asking is profoundly colored in my thinking by the way you are going about things."

"How should one go about them?"

"I don't think that, with someone of your intelligence, I need to define all the channels open to you."

"No, Eminence, but they take time. And haven't Catholics everywhere run out of that commodity? And patience, too?"

"That may be," Ignatius countered, "but we may be stuck with that, although we can always hope we are not. I have worked hard most of my years in the Church for some of the reforms you advocate in both Church doctrine and canonical law where they concern papal infallibility and election reform, but I must tell you that you could bring about the exact opposite of what you want. Ignoring all established procedure is beginning to play directly into the hands of Vatican right-wing extremists— yes, Cardinal Mancini, if you wish. Regrettably, he and his Traditionalists would seem to be trying to ally the Church, in America, at least, with the extreme fundamentalism of the Christian Far Right."

"Eminence." The priest spoke without his usual gentle smile. "Is it the faithful around the world who asked the Vatican curia to get itself into the sort of political turmoil that has caused the Eucharist to be given second priority, if not actual lip service?"

Ignatius thought this unfair and said so. "You speak, Father," he answered rather waspishly, "With little regard for history."

"Oh, I don't disregard it," Father John said quickly. "I know enough of the Church to know that the early popes were forced by circumstances of the time to become secular in their thinking as well as in their actions. To maintain any Church at all meant the maintenance of an army to protect it as well as endless politicking with its neighbors."

"All that is true."

"Armies today, however, at least where the Church is concerned, are hardly necessary, but unfortunately many of the attitudes of power and regency from centuries ago are still with the Church today. What better way to protect or to destroy than with vast wealth? That's if one wants to say that the business of faith needs such power or regency to survive."

"In a way it does," Ignatius countered. "The one billion faithful in the world have needs. And their needs have to be seen to."

"What needs other than the Eucharist?"

"Churches. Priests to administer the sacraments."

"Oh, I don't disagree with that. By necessity, the Church, I suppose, has to be a vast business machine of sorts, and I don't think for a moment that part of it should be dismantled." Father John paused a moment, then went on. "But we've strayed from the argument.

The argument is that much of the Church doctrine of today reflects secular circumstances of the past. This should not be allowed, especially when the doctrine is so at variance with the Eucharist. I'm afraid that Rome has too often lost sight of that. The papal curia needs to remind itself that insofar as the Eucharist is a reenactment of Christ's sacrifice, it makes holy a mortal life which stood against nearly every aspect of Church doctrine today.

"In saying to Peter, 'I will give you the keys to Heaven,' our Savior meant keys to all that He Himself was. He meant Father, Son, and the Holy Spirit. He did not mean the keys as a means to uphold ruthless dictators, banking scandals, and the election of popes by a narrow elitist group with little connection to the living realities of their constituencies. He also did not mean keys to an unaccountability and infallibility he himself did not possess."

On returning from dinner, Ignatius wrote further in his diary:

As far as I could tell, Father Zacharias listened to what I had to say with no hostility at all. But as I'd feared, he didn't bend an inch. Within himself, he clearly saw no reason to argue, or, more importantly, to defend what he felt right. With Zacharias, ideology denies most realities. The politics of the Church are of no interest whatsoever—there shouldn't be any. There is the Church and there is Christ and they have to be one. Thus, where any negotiations were concerned, I felt to press him further at this time would be counterproductive.

It did indeed stop there. Before the end of the first course, Ignatius realized that he was going to get nowhere. He said so, and, hoping it wouldn't sound condescending, also said, "Regardless, John, of the outcome of all this, we always should be able to talk to each other, you and I, no matter what."

He turned to Francesca, who for most of the time had remained silent. "And I count on you to persuade him if he's reluctant."

He was rewarded with a warm smile. She'd relaxed, finally, and accepted that he was not a danger to the priest. Were they lovers, he wondered? He decided not. Father Zacharias would probably refuse such a relationship, not for his own sake, but for fear of jeopardizing her rejection of her former life and her spiritual rebirth.

He wondered, too, what had brought them together, what act of God, for there was an affinity between them that made them seem like one person. Perhaps, he thought, some need in her had been matched by some need in him.

Rupert poured the wine, and Ignatius, relieved that neither Francesca nor the priest seemed anxious to continue their discussion, moved the conversation on to great vintages and great food and to the terrible problem of pedophilia in the priesthood.

"Perhaps a Church that was truly in the image of Christ might not attract such people," the priest commented, and Ignatius found he had to agree.

There was coffee and a liqueur, and the evening finally came to an end with nothing resolved, but, Ignatius thought, at least with contact made. He was certain that the ailing Holy Father expected little more. Pope Gregory would know that no progress could ever be made without a beginning, and that beginnings took time.

When Father John and Francesca departed and he shook hands with the priest, Ignatius held the priest's hand in both of his a moment to emphasize his feeling of warmth toward him. "I am deeply indebted to you, John, for your coming tonight." He turned to Francesca. "And you, too, Miss Berenson." He was gratified to receive the same sentiment from them both.

Waiting for Rupert to come back from seeing the priest and Francesca to their car, he reflected that, in an odd way, the whole evening had been symbolic of the history of the Catholic Church in America, with Rome and the New World seemingly at insolvable loggerheads, and with himself trying to negotiate some sort of common ground.

Could it be that compatibility was actually impossible? Great historical divisions in the Church crossed his mind, whether from differing religious viewpoints or from political secularism. The two papacies, one in Avignon, one in Rome, a time he had so successfully written about: a second papal throne established far earlier in Constantinople, dividing the Church into East and West, the breakaway by many, under Luther, to Protestantism.

Would there be that sort of schism between Rome and America, where already the practice of Catholicism among the laity was so different, more serious and conservative in some aspects, more liberal in others?

He spent a wonderfully nostalgic hour with Rupert when the chef came back, reliving old days at college before the hard realities of life had set in, and catching up on each other's lives ever since. But back in the little guest room and listening to the night sounds from the park— the distant and haunting blues someone was singing, the closer call of a mockingbird—a strange anxiety began to overtake him, one he had avoided until then.

He realized he'd felt an unexpected empathy toward Francesca. The feelings she had engendered within him, however, were not the nearly unleashed libido Merrill Christie had aroused. The attraction had been different, stronger, and one he felt was dangerous, but could not identify. It was an attraction that left him with a deeply uneasy sense of the familiar, yet somehow unknown; an attraction that left him with a feeling of guilt and shame out of proportion to the experience.

Just as troubling was his realization that he had felt jealousy, too, for the closeness he'd observed between her and Zacharias; a jealousy that was also somehow familiar. Was it the same jealousy he experienced in the confused and nebulous dream, repeated so often for so long now, in which he lusted after a faceless woman, only to be rejected by her; the dream which alone among all of his dreams he could never clearly recall, only clearly remembering, when awakening, the sense of the most terrible betrayal imaginable?

Laying awake, he tried as always, to "see" the woman, to understand why she refused him, and whom he had betrayed, but to no avail. After a while, he gave up. Perhaps he was just imagining what he thought. He lay a moment thinking of nothing until he heard the mockingbird call again. Then he began to relax and, accepting the beauty of the surrounding night, he listened for the call once more.

CHAPTER

20

One moment there was the call of a mockingbird, and the softness of the southern night. The next, Ignatius was asleep.

Then the dream began.

He was in a medieval castle. He recognized the architecture at once as pre-Norman and eleventh-century Breton. It was a late summer's night. He was standing at the narrow window of his bedroom, high in the donjon that towered up from the castle keep. A full moon brightened the forest and fields of the surrounding countryside into a pale and mysterious softness. In contrast, the castle's inner courtyard, directly below, was fetid with the stench of ox and horse manure and of human excrement and refuse. It waited for a storm to wash it all down into the surrounding fields.

The moon brightened the several score of thatched roofs of the sleeping bourg, clustered for protection close against the yards-thick, fortified walls encircling the castle. He took pride in those walls. Thirty years ago, in 1036, when he'd come to Brittany to be Bishop of Vitré, the castle had been encircled only by a palisade of pointed wooden stakes and was vulnerable to any besieger. The fealty owed him by the burghers of the town, as well as the peasantry for miles around, enabled him to build in stone.

In return, his vassals received the protection of his armed force: nineteen hundred men at arms, pikesmen and archers and a score of mounted knights; a disciplined body that thrice with the help of his neighbor, William, Duke of Normandy, had repelled the Capetian King, Henry of France.

Henry bore him an old grudge and saw, if ever successful in defeating him, a sure way to be a thorn in the flank of William, for the Norman had become far too powerful for his liking.

There was no love lost between himself and William, either; their alliance was but one of expediency. Each was less dangerous to the other than Henry. And Henry was less a danger to each if they chose to stand against him together.

He at first ignored a knock at his heavy, oaken door, its rough-hewn timbers held together with forged nails. His mind was in a turmoil, his head pounded. William's son, Rufus the Red, slept a drunken sleep below as his trusting guest. What to do with him tomorrow? Hold him as hostage to extort concessions from William? Cut his unsuspecting throat? Send him on his way?

The knock persisted. He turned from the night into the damp gloom of his room, lit only by one resin torch, and cried, "Enter!"

The door creaked open on its massive iron hinges; his body servant appeared, an elderly, hunchbacked monk who bowed abjectly.

"The lady awaits, sire."

"Lady?"

"The armorer's daughter, sire. Her name is Christine."

He remembered then. Some young maiden of the bourg. Her marriage ceremony had been that day. Her nuptial bed had already been blessed by a priest, but her husband would have to wait until she had fulfilled her wish to be first bedded by himself. For if she were fortunate enough to become pregnant, this would bind her entire family to him by blood and give them his protection. And if the child were a boy, he would become a knight and carry his father's coat of arms on his shield with the bar sinister.

He cursed. Tonight Rufus the Red was everything. He wanted no woman in his bed. "Send her away," he told the old monk.

"Would that be wise, sire? Her husband has boasted to the whole bourg of her coming here. And she has seen a witch, I've heard, who gave her love potions and magic words, and promised a curse if you refused her."

"Enough! Away!"

"And in coming, sire, she has defied her father," the old monk insisted slyly, "who does not wish to be bound to you."

"Not bound? The armorer?"

"A faithful man, sire, but a free man by your own agreement."

"Ah?" He remembered then. The armorer, a crafty Helvetian from the far-off bourg of Zurich, had refused to swear allegiance, fearful one day he might be unable to switch to some invading conqueror in time to avoid a blade through his throat. Rankled, he had taken him on, but only because of his great artisanship.

"Defied him, did she?" He liked that. Such filial rebellion could enable him to revenge himself on the humiliation, slight though it was, that the armorer's refusal of allegiance had dealt him. He laughed and scratched at the heavy gray mat of his belly and chest hair exposed by his open woolen robe.

He tried to remember the girl. "How old is the lady?"

"Fourteen, sire. Just this last week."

He frowned. Twelve or thirteen was the usual age to be married. Why had she dallied so long in accepting a husband? Or was she ugly and undesirable with perhaps scant dowry from her father?

"Fourteen? Is she then not fair?"

The monk smiled. "Nay, sire. She's as fair as the sun."

He grunted his doubt, but nodded his permission. When the old hunchback withdrew, he pulled an iron brazier filled with glowing embers close to a table where there was a skin of wine. In spite of the warmth of the night outside, the bare stone of the donjon was damp and chill from a recent cold rain.

His eyes fell for a moment on his bed with its rough linen sheets covering the straw mattress and with its blankets of softened wolf fur, where he had lain with so many a woman, but never a wife. It was long and wide, for he was a big man likened by some to a grizzled ox and by others to a great bear, and one who, always restless in sleep from tormenting dreams, needed space in which to toss and turn.

He looked, but hardly saw. His eyes moved across the room past the wooden tub in which he washed, and past the long perch pole from which he hung his helmet and chain mail, his sword and battle mace, to then rest on the only decoration on the barren stone walls: a massive iron crucifix where the face of Christ so often appeared to him, eyes filled with the sorrow of accusation.

Staring at it, he barely heard the faint tapping at the door and the sound of it opening when he sensed her presence. He turned and saw her and had an impression, suddenly, of a wood sprite or fairy. The resin torch behind her made a halo of her long hair, which spilled like spun flax down over the shoulders of the cloak she clutched tight across her chest. Her arms and legs were as slender as a child's. He felt brutish then, and old, and, with his guilt, almost an ogre.

He filled two silver beakers with wine and gruffly said, "Come now, beside me. I am not that ugly, and you are a married woman today and here of your own will."

She came and sat near him and presently unfastened her cloak to let it slip from her shoulders. She wore only a thin white linen tunic tied at the waist with a narrow belt of twisted gold cloth, and the discomfort he felt at her fragility increased. Through the cloth, he could easily see the slenderness of her waist and the contours of her young breasts with their virginal nipples. She had come there like a lamb eager for its own sacrifice.

They were silent some moments, but finally she spoke, her voice docile. "Does your lordship not find me favorable?"

He did not answer. His mind had gone once more to Rufus, sleeping below.

She spoke again, and in her voice, there was an unexpected shrewdness not common in one of her age. "They say in the kitchen and barracks you know not what to do with Rufus the Red."

He looked up slowly from his wine. "Aye? And what do you know of Rufus?"

"He sleeps trustingly, my lord."

"And, if so, why would I not know what to do with him, but send him on his way at sunrise with my blessing and messages of friendship for his dear father?"

This time, it was she who did not answer. She seemed suddenly distracted by a board of *shatranj* with its carved ivory castles they called rooks, and kings and queens and bishops and little soldiers they called pawns. It was a game from Persia that was now sweeping all Christendom. His was a present from the Patriarch of Florence, brought in a caravan that had crossed the Alps after the snows had melted.

Without a word, she swung the board around, moved a pawn and said, "Because, my lord, you think instead to have Prince Rufus sleep in your dungeon tomorrow night, perhaps in irons."

He was speechless. Had the witch also given her the power to read his mind?

"Your play, Sire."

His surprise turned to anger. What nonsense was this? He tried to pull the board away. "Enough, child. This game is not for women."

She held it fast. "I am champion of the bourg, Sire."

Seething, he said, "Why speak you such of Prince Rufus?"

"I speak not so much of Rufus, my lord, as of your oath of friendship with King Harold of England. A far greater friendship," she added, pointedly, "than you have with William."

"Harold of England?" Even more surprised, he could only stare. She reached across the board, moved his pawn and one of her own, then again his. "You would have moved thus," she said, "and I, thus." She moved a rook and stared intently at the board. "And you thus, I suppose." She moved his knight.

He found his thoughts and was wary. How much did she know? "What friendship is this you tell?"

"He saved you from drowning, they say. When a great wave swept you away as you swam together on the beaches at Dieppe."

He cursed in his heart then. His closest secret. Someone had talked, and he would never know who, even if he put a score of men and women on the rack. In frustration, he struck the table with his fist. A beaker flew away. "They? Speak up! Who are they?"

She smiled mysteriously and moved her bishop again. "William sails for England next week," she answered, "with an army of five thousand bowmen and mounted knights. If Rufus were to remain here, William might not dare sail. He'd have a dagger at his back. Nor, with Rufus as your hostage, would William dare to revenge himself."

Blindly, he moved one of his rooks himself.

"And a grateful Harold," she continued, "would surely reward you with some English dukedom." She paused, her hand poised over her queen. "But then," she added, "such a prize might never be claimed, for you fear King Harold would never cross the channel just to help you fight off Henry. And the French king would be sure to defeat you with William no longer your ally, but your enemy, and you thus standing alone."

She moved her queen to protect her king and glanced shrewdly up from the board. "A pretty dilemma for you, my lord. But sire, there is a way out. If you were to sail with William, Henry would stay in Paris. For with your powerful force joining William, Harold's defeat is all but guaranteed, and a dukedom in France would be your prize, or a cardinalate in Rome, perhaps. For William, as you know, is close to the pope."

He burst out harshly. "And my oath to Harold?"

Her answer was a knowing smile. "Oath, sire?"

He struck the table once more. Harder than before. "And what is all this to you?"

Her smile disappeared. Her eyes held his. Her face had changed and was the face of a woman and there was a woman's cold purpose in it. "I am here, my lord," she answered softly, "to tie my firstborn to you by blood. You do me no good dead."

"My word has always been my bond."

"And Harold's word? Have you ever thought, Sire, that your nearly drowning was perhaps a useful stroke of luck for him? Some say he only saved you from the waves to lessen your loyalty to William."

His heart tightened. Was this true? No, Harold's love for him surely was pure. The girl goaded him.

She moved her queen again. "Check," she said. "And two moves hence it will be check again, whatever you do, and mate. Surrender, my lord."

Anger nearly choked him. Blind rage. Bitch of a child who would tell him how to act. Had the witch given her authority to preach, too? In a gale of fury, he swept board and men away and then, violently upending the table, roared at her to leave.

And when she didn't move, he seized her by the shoulder and threw her bodily toward the door and stumbled across the room to fall heavily to his knees before the crucifix.

There, head bowed, he thought of Harold and the love they had always shared; he thought of their young bodies that day, like plunging, white arrows in the waves until the beauty of the moment had turned nightmare and he was swept helplessly away. And he thought of Harold thrashing the angry water to reach him. "Guy, Guy! I am here."

And he thought of later, too, when kneeling in the sand, he swore his love and loyalty to Harold forever. Even now his heart burst with love for him.

And finally he thought of Henry of France. For if he betrayed William, the vile Capetian Henry would come to defeat him and hang his flayed-alive body from a gibbet outside the gates of his Paris kingdom.

He tore away his robe, but even as the first hissing blow of his whip lashed into the torn and tender flesh of his back, he felt his arm stayed.

"My lord?"

He looked up. She stood there, close to him, bare thigh against his naked shoulder. She had taken off her linen tunic, and he could smell her body, her woman smell and the soft sweet scent with which she had bathed her skin. Her hair made a halo for her face, and her virgin breasts were firm and young, and close to his eyes was her smooth, rounded belly and below it the soft cloud of hair that beckoned.

The warmth of her enveloped him. Blood pounded in his ears and he rose slowly to her, the cross and the scourge forgotten.

At dawn, she slipped away as quietly as she had come, and with heavy heart he went below to bid farewell to Rufus and send messages of fealty to William, his father, and swearing his help when William invaded England.

"Oh, Harold, Harold!" Within an hour, terrible guilt brought him to send a body of horses after the Duke's son, but it was too late.

The next night, his betrayal drove him back to the great iron crucifix. The sorrowful face of Christ appeared. He fell before Him and prayed forgiveness, and when his prayers went unanswered, took up the scourge once more and lashed his back until the blood ran down between his buttocks to redden the rush-covered floor.

To no avail. His love for Harold crowded in on him and there was the cold voice of God, damning him forever for his betrayal.

At home. VII April Anno Domine MMX. In nomine Patris et Filii et Spiritus Sancti: Amen:

Last night in New Orleans, I dreamt I again was Bishop of Vitré. I awoke with the memory of young Christine as though yesterday, her body warm against mine. God rest my fantasy of her. And today, I am still haunted by Harold in my dream, too, when in the evening after the great battle at Hastings in England, I find him lying amidst a heap of his fallen men-at-arms, his one remaining eye still open and staring up at me, and the shaft of the arrow of death that filled his other eye pointing at me accusingly.

CHAPTER

21

On returning home, Ignatius was informed that Sister Jessica's mother had died the day before and that Sister Jessica had been given permission to return to her home in Mountsberg, West Virginia, for the funeral. He remembered only too clearly his own father's and mother's deaths and without a second thought, and since there was no telephone or computer for email at Jessica's home, he put on his black suit and Roman collar, threw his cardinal's waistband and biretta into a suitcase along with his cassock, and made travel arrangements.

He knew how much it would have meant to Jessica's mother, with her devout faith, to have a cardinal help officiate at her funeral. But more importantly, he wanted to give Jessica as much help and support as possible. He knew that she was very close to her mother and unquestionably would be grieving deeply. She was perhaps also having to bear the burden of most of the funeral arrangements. Her father, he knew, was an alcoholic, and from pictures on Jessica's desk of numerous younger brothers and sisters, he'd surmised that the family was desperately poor.

He caught a flight to Atlanta, where he changed for another to Charleston. There, he rented a car and set off for Mountsberg.

It was raining, and the roads were slick. He drove for an hour before turning off the main highway onto the winding county road that led down into the darkly depressing valley that harbored the town.

The coal towns of West Virginia always seemed worse to Ignatius than he remembered them to be. Mountsberg was no exception. On its outskirts, many homes were nothing more than shacks or old trailers scattered about what had once been pastures. Most had battered pickups and half-rusted cars strewn around their unfenced yards. The town itself, deep at the foot of the somber, shadowing hills, consisted of a main street where a few dilapidated shops showed the effects of a shopping mall some miles away, and coal-grimed frame houses stared bleakly at each other across three or four narrow intersecting streets. One such frame house was Jessica's former home.

Five children, aged six to twelve, sat on the stoop and stared at Ignatius as he got out of the car and remained warily silent when he said hello. In the dark hallway that smelled from damp and human sweat, he came face to face with Jessica's father. The miner, who'd hated his wife's religion and had been bitterly opposed to Jessica's taking vows, looked smaller than Ignatius expected. He was stooped over from a life of hard labor and too worn to care much about anything. There was a line of coal dust around his sideburns and on his wrists and he smelled strongly of whiskey.

"If you're the preacher feller, she's in there." His voice was slurred. He jerked a truculent thumb toward the back of the hall and shuffled into a side room where there was a television set and a shabby old couch and chairs.

Ignatius went on to the kitchen, a back room with a patched linoleum floor. A single window looked out across an alley at the side of another house. Jessica was at an old coal range stirring something in a large pot. In a plain cotton dress, she looked different than what he was used to. She looked so much a woman, not his young assistant. She looked like a housewife and mother, and for an instant Ignatius wondered if there weren't times when she regretted her vocation. There was another with her, standing by the single cold-water-faucet sink. Ignatius remembered Jessica mentioning a sixteen-year-old sister. She looked thin and unwell, her eyes dark-shadowed and her hair without luster. She saw him and nudged Jessica, who turned.

Seeing Ignatius, her hand went to her mouth in surprise. "Father Ignatius!"

"I thought your mother would have liked me to come down," he said. "And maybe help out at the service."

He felt awkward—would she perhaps resent his coming? Young women her age were still often trying to shed parents, he knew, in their need for independence. She might think he'd decided she couldn't handle a death and funeral by herself. But then he found himself almost embarrassed. With tears in her eyes, Jessica poured out her gratitude and, clearly more than happy to see him, rushed about to get coffee and be sure he needed nothing more.

The funeral would be in the morning, he learned, and ten miles away, where the only Catholic church in the valley was visited once a week by a priest. The rest of the day was then a blur. Jessica's father sat in the parlor, drinking, and Jessica, along with her sister, on whom now would fall the burden of keeping house, was fully occupied making all the necessary arrangements.

Ignatius did the best he could to help her. He ran errands in his car and took the younger children off to the distant mall to buy them proper clothes for the funeral, as they had next to nothing. Like the home they lived in, they suffered from their father's failure of responsibility.

Late in the afternoon, the undertaker brought Jessica's mother home. The plain, dark-wood coffin Jessica had picked out was placed on two trestles in the living room, its lid open, the dead woman in it a frail, white wax-faced figure dressed in black and holding her rosary with its crucifix in bone-thin hands resting on a shrunken breast.

Neighbors came all evening, most of them women alone, although a few with their husbands, nearly all coal miners. They brought flowers and some came with food. Many stayed for hours, sitting on anything available, and talking together in low voices.

Ignatius spent the night in a motel thirty minutes away. In the morning, an hour before the funeral service, he went to the little valley church to see Father

Kiley, the officiating priest. He found him a pale and intense young man who had been ordained only three years before. Although he showed Ignatius all the respect and deference due his rank, Ignatius was quickly aware that Kiley resented him. He at first thought this was due to his authoritative presence undercutting the young man's role. Halfway through celebrating mass, however, he realized that it was the Church's entire hierarchy, which his rank represented, that was the object of the priest's hostility.

Later, her mother interred in a bleak local cemetery, Jessica told him that this was the young priest's last mass. He was renouncing his vows and returning to secular life.

Remembering his own early years, Ignatius knew why only too well. How often, when the burden of loneliness became so great, had he not wanted to give up, too? The gulf between so many who tended daily to the spiritual needs of the millions and millions of exploited poor the Church claimed as its own and those who dictated their lives from Rome was too great to mentally bridge. More than a thousand priests a year were leaving the Church, many disillusioned at its failure to meet the realities of their parishioners. The need for the sacraments by the laity could often not be met in many places. Unless the hemorrhaging was stopped, the Church would eventually cease to exist as a viable force in people's lives.

Back at the house, when friends and neighbors came again to remember the dead woman with much-needed food and drink, Jessica kept up a soft smile for all, and

Ignatius found himself wondering once more at her inner strength, which he knew would stop her from following the young priest into an easier life.

When he told her he'd be flying back in the morning, Jessica insisted she return with him. "There's no point in my staying here, Father. I've done everything I can. You'll need me in the office."

He could see it was useless to argue. Save for Jessica's father, the whole family went to the airport to see Jessica off, using her departure as an excuse to enjoy a rare excursion. Ignatius, in his rented car, took four of the younger ones, all wildly excited to see airplanes take off and land. The others drove with Jessica and her sister in their father's pickup.

At the airport, he bought them all lunch and presents to take back home, and, when it came time to say goodbye, he stood to one side as Jessica held and spoke to each one of the children in turn and then talked for a few minutes with her sister, who would be their mother now. Barely sixteen, she suddenly seemed impossibly young: frail and small and virtually breastless and still in her loose-hanging dress that was a size too large for her. Ignatius felt anger well up within him—at the government, at the Church, at life. In a nation almost overwhelmed with wealth, and belonging to a Church whose riches were so great as to be beyond description, this girl would have to quit school to look after the younger children. If her father stopped working, which would surely happen soon, she would need to get a part-time job to supplement the family welfare check and whatever was decided to give her by whatever Catholic charities took interest in her plight. There'd be few if any dates or fun with young people her own age. In one stroke, death had slammed a door on her youth and had thrust her into the full responsibilities of adulthood.

She and the little group of children looked touchingly vulnerable as they finally walked away toward the old pickup, the oldest carrying the youngest on her hip in the instinctive manner of all women through all of time. Ignatius, watching them, heard a stifled sound from Jessica. Turning quickly, he saw a look of terrible pain on her face and heard her say in a low, broken voice, as though only to herself. "What have I done? Oh, God, please forgive me." Then she looked at him. "Father, they're all alone. I left my mother and now I've left them. Father, what have I done?"

He said, "You've chosen to serve God, Jessica."

It sounded utterly heartless to him, and stupid, but for a moment, he could not think of what else to say. She was torn between her deeply devout faith and her family's need of her, but she had made her choice long ago, and it was too late to turn back. She shook her head and covered her face with her hands. But not until he'd seen her tears and felt all the helpless agony of a loving parent for a child's first major blow from the brutality that life could deliver.

Impulsively, he reached out to comfort her. "Don't cry, my child. They'll be all right, you'll see." He held her close. "They'll be all right. They won't be alone. We'll take care of them, both of us will. Count on it."

When he raised her chin to kiss her tearful face and try to reassure her again, a local news photographer happened by. He'd come to the airport to take pictures of a rock group scheduled for a Charleston concert. Unexpectedly seeing a priest embracing and kissing an attractive young woman, he put his camera to work.

"Who's the lady, Father?" It was an insinuating leer. It was open season on priests these days.

Ignatius didn't answer. He put a protective arm around Sister Jessica and hurried her away to the boarding gate and then onto the plane, unaware that the persistent newsman would soon find out Jessica was a nun, he a cardinal, and would be on the phone to his editor.

CHAPTER

22

Ten days later, Cardinal Mancini boarded the Vatican helicopter for Rome's Ciampino airport and a flight to Zurich to meet with Swiss bankers.

Benetto and Brother Demetrius had accompanied the secretary of state to the helicopter pad in the northwest corner of the Vatican gardens. There, before boarding, Mancini issued last-minute orders, unaware that Benetto planned to take full advantage of his temporary absence to lunch with his friend Luciano. While Benetto listened to Mancini, Luciano, who was pasty-complexioned, flaxen-haired, and plump, lingered out of sight at the edge of the small crowd of priests and lay workers gathered by the helicopter pad.

The moment the helicopter rose up above the trees to clatter noisily away over the great dome of St. Peter, the two friends joined up.

Guessing the priest planned to duck out of work, Demetrius intervened. "Where are you going, Father?"

"To lunch."

The monk took no pains to hide his disapproval. "Did His Lordship grant his permission?"

Benetto considered Demetrius, a lowly monk, far beneath him and loathed Demetrius for his ever-pious submission to rule. He answered with an offensive sneer. "Why don't you mind your own business, old man? Or is it because you don't dare sneak off, so nobody else should?"

"God is your judge, not I."

Benetto laughed and, ignoring the look on the secretary's cadaverous face, walked off with Luciano toward the Viale dell'Osservatorio, the great gate in the ancient east wall of the Vatican gardens leading to the city streets of Rome.

The beauty of their surroundings, the narrow paths amidst Lebanon cedars and cypress trees, the broad walks bordered by lawns and beds of flowers now in the full bloom of spring, held little interest for either young man, however. Nor did the Vatican Palace, whose hoary Medieval and Renaissance walls enclosed the masterful genius of Michelangelo, Raphael, Botticelli, and scores of other greats, along with a priceless treasure of illuminated manuscripts and galleries of Greek and Roman statuary.

Their minds were elsewhere. The moment the monk was out of sight, Luciano, who had been giggling like a schoolboy over his disapproval, looked around almost furtively and burst out, "All right, let's see them."

The papal nuncio in Washington had emailed three American news photos to Mancini that showed Ignatius embracing Jessica at the Charleston airport. Benetto had promised to bring them to lunch and had filched them from Mancini's desk.

"Not here." He seized Luciano's arm and hurried him through the Nympheum, an open elliptical courtyard separating two small Renaissance buildings, where they often ate a sandwich lunch by a bubbling fountain.

The shortest route took them hurrying to the imposing Pinacotteca just inside the Leonine Wall. Oblivious to one of the greatest and most priceless collections of Christian and Italian painting in the world that graced the imposing building's fifteen marble halls, they cut through the ground floor devoted to restoration and, quickly reaching the giant gate, hurried out into the bustling streets of Rome and headed for Luciano's apartment, several blocks away on the Via di Porta Angelica.

"If they're half of what you say," the clerk insisted, "the only thing more scandalous would be a picture of Monsignor Pasternelli enjoying himself with an Oratorio choir boy." It was well known that Pasternelli frequented a certain private house in Rome that offered clerical clients every possible sort of hedonistic pleasure between men.

"It shouldn't be difficult to take one," Benetto agreed. "Does he ever do anything else?"

Ten minutes later they were in Luciano's expensively furnished living room, where an Impressionist painting of nude young men bathing in a river hung above the marble mantle of the fireplace.

Benetto produced the newspaper photos from inside his cassock. "Here you are," he said. He spread them out on a glass cocktail table.

Luciano squealed and pounced. "Well, well! So much for celibacy."

In one picture, Ignatius was holding Jessica's chin up with one hand and looking into her eyes. In another, he held her close and was kissing her forehead. In the third, he was walking her to the plane with his arm around her.

Luciano sniggered. "A cardinal and a nun! I don't believe it. She's half his age, too. That's borderline pedophilia." He put a finger on Jessica. "Are you sure she's a nun? She's not wearing a habit."

Benetto laughed. "Most of them over there don't anymore."

"Really?" Luciano studied the clipping further. "Silly me, I always thought the American clergy only liked little boys. What does the caption say?" He couldn't read English.

Benetto translated it into Italian. "It's headed: *Love in the Church?* Then it says: *His Eminence, the most Reverend Cardinal Heriot, at the Charleston airport with a woman identified as Sister Jessica Pace, a nun of the order of the Little Sisters of St. Agnes of Tours.*"

"But was this a secret weekend or what?"

"No, no. He went to officiate at her mother's funeral. I heard Mancini talking about it on the telephone with our nuncio over there."

Luciano held up one photo. "Just look at them. What a great poster this would make. Sacred love!"

Benetto laughed and agreed.

The doorbell rang. Luciano went to admit a catered lunch of cold delicacies along with champagne. Then, while Benetto laid it out on the cocktail table, the clerk went into the bedroom to shed his street clothes and put on a silken dressing gown embroidered with butterflies and flowers.

Coming back, he asked, "What does Mancini plan to do with them?"

"What can he do? Heriot can always say he was simply trying to comfort her. After all, she'd just buried her mother. That's innocent enough. I think the nuncio sent them over only for fun. He knows how Mancini hates Heriot."

Luciano gave the photos a last look and shrugged dismissively. "Too bad." He turned his attention to opening the bottle of champagne. "It would have been such a fun scandal."

Benetto tried mentally to shrug off the regret he heard in Luciano's voice. Luciano lived for scandal. He was always talking about the younger princes of the court, too many of whom he'd slept with himself.

Luciano poured the champagne. Taking his glass, Benetto forced down a twinge of jealousy at the thought of Luciano's endless promiscuity amongst the Roman nobility. He put up with it only because he knew he was number one in Luciano's life, just the way Luciano was in his. Not because of love, although he could pretend real love for Luciano just the way he was sure Luciano's undying love for him was pretended. But because what they had together—using each other to get ahead in life, to get what they wanted—was of far more importance to both of them than mere love.

From Luciano, Benetto got inside information on all the illicit dealings of the Vatican Bank, from laundering money to supporting dictators who protected Vatican property. He garnered information that, even when untrue, he could use one day to further his own career.

And from him, Luciano gained similarly useful knowledge of Vatican affairs abroad, which could help with his private investments as well as to maneuver his way upward in the bank. How useful their mothers' ambitions for each in separate careers, the Church and banking, had turned out to be.

They ate lunch, and then Benetto said he had to get back. Mancini might telephone with some new order he'd forgotten when he left.

Luciano's hand rested on Benetto's knee, his voice insinuating. "Just today, can't Mancini's work wait?" He smiled and refilled Benetto's glass.

Benetto studied the pale amber champagne, its little surface bubbles hissing gently into eternity. Luciano was right, he thought. If Mancini did call, he could always say he had gone on some errand or other. Or to pray in the Basilica. Right now belonged to him.

He sipped the champagne and sank back against the couch cushions. "You're incorrigible," he murmured.

Perhaps the very last thing on Benetto's mind as he surrendered to Luciano's blandishments was that his insulting behavior at the helicopter pad had so shocked Mancini's skeletal valet as to set in motion a chain of events

that would produce a greater scandal, although of a different kind than either Luciano or he had ever envisioned.

———◆———

Everything about the young priest profoundly horri-
fied Demetrius. Bad enough his appointment as Mancini's
secretary due solely to wealth and privilege. Bad enough
the endless daily manifests of anti-Christ behavior.
Benetto, he was also certain, was also guilty of the mortal
sin of sodomy.

The monk came from a peasant family in the poverty-
stricken region of Calabria in southern Italy where the
only relief from utter misery in a life of unremitting struggle was devout faith and service to God. He had become
Mancini's valet through a series of happenings over which
he'd had little control. As a brother in an obscure
Dominican order in Calabria, he had been sent to the
Vatican by the order's Superior with a letter begging temporary relief from interest on a loan from the Vatican
Bank. Testifying to his order's poverty, he had so amused a
presiding cardinal with his rustic appearance and explana-
tions that he was offered a recently vacant clerical position
in an accounting office with the thought that such simple
provinciality might, through comic relief, improve the
mood of the workplace.

At first, unaware he was an object of fun, awed by
being in the very heart of the Church, and reverently
devout in his profound love for Pope Gregory, he had
readily accepted the position. During the year that followed, however, his role as butt of all office jokes became

obvious to him and wore thin. When he proved incapable of executing anything but the simplest task of accounting, his superiors sought to place him elsewhere.

Fortuitously, Mancini's elderly valet was forced to resign due to illness at that time, and Demetrius was sent to be one of many interviewed by the cardinal. To everyone's surprise, Mancini took him on, seeing in the monk's simplicity and devotion a man who could be trusted to safely guard the most intimate secrets of his personal, as well as official, life.

Mancini's arrogant disregard of what Demetrius believed was true faith in Christ pained the monk deeply. He performed his job perpetually distressed by this and by Vatican politics and materialism. And, listening to Mancini's haughty dismissal of Father John Zacharias as a heretic for what he saw only as true following of the Lord, Demetrius found himself, in his heart of hearts, allying himself with the American.

Several days previous, while tidying Mancini's bedside table, he had stumbled on an exchange of memoranda between Cardinal Carezza and Mancini that clearly indicated that a way was being engineered to bypass the desperately ill Pope Gregory and excommunicate Zacharias. If Gregory died before a means to do so was found, and Mancini became pope, such a move would be a certainty.

Ever since his discovery, Demetrius had gone about his tasks with a heavier heart than usual. He drew more and more deeply into himself. He obeyed orders mechanically while trying not to think of what he saw in the memoranda as being profoundly irreligious as well as unjust.

Until now. Returning to Mancini's suite and his small service room with its ironing board, sewing machine, and special storage arrangements for Mancini's ritual vestments, he sat for a while burning with resentment and anger at Benetto and his foppish friend and wondering what he could do to remove such a cancer from the bosom of the Church. Exploring every possible avenue, he could find no way. The only person who could do such a thing was Mancini.

That thought, and all the storming emotion in Demetrius, triggered a sudden change in the target of the monk's resentment. Mancini superseded Benetto, and every feeling Demetrius had harbored for so long against the Cardinal erupted.

With it came an overwhelming desire to protect the one person who, in the monks' eyes, truly followed the Lord and behaved in His image. That person was now in mortal danger of an act that was anti-Christ. But what could he do, a lowly monk with no rank and no power? He thought of Jesus and what he had done, and of all the saints and their sacrifices, and felt ashamed. They had not hesitated. And they would not now. Father Zacharias was pure, and they would not have sat idle and let him be denied access to God.

Thinking of them, Demetrius felt a determination he'd never felt before. Nor would he sit idle. He could at least warn the priest. Getting out pen and official Vatican note paper from Benetto's office, he hesitated a last moment, then sat down and, trying to remember how to spell English words correctly, wrote in his almost childlike hand:

Dear Father John:

I know about certain secret communications and meetings in the Holy See. They plan your excommunication without the knowledge of His Holiness. This will also certainly happen if His Holiness suddenly leaves us and Cardinal Mancini becomes pope. I have not the power to prevent this. You must act as soon as possible to defend yourself. May the Lord continue to bless you and always shed His light upon you.

Without signing it, he folded the paper carefully, put it in an official Vatican envelope, and addressed it to Father John Zacharias at a Chicago address for the priest that he found in same file as the memoranda between Mancini and Carezza. Putting a Vatican stamp of required value on the envelope, he tucked it carefully away against his heart inside the cotton shirt he wore beneath his monk's robe. After going to the Basilica to pray in one of the chapels, he then went to the Vatican post office and, without hesitation, mailed the letter.

CHAPTER

❖23❖

The third day of voting in the conclave was over, with the tally of votes little changed from the first and second days. Mancini received forty votes, Ignatius thirty-four, Berssi twenty-eight, and Ngordo eighteen.

In the Sistine Chapel, chemicals were tossed into the old iron stove, and black smoke rose into the sky above the tiled roofs of the Apostolic Palace to inform the outside world once again that a pope had not yet been elected. The junior cardinal lifted the ceremonial chain from the chapel side of the door, the locks on the other side were turned. The cardinals rose from their thrones and filed out. As after the previous two days' voting, the corridors and cells around the Sistine buzzed with forbidden lobbying. There were whispers of a possible deadlock. There was talk by the ultra-right Traditionalists of making a deal with some of the Third World cardinals. Their particular targets were those they knew were fearsome of left wing coups d'etat in countries under rigid authoritarian rule. Through corruption and bad management, such countries were more often than not in economic chaos, with the general population suffering severe hardship. Besides endangering Vatican investments, a coup could wreck the narrow elitist and privileged social world surrounding those in power and to which a colleague, thus the Church, was invariably attached. Through diplomatic and financial leverage, a Traditionalist papacy could be instrumental in helping to forestall such coups.

Equally, there were those in similar countries, but under left-wing governments, where Vatican help in a rightist coup would be welcome in reestablishing Church influence and thus the well being of those who served it.

Once again, Ignatius took no part in any of it. He quickly retreated to his little garret room. There he barred his door, filled in a page of his diary, knelt in prayer at his *prie-dieu,* and then sat looking out at the gathering evening in the sky above the huge dome of the Basilica.

Although distancing himself from his colleagues physically, he was unable to avoid reflecting on the deep divisions in the Church that Father Zacharias had brought to the surface. He again felt all the discomfort he'd experienced in his meeting with the priest and Francesca in New Orleans, as well as with the president and his family, when he had defended the Church's position on so many current vital issues. There was pain in recalling some of the specious arguments he'd used. He thought, too, of his discomfort, save for defending the papacy, in rebutting Father Zacharias on television.

Had he been guilty of misguided loyalty in defending what an inner voice told him was wrong? Had he perhaps been justifying all his years of toil as a worker priest and since then as bishop, archbishop, and now cardinal, protecting every stand the Church took? If so, it would make him as culpable as those of his colleagues who would defend the rotten governments that gave them a lifestyle and power they did not want to sacrifice, and the Church, via the Vatican Bank, privileges it would not otherwise have.

And if he had indeed been misguided into hypocrisy, why had he been? In the back of his mind, there constantly nagged the thought that there was some elusive reason, some ulterior motive, that had constantly guided him all these years, which his mind was carefully avoiding.

Reverse himself now, and the papacy could well be his. That was clear. He had only to speak out for the maverick priest and it could be his to get the Church to surrender its dangerous idolatry of archaic theological thinking, to recognize the capriciousness of its own checkered history, and, instead of giving opulent and often fraudulent lip service to Christ, to truly act in His spirit.

One word, and with it could also come the chance to make the Church the great creative force in the world he knew it could be; to meet such daunting challenges as the population explosion, nationalism, and ethnic violence, the destruction of the environment, the terrible plague of AIDS, the tragic divisiveness between Christianity and Islam.

Yet he could not speak out, and would not. To do so and court the papacy with the terrible secret burden of sin he carried would be an insult to God.

Leaving the gathering night, he returned to his desk to open his diary and read what he had written the day after the pope's funeral.

Rome, XI May, Anno Domine MMX. In nomine Patris et Filii et Spiritus Sancti: *Amen:*

> *This day, I walked in the gardens, and was found there by that dearest of men, Ngordo, as deeply saddened by the loss of our dear departed friend Petrucci as I. We went to San Giovanni's tower at the head of the old Leonine Walls. There, we seated ourselves awhile in the warm sun on one of the old stone benches at the tower's base, and Ngordo begged me to make known my interest in the papacy. I was saddened when I told him I could not, and would give him no reason why a year's hard work by such a dear friend rallying Third World and other liberal cardinals on my behalf had been time wasted. And depressed, too, that Ngordo seemed not to take my word as definitive. Afterward, needing to be alone, I visited St. Peter's, hoping to have the rare opportunity of once again praying at the sepulchre of the First Apostle.*

It was early dawn. The little candles on the *prie-dieu* had long guttered out, but Ignatius did not sleep. More than ever, he was disturbed at the dilemma Ngordo faced because of his silence

Even worse was what he had learned about himself in

Washington only days before Pope Gregory died. Years of searching libraries for the sources of his dreams had finally led him to one that questioned the fallibility of his very existence in the Church, if not indeed his whole life.

CHAPTER

24

Washington, three days before the death of Pope Gregory and three weeks before the third day of voting in the conclave, was enjoying soft spring weather. The cherry blossoms were out, runners were back on the Mall, tourists were lining up to see the State Rooms of the White House.

Late in the afternoon, as all of the city was shutting down for the day, Allegra Shaw left the Library of Congress Annex complaining to herself that she was missing such lovely afternoon weather. She'd spent several hours researching for the novel she was currently writing. Heading across the broad sidewalk separating the library from Third Street, she stopped short in surprise on seeing Ignatius, dressed in a plain black priest's suit with a white Roman collar and waiting to cross the street. He was the last person she ever expected to see. What on earth was he doing in Washington?

The light changed, others crossed the street, but he didn't move. She quickly joined him.

"Ignatius. For heaven's sake. What are you doing here in Washington? Were you in the library? I was just there myself. Why didn't you let me know you'd be in town?"

He turned, but seemed not even to see her.

"Eminence! It's me, Allegra."

He mumbled some reply, his words drowned out by a passing truck. Then she saw he was sheet white and looked almost as though he were in shock.

He slowly focused on her and mustered a weak smile. "Sorry. I should have called you, but I didn't know myself until last night." He'd begun to sweat.

"Darling man, are you sure you're all right?"

"Yes, yes, of course."

That didn't wash with Allegra. "You're not. You look like you've seen a ghost. Come sit down a moment. I'm parked just a block away."

She took him firmly by the arm and marched him, unprotesting, across the intersection and up a side street to her car and steered him into it.

"Now sit back and relax. Do we need to get you to a doctor?"

"No, no. I'm fine."

"No heart problem you've been hiding?"

"No. Honestly. You just caught me when I was miles away."

"Pains in your chest?"

"No. Good heavens." He laughed, finally more like himself.

"Then for God's sake, tell me what's happened. You've had some kind of a nasty shock, am I right?"

"I suppose so. Well, yes. It's a long story." She studied him. Besides looking ill, he wasn't responding like himself at all. He was hiding something, she knew, and she suspected the something was bad. For his own good, she decided she'd try to get it out of him. "Where were you headed just now?"

"I'm at the Georgetown Hotel."

"Well, you can worry them later. Right now you're coming home with me. You didn't have plans?"

"Just to get a night's rest. I'm on my way home from New Jersey. Princeton. A conference on the environment. But look, I don't want to interfere with anything you might have going on."

"You're not. Amory's out in California arguing genetics with some equal egghead, and I don't like dining alone."

They drove in silence except for Allegra's occasional muttered threats at other drivers in the heavy rush-hour traffic. Some of the dream for which Ignatius had found a source retreated a little. Enveloped in the protective body of the car separating him from the world, he felt momentary safety. He thought of all the long years of friendship, the conscious slot of time in a brief moment of eternity that he and Allegra and Amory had been fated to share. He felt a profound sense of privilege and gratitude for it.

At her house, Allegra took his hand and led him through to the flagstone terrace in the back yard, where there was comfortable garden furniture and a barbecue. He sank down gratefully onto a hammock couch and closed his eyes. He'd lived a nightmare at the library that had left him feeling almost beyond exhaustion. At the intersection at Third Street, he'd thought he might collapse. And while he was mortified at needing assistance, he silently thanked God for the unexpected appearance of Allegra. One moment he was alone with terror, the next she had been there at his side. Like some sort of guardian angel.

He watched her fix them both drinks and when she came and sat by him he wondered an instant at the quality of caring in so many women.

"Now," she said firmly. "Tell me what's wrong and don't tell me nothing is."

He realized there was no point in fencing. He had to tell her. This was Allegra, who could see through almost anybody. Including himself, he thought with a wry inner laugh. And this, too, was a woman who, though on opposite poles from him on nearly everything, was someone he was safe with.

It was hard at first, and he began almost hesitantly, telling her how he had taken advantage of a spare day on his return to his diocese to visit the Library of Congress. He'd wanted to look, he told her, for a source, in something he'd once read and forgotten, of a recent and horrifying nightmare in the hope that this would reveal why he'd ever had such a dream in the first place. Even weeks after he had suffered it, every moment remained in his memory with vivid clarity.

"I don't know why I bothered looking in the Library, actually. I didn't really think I'd find anything. I've never read much of American history and in the dream I was a young French priest in New Orleans soon after the colony was ceded by the French to the Spanish. I think that was around 1750. Maybe a little later.

"I got there from Acadia, the French colony on Canada's Atlantic coast, from where I'd only just escaped when the British invaded and seized it for their own colonists. I'd heard there were French in New Orleans and, in my dream, I caught a boat in Boston for Savannah and from there rode or walked the rest of the distance."

He went on to tell her how he had been befriended in New Orleans by a wealthy plantation owner, a giant Haitian freeman who was a leader among the French people of the colony.

"But then I developed a passion for the Haitian's white wife. She was French and the mother of two illegitimate children by a French nobleman. She was disgraced in France and had come with her children to the new world to start a new life. She married the Haitian to give the children a name and an inheritance."

Hesitantly, he described how they had fallen in love and consummated their love at the very altar of a chapel the Haitian had built for him.

Afterwards, knowing that the child she bore by him would by its color, when born, reveal her as an adulteress, and terrified for his life if she confessed that he was the father, he'd broken the sanctity of the confessional and revealed to the Spanish governor of the colony a seditious plot against him by the Haitian. "I thought only to have the giant arrested and jailed long enough for me to dispose of the child. But it didn't work out that way."

"What happened?"

The Haitian was arrested, he explained, at a state dinner and executed, then and there, right in front of his wife
and all the other guests as an example to others who
might plot.

Ignatius was silent a moment, too tormented by
memory of the dream to continue. Then he told how the
Haitian's wife, along with her adolescent daughter, was
turned over to Spanish soldiers for their sexual pleasure,
and afterward, with her daughter, how she escaped and
drowned herself and the child. And how her young son
was sold to the owner of a northern male brothel. For his
treacherous loyalty to Spanish authority, he himself was
awarded all of the Haitian's property.

"I'd almost given up finding anything when in the
middle of the afternoon I unexpectedly came across
something I knew I'd never read before. It was in a biog-
raphical paragraph about a wealthy merchant later on in
New Orleans, a man who financed the construction of
the New Orleans cathedral. There was a personal detail
that caught my eye."

Indeed, it was a passage that he would never forget.

"I made a copy of it," he said. He pulled a folded sheet
from a pocket and handed it to Allegra.

She read it quickly.

*There is a story connected with the completion of the cathe-
dral in 1794 after the great fire of New Orleans that year,
which miraculously left it unscathed. Where it stands in the
ancient Place des Armes, there was once a small church offi-*

ciated over by a French priest, one Father Claude Gregoire, who had reputedly become wealthy by once betraying the confessional and informing Spanish authorities of a seditious plot by French leaders. Interestingly, the first official ceremony performed in the cathedral was the wedding of a Claudine Pinard, one of several illegitimate daughters of a Creole housekeeper said to be by this same priest whose remains were found at the altar of the church when the church, less lucky than the cathedral, burned to the ground on the day of her birth.

Claudine Pinard's groom was one Henry Heriot, an English adventurer who later became one of the first commission agents shipping agricultural produce from Ohio and Illinois via the Erie Canal after it opened in 1825.

When Allegra finished reading, she was silent a moment, then handed the paper back to him. "Are you sure you never read about this before?"

"Positive."

"What about the Englishman? Heriot."

"He was my great-great-grandfather."

"Oh? You know that?"

"His name was at the top of a family tree we had on the wall at home when I was a child."

"But Ignatius, Heriot is not an uncommon name. That could be a coincidence."

"I'm afraid not. My great-grandfather, Michael, left a diary he'd kept. It was a family treasure. In it, he told how his grandparents, Henry and Claudine, had married in the new cathedral in New Orleans. He mentioned, also, how his grandfather had made a fortune with the opening of the Erie Canal and then lost it all gambling in St. Louis."

Allegra stared at him a long moment, then rose to walk about restlessly, thinking.

"Ignatius, you must have at least heard about this priest at home, some time or other, perhaps when you were very young?"

"No, never." For a moment, his dream returned, first shadowy, indefinite, then sharper. The Haitian's wife, his passionate possession of her at the altar, the church, the dark face of the Spanish governor, the Haitian denounced during the grand ball, forced to kneel and receive a Spanish bullet that shattered his head, the terrified women in their ball gowns screaming at the horror. Ghosts.

"Eminence?" Persistent. The blood-drenched horror of the dream faded.

He found himself looking into Allegra's intense eyes.

"Never, or not that you remember?"

Pictures in his mind flickered. Family dinners. His grandparents. Great-grandfather's diary on the Thanksgiving table. Sacred. *Don't touch, children.*

"You're not absolutely sure, are you? "

Was he? Was anything absolutely sure? "I guess not."

She looked at the news clipping. "You know, for an historian and a researcher, you ought to be ashamed of yourself. 'Reputedly become wealthy,' indeed. Unverified rumor, right? I can see the old men sitting in the sun and smoking their pipes and speculating on it right now. And 'said to be by the same priest'—women's marketplace gossip, Ignatius, and you know it. They probably had him fathering every child in town."

She looked at him intently again. "Darling man, you're holding something back, aren't you? I mean, you're far too strong a person to be thrown by finding you might have had such a monster priest among your ancestors and that, conceivably, you might have some of his genes in you. You were in a state of shock back there at the library when I found you. Am I wrong?"

"No. I guess I did feel a little shaky."

"Let me ask this, then. Why on earth were you trying to find a source for the dream in a library? I mean, I don't know anyone who rushes to one after a nightmare to try to find its cause in something they once read."

He knew then that he had to tell her everything, and with every revelation he felt the easing of a burden he'd found it almost impossible to carry any farther, one he'd never found lifted from him in confessional. He told her about Seth drowning, how it had happened, the guilt he'd suffered, and because of it the endless reliving of it in nightmares, night after night. And all the years of other ghastly nightmares that followed.

"Ignatius, that's just awful. You poor thing. Did you ever think to see a psychiatrist about it? Or does the Church still not hold any truck with Sigmund Freud?"

"The Church is not as hide-bound as some of you humanists might think. Of course I saw someone. Years ago. I underwent therapy for about six months. That was before I became a priest." Ignatius paused, remembering the psychiatrist and the irony of a Catholic seeking insight into his troubled soul through the help of a Jew. It had been a wonderful and warm experience that had given him an unusually intelligent and caring friend and a new appreciation of Judaism.

"Did it help?"

"Not a great deal. The psychiatrist told me I had to stop feeling guilty about my brother. A lot of our dreaming came from guilt, he said. He thought mine certainly did. And I understood that. But I kept dreaming about Seth just the same."

"How about the other dreams?"

"They came much later."

"They weren't mixed up with the Seth dreams?"

"No, no. They started and took over after I was ordained."

"Oh?"

"Oh what?" Ignatius had heard surprised reaction in her voice.

She didn't answer directly. Instead she said, "Did you go back to the shrink for them?"

"Yes, I did. For a while, anyway."

"And?"

"I didn't get anywhere. I kept running into a complete mental block about them and finally gave up. It was like a solid black wall inside my head that, no matter what, I just couldn't get by. I felt guilty, and have ever since, but about something I couldn't identify, no matter how hard I tried. I think the doctor gave up, too. He said it might take years to get to the bottom of it all. I didn't have years then. And I have fewer now."

"It's the same with everybody," Allegra said. "The years just disappear and one day you wake up and say, 'Where did they go, where was I?'"

"I keep trying libraries," Ignatius continued, "but I don't seem to be getting anywhere."

"Libraries? You mean this dream you had the other night about your ancestor, that wasn't the first time you tried to pin a dream on something you'd read?"

Ignatius's laugh was hollow and weary. "I'm afraid not."

He told her about the countless hours he'd spent at libraries everywhere, looking for things he might have read that could have triggered other dreams and perhaps put an end to them.

When they'd come in, she'd put chicken breasts on the barbecue and had made a salad. She served them up and came and ate with him, balancing her plate on her knees, her expression earnest and caring. The soft garden light glinted from her tousled, graying hair, and Ignatius thought of all their years of friendship and trust and felt blessed.

"Let me get something straight," she said. "You spend your life tortured by nightmares. You arbitrarily decide, because you're an historian, that the nightmares with all their vivid reality and accurate historical detail must have been kicked off by something you've read and perhaps have decorated up a bit. Am I right?"

"Yes."

"And if you can prove enough of them match up with something you read or studied, it might put an end to them? They'd be the source of your dreams, not some unidentifiable guilt."

"Something like that. Yes."

She put down her plate and smiled and said, "Cardinal Heriot. Do you want me to speak honestly?"

"Of course."

"Say what I really think? Okay. For God's sake, Ignatius, give up the damn libraries. You must have read enough in your lifetime to provide you with material for ten thousand dreams. All you will do is end up torturing yourself. A dream could come from something obscure that you have read and have forgotten that it's like looking for a needle in a haystack. Or it could come from something you may have read and elaborated on or changed or mixed up with something else as to make whatever it was impossible to recognize. Like this stupid news item. It doesn't say anything definite about your great-great-grandmother being this priest's daughter, or the priest being the horror your dream said he was. All that rape and murder. Does it? Myself, I doubt any of your dreams did come from your reading. What's your record so far? Zero, right?"

He admitted it and said, "Okay, maybe no libraries. Where does that leave me?"

"*Us*, Ignatius. Where does that leave *us*. I should think that would be obvious. It leaves us with that dinner conversation we had the night Merrill Christie set her sights on you."

"Sorry, I'm not sure I follow." But he did. He knew where she was headed even before she spoke further.

"We talked about *déja vu*," she said, "and I told about the strange sensation I had of sitting on my own grave in an English churchyard, remember? And you said that you didn't believe in previous lives."

"And don't," Ignatius asserted firmly. He felt far better, far more positive, for unburdening himself to her, even though they seemed to have gotten nowhere.

"Are you sure you weren't in such a state of shock when I found you because you'd begun to change your mind?"

Had he? His mind balked at the thought. "I was in a state because of an irrational terror of a possibility. The priest, my great-great-grandmother—it was all so close to home."

"Some of the genetic people, like Amory," Allegra said, "think we have locked away somewhere not just a record of every single thing in our present checkered lives, but a complete memory of everything we've ever been or done since we were one-celled amoebas floating around in some pregeological sea. So why not more recent people?"

"I don't believe in reincarnation, Allegra. You know that."

"Yes I do, and it's too bad, because if you did, you might very well accept your horrible nightmares as memories of other lives. Distasteful as that may be. And frankly, you'll never convince me they're anything else."

"What convinces me," Ignatius said firmly, "is how right my psychiatrist was. My dreams are caused by guilt. I've finally realized that. And not because of Seth. I long ago learned how to handle my guilty feelings about him. My dreams since I became a priest are because of some other guilt I can't identify. Somewhere, somehow, I've done something far worse than betray Seth. And my nightmares are punishment for it."

Allegra didn't reply, and they were silent a few minutes after that, each with their own thoughts. They had finished eating, and she poured them coffee and sat back down next to him, cradling her cup thoughtfully between two hands. "You know, the one thing I can't understand is why, in all your so-called dreams, you are such a loathsome beast, when in reality, in this life, you're such a nice guy."

Ignatius smiled. He was relieved she'd gotten off her reincarnation nonsense. "My life isn't over yet. I might surprise everyone and end up a serial killer."

"Don't be facetious, Eminence."

There was sudden sharpness in her tone that brought him up short and wiped the half smile from his face. Her expression was unusually somber.

"Or maybe you're not such a nice guy," she went on evenly. "Even though we do all love you. Maybe you're a serial betrayer. In every dream of a past life you've betrayed someone. Who are you guilty of betraying in this one, Cardinal Heriot?"

It caught him off guard and made him abruptly uncomfortable, dispelling any warm feeling at having unburdened himself. He tried to think and couldn't. "You tell me. After Seth, which wasn't really betrayal, I can't think of anyone."

"All right, let me ask you another question. Why did you become a priest?"

He swallowed at being talked to like a schoolboy and said, "That's easy enough to answer. I chose priesthood, I suppose, because like many others I felt the need to devote myself to something higher than the confusion and misery of mortal men."

But he himself could hear how glib that sounded, and he knew at once from her expression that she wasn't going to let him get away with it.

"You mean God. But why?"

"I don't think that's a question any priest can rationally answer, Allegra. We've argued this one so many times over the years. It's a question of faith. Or, to put it another way, it's simply God's will that we should feel that way."

But was it? he wondered. The discomfort he'd begun to feel increased. The feeling of guilt. He felt boxed in. Not so much by her as by his inability to come up with anything other than clichés as answers. He thought once more of his vacillating explanation to both the president's daughter and Father John Zacharias as to why he thought the priest was wrong.

"You didn't just find priesthood a means to an end?"

"What do you mean? What end?" But he suddenly knew and wanted to tell her to stop, that he didn't want to hear any more. But he couldn't. It was already too late.

"I'm not sure," Allegra replied. "But it crossed my mind that the person you are betraying in this life might be God Himself."

It stung. Ignatius found it almost impossible to think about it, about what she'd said. For a moment he could find no reply. Then, in defense, he forced a smile. "I thought you didn't believe in God." It was a last effort to avoid what he knew she was going to say next, while at the same time knowing he couldn't.

"I don't, but you do," she said, "And I'm wondering if you might have become a priest not for devotional purposes or from love of God, but because you thought that would be the way to rid yourself of your dreams about Seth, something the shrink couldn't do. And that this is the very reason for all the other dreams that you've been stuck with. Good heavens, if I believed in God and thought I'd betrayed him of all people by using Him like that. Talk about guilt and nightmares!"

Ignatius looked away from her steady gaze to stare into the darkness beyond her. His mind went back to his first year at medical school, to a lecturing professor describing the peripheral nervous system. He'd had a terrible dream the night before about Seth and was desperately trying to erase the memory of it so he could concentrate on what the professor was saying. He remembered a picture had flashed through his mind of himself praying in church to God to erase the awful memory. It was just at that moment, he knew, that he'd decided to quit medicine and become a priest, in a sense to spend his entire life as a prayer for help.

Had he indeed chosen self-denial and devotion only to gain God's mercy and bring an end to his tormenting dreams? It would make his whole life a lie.

He could find no relieving answer. Deep inside, he felt a dark and growing coldness that had begun to spread throughout his body. He couldn't think anymore.

Allegra saw the distress in his expression and came to sit beside him. "Ignatius, I'm sorry. I've upset you. And you know, I could be mistaken." She took one of his hands in hers.

"Yes, you could be." Even as he said it, he knew the chances were slim that she was.

In her dismissive, husky laughter at herself, there was apology. "I'm really doing exactly the same thing I've accused you of doing, aren't I? Starting with a foregone conclusion, and then coming up with every fact possible to prove it. Let's not talk about it anymore."

"I don't mind," he said. But he did. He'd had enough. He felt as though he'd been looking into hell.

"I do. You trustingly reveal to me all your troubles, and what do I do? Tell you what makes you tick. As if I really knew. Trying to play God. When I'm not even a believer. I'm sorry, Ignatius."

She'd brought out a vintage Armagnac and filled two delicate liqueur glasses. "Anyway," she said, "we're both too tired to go on tonight. Let's save the next round for a nice sunny-day walk in the country sometime. And, Ignatius, please understand how very much I love you for trusting me with all this. I'm sorry I haven't helped more."

He knew she was opting out for his sake and he appreciated it. What he wanted to do now was be alone and think. He tried to restart, to be positive and cheerful. They talked about other things for a while, people they knew, the state of the world, and then he said good night.

At the door, and when he'd thanked her over and over for her kindness, she said, "Ignatius, if you need me or my Amory at all, anytime, day or night, we're here, okay?"

"Okay." He kissed her cheek. "If you weren't so beyond redemption, I'd give you my blessing, but I'd be wasting God's precious time. I'll just say thanks." She laughed, blew him a kiss. The door closed. He was alone with everything she'd said, with all the doubts she'd raised.

He walked a long way through the dark and quiet suburbs before hailing a taxi to take him to the hotel. That night, he wrote in his diary:

Washington, XVIII April, Anno Domine MMX. In nomine Patris et Filii et Spiritus Sancti: *Amen.*

Today in the library, I was profoundly shocked to discover a virtual description of a dream that I was certain I never read about or heard of before, and that made me fearful that I might possibly be directly descended from a real person, myself in the dream, in which I was a priest who was a rapist and despicable murderer. The very thought of such a thing made me feel like my whole world was going to pieces. Everything went dark and icy cold and I felt as though thought I had embraced the ultimate in evil.

I was rescued by my dear novelist friend, who used the occasion to insist that all my dreams were memories of past lives, an idea that I of course dismissed. With best intentions, however, she has raised in me tormenting doubts about myself, bringing me to wonder if I became a priest not from devotion, but for selfish reasons, and that in doing so I lied to God. The thought that this could be possible raises in me such despair as to make every waking moment for me unbearable. I know not where to turn except to try to find an answer in prayer.

CHAPTER
25

In Rome, Benetto, who had the evening off, dined with his friend Luciano at one of Rome's more expensive and exclusive restaurants. There was excellent food and equally excellent wine, there was candlelight giving the place a romantic air, and there was impeccable and obsequious service that did justice to the price of the meal.

Both the young men felt their usual relief at getting away for an evening from the narrow confines of the Vatican. Both had been born into a world that knew little other than what went on in their own privileged social circles, and, except for exchanging any gossip of importance picked up at their work in the Vatican, their conversation was almost entirely about their various friends in Rome, Venice, and Florence.

Over coffee and brandy, however, Luciano once more began to giggle over the photographs of Ignatius and

Sister Jessica and to insist in humorously barbed remarks, most of them thoroughly indecent, that there had to be more to the relationship between the cardinal and the nun than it appeared.

Benetto, as he'd done before, laughed off any suggestion, but back at the Vatican after the evening was over, and still partially under the spell of Luciano's insinuations, he began to have second thoughts. Where there was smoke, there sometimes really was fire. Might there conceivably be a chance, no matter how remote, that Luciano was right, that there was indeed something illicit going on between the American cardinal and the little nun? If there was, and if it was uncovered, it would ruin any chance at the papacy that Heriot might entertain. That was a given. And if it were due to his effort, Mancini would be quite indebted to him. With added pressure from his mother, he could certainly demand and receive a better position than a secretary, one that would free him, at least partially, from Mancini. He might even be successful in getting the position of nuncio in one of the more lucrative South American countries where there was always opportunity for economic advancement on the side.

Quietly entering his little office high above St. Peter's Square, he once again studied copies he'd made of the photographs of Ignatius and Sister Jessica and secreted in one of his own files. And he thought, *Yes, why not indeed be suspicious?* Was it possible not to entertain suspicions where these so-called "new" nuns in America were concerned? With so many American priests engaged in pedophilia or admitting to a mistress or a child fathered, what was to stop a nun from looking for sex, too? So many attended universities now, did what they wished, and, displaying all of women's weaknesses and failures, had the outrageous effrontery to demand to be ordained as priests; others, in droves, left their vocation for love affairs, or marriage, or to compete with men in business and law and politics, rather than submit and remain in the role God clearly intended for them.

Thinking further, Benetto decided that if indeed such an illicit liaison did exist, the right place to start looking for it would be with one of the sister's fellow nuns. Remembering his mother and her endless *tête-à-tête* with her friends, he reminded himself that women often tell each other their most intimate secrets, revealing every detail of love affairs and endlessly comparing lovers.

It was past midnight in Rome. It would be six hours earlier in America. Settling himself by his telephone, he had no idea what a call would produce. He couldn't have a plan for something like this—he'd have to make one up as he went along.

It took him but a few minutes to find out the residential number at the diocese of the Little Sisters of St. Agnes of Tours. He put in a call.

Even as the phone rang, he decided he'd begin with the Mother Superior. Almost certainly she would be an older woman. Her attitude, then, toward her pretty young charge would either be one of slight jealousy—or, she

might be motherly. Either way, she would be always concerned with the moral character and behavior of the
younger woman.

When the phone was answered, he asked for the
Mother Superior, and when Sister Andrea came on the
line, he introduced himself as personal administrative assistant to His Eminence, Cardinal Mancini. Then, quickly
sensing that Sister Andrea was impressed, he explained the
reason for his call. "I understand there is a Sister Jessica in
your charge."

"Sister Jessica? Yes, Father. That's correct."

"There was, I believe," Benetto chose his words carefully, "a recent and slightly unfortunate photograph of her
and His Eminence in some of the press."

"Yes, Father. We know about it."

In those few words, Benetto, acutely sensitive to the
slightest nuance in others, clearly heard a distinct touch of
frost. Jealousy.

Again he was careful. "We understand that this young
woman and his Eminence work very closely together."

"Yes, Father."

"We supposed that there would not be much contact
between them outside of work hours, however."

The moment's silence before she replied at once suggested to him that the older nun might be trying to frame
an answer that would imply an improper relationship
without actually saying so. "I'm not certain, Father," she
said finally. "I would hardly know anything of His
Lordship's private activities. Or what Sister Jessica does in
her free time. She is not under my supervision when at

work and, of course, she is often alone with Cardinal Heriot when she chauffeurs him to engagements or to the airport. Perhaps, though, I can let you know if anything specific comes to my attention."

Benetto suppressed a laugh of pure delight. This time, he'd heard an interesting combination of cautious innuendo and spitefulness. The Mother Superior might well turn out to be more useful than he'd anticipated. Well, let her get on with spying, by all means, for he was sure she now would. If she didn't turn up anything specific, he felt quite certain she could eventually be coaxed into inventing something that would insinuate, if not the forbidden, at least the improper.

"If you would, please, Sister," he said. "We would much appreciate it."

He told her to contact him directly and gave her his extension number so the call would not come through to Mancini or to Brother Demetrius.

Then, thoroughly pleased, and with the rungs of the golden ladder to the top of the Vatican curia seeming suddenly less in number, he went about the business of preparing to go to bed.

———◆———

At about the same time, Sister Jessica was finally able to abandon her desk. She didn't want to be late for evening prayers and get a lecture from Sister Andrea, and she hurried for the old brick building that housed the little community of nuns. She was surprised, then, to see Sister Andrea standing in the hall just inside the doorway with a welcoming smile for each sister coming back from work. It was something the older woman never did unless some new rule was to be imposed, a ruse that didn't work because all the nuns knew that Sister Andrea was trying in advance to lessen her charges' annoyance with her later.

Tonight, however, it seemed to Jessica that the Mother Superior's smile was slightly more deliberate than usual. As she headed for the small, barren room she called home, she suspected trouble of some sort was brewing.

She was just opening her door when she was stopped by another nun. "Sister, did you hear about Sister Andrea's phone call?"

Sister Jessica said she hadn't and wondered what would come next.

She didn't have to wait long. The nun was suitably awed. "It was from the Vatican. I answered the phone myself. Sister Andrea spoke to a Father Benetto for several minutes. What on earth do you suppose he wanted?"

"I'm sure I can't imagine."

But the news put Jessica's head in a whirl. When the nun ran off to tell someone else, she closed the door of her room behind her, sat down on her bed, and tried to make sense of it. Father Benetto? It was one thing for him to call Cardinal Heriot about a gift, but Sister Andrea? What on earth could be going on?

Thinking of Sister Andrea's smiling welcome, she felt an uneasy foreboding. Could the call have been because of the photographs of herself and Father Ignatius? If so, might it mean that steps were being taken to get her transferred to another community?

She had no way of knowing that separating her from Ignatius was, at this moment, the last thing Benetto wanted.

CHAPTER
❖26❖

After the meeting in New Orleans with Ignatius, and after Father John Zacharias had gone on to address large crowds in Miami, Louisville, and Memphis, Francesca left him with Fathers Howell, Graham, and Berthold and five other priests who had recently joined them, and flew ahead to Baltimore. There were television and radio interviews to line up and, in addition, there were final arrangements to make for the Orioles stadium, where a crowd of more than thirty thousand was expected.

Arriving mid-evening, Francesca collected at her hotel desk a small bundle of mail forwarded to John from Chicago. Leaving it unopened, she went down to the dining room for a late dinner, where she was made vaguely uncomfortable by the kind of stares from single men she had once invited.

She quickly finished her meal and fled. Hoping to pick up a newspaper to check on John's advance publicity, she found the newsstand closed and reluctantly went to the bar after a bellboy told her the bartender always had one.

The barroom was invitingly dark with indirect ceiling lights, plush carpeting, and a gray-haired pianist playing nostalgic old hits. It was now mostly empty, with only a few couples at tables and three or four single men spread out on stools, watching television.

The bartender, a young black man, welcomed Francesca with a smile, produced a well-read paper and, without giving a reason, offered her a drink on the house. Surprised, and out of politeness, she accepted a Coke and sat at a table, fighting memories of when she had cruised bars with abandon, downing one vodka after another and looking for the most likely bed prospect for the night. She hurried through her drink and was about to leave when a young man came over from where he'd been sitting at the bar with a friend and tried to pick her up.

"Hi, can I buy you another?" He was in his late twenties, with an expensive suit and hair that was perfectly styled. His eyes were all over her, and when they fixed on her bosom, she felt as if she were exposed.

Francesca dismissed him with a polite, "Thank you, not tonight," and rose to go.

The young man grudgingly retreated, but halfway to the door she was confronted by his friend, who was older and coarser looking. He had a large double Scotch in his hand and had already drunk too much. "Hey, my friend asked you to have a drink. A working girl like you ought to have better manners."

It was a moment before she realized that he took her for a hooker. She silently tried to go past him. He blocked her way. "Listen, let's cut the hard-to-get shit, okay? Name your price."

Later, she could hardly recall slapping him. But she remembered his cursing: "Why, you lousy fucking little bitch. The same to you." And his throwing his drink in her face.

The bartender was suddenly there, his huge presence looming. "I'll take care of this for you, Miss Berenson." He seized the man's arm. "Okay, get lost. Got that?"

Muttering, the man rejoined his friend.

Helping her wipe off the Scotch, the bartender apologized; the hotel would have her dress cleaned by morning. Francesca asked how he knew her.

"I recognized you. I went to hear Father John speak when he was in Philadelphia. You were sitting up on the platform with him and I remember thinking at the time, 'That lady up there, she's just like Saint Mary who went everywhere with Jesus and was there when He died for us.'"

Francesca was deeply touched by the comparison to Magdalene, who had abandoned her dissolute life to follow Christ. Back in her room, however, she found herself shaking. She felt defiled. They'd thought she was a hooker. Why, why?

She went to a mirror to stare at herself through sudden tears that smeared her eye makeup. She brushed them away fiercely. Same old face. Or was she kidding herself?

Was it true, once a whore, always a whore? She picked up her dress from the floor where she'd shed it. Was there anything about it that had been a come on? No. The skirt was well below the knee and no cleavage showed.

She put the dress into a hotel laundry bag and hung it outside her door. And, looking down the empty hotel corridor, felt fear unexpectedly clutch her innards. The corridor empty, herself alone, would one of those men suddenly leap out from somewhere and rush her before she could close the door? She shut the door fast, and double locked it. And then she thought of Dominic for the first time in days. Had she been living in a fool's paradise? Would he somehow actually chase her down? She might answer the door for breakfast coffee and instead of the hotel waiter find Dominic standing there, ready to push his way in.

Francesca desperately struggled to assuage the fear. Dominic wasn't there. The door was locked. There was a telephone to call for help on if he ever did show up. Perhaps she was only frightened because she hadn't heard from him for so long that it seemed strange— ominous, really. But she was all right. She was safe. She wasn't the old Francesca anymore, the whore who lived in terror of herself and submitted to almost anything in trying to ease the terror. She was someone else now, someone Dominic couldn't possibly ever understand or know. She was with God now, and safe. Even if Dominic were to come and shoot her, he could no longer hurt her. Slowly she got things back into perspective. The fear went away. The two guys in the bar had done it. It wasn't her. It was them. And the two guys were the kind of jerks who think that any woman alone in a bar is there just for them. She removed her makeup, took a shower and, in spite of the late hour, sat down at the desk to prepare for the meetings she had the next day.

But something began to nag, a vague and different feeling of anxiety. She couldn't at first put her finger on it. Then she realized that it had to do with the New Orleans meeting. A week had gone by, but the dinner at the country inn seemed only last night. She could still feel how desperately nervous she'd been about meeting Cardinal Heriot and her relief at his obvious effort to make her feel comfortable. Relief and surprise at his being so conciliatory, so fair minded. She'd found humanity in his face, so sculpted by his years as a worker priest. At the same time, he radiated a strength and authority that could not be questioned. *He is a true priest, like John,* she thought.

How had he seen her? He had to know of her past. Did he see her still as the men in the bar did? Did he think she and John were sexual partners? Strangely, she thought that perhaps he saw her only as she was now.

She ordered up coffee, and when it came made herself concentrate on her other impressions of the meeting. It was obvious that Cardinal Heriot had been asked by the Pope to see if there wasn't some way to conciliate John. He had failed to do so, and that such an attempt should ever have been made must have infuriated the reactionary curia, especially Cardinal Mancini.

Hadn't it been the same with ancient Rome, she wondered? For fear of causing an open revolt against its harsh rule over the Jews, Pontius Pilate, the Roman procurator, had hesitated to suppress Jesus when He first began preaching. Rome had continued to ignore and conciliate until the very last minute before it finally decided enough was enough. Although Jesus, betrayed by Judas and arrested for blasphemy, was not condemned by a Jewish religious court under Herod Antipas, the Jewish Tetrarch, he was ordered crucified by Pilate in civil court when the Roman procurator finally decided that continued preaching by Jesus might indeed lead to armed insurrection. Now, John was up against Rome the same way Jesus had been. A different Rome, to be sure, but a Rome that still dominated every aspect of people's lives while refusing to heed, let alone understand, their needs. And, like Jesus, wasn't John also arousing the multitudes with the truth? In his insistence on a Church that would truly be in Christ's image, had he not frightened Rome at first into taking no action against him for fear confrontation would give him added strength?

Now it was too late. His popular support was too great. Would a day then come when the Vatican would seek to destroy him, just as Rome had finally decided to destroy Jesus? The thought provoked the specter of excommunication and terrified Francesca. Could such a living death, all hope of God's mercy gone, possibly depend on Cardinal Heriot as a confidant of the pope? Or, if ultimately, as many wanted, he became pope himself?

She tried desperately to remember anything said during the New Orleans meeting that would give her a clue. She found nothing. Her anxiety still gnawing, she began opening the mail that had been forwarded from Chicago. She examined three or four letters and then came across one in a Vatican envelope with a Vatican stamp and a handwritten address. From whom could it possibly be? It didn't look official at all.

She opened it carefully and extracted a sheet of Vatican note paper with a handwritten message. There was no signature.

Time stopped. She carefully hid the letter, and when she went to bed much later, it was to lie awake most of the night desperately trying to think of some way to rescue the man who had rescued her.

CHAPTER

❖27❖

It was noon at the archdiocese. The air was chill, with the sky darkening over the cathedral and promising cold sleet and rain or even a last flurry of spring snow.

Ignatius, who had returned the day before, had forsaken his office and had gone out onto the small terrace that led to the lawns between the chancery and the cathedral. Sister Jessica, straightening his desk, answered the telephone.

The call was from Francesca, who hesitantly asked if she could speak to Cardinal Heriot.

Surprised, Sister Jessica put her on hold and went outside to Ignatius. "Father?"

He didn't answer. His shoulders were slightly hunched, his hands shoved into his pockets, his expression withdrawn, and he seemed oblivious to the chill air, unseasonable for the first week in May. Jessica had never seen him like that, and it worried her. Whatever was bothering him, she felt it had to be something personal he wouldn't want to talk about. She wondered if it somehow had to do with his stopping off at Washington on the way back from Atlanta.

"Father?" she said again. He turned. "Miss Berenson is on the line."

"Berenson?"

"Yes, Father."

"Thank you." His somber expression changed to one of puzzlement. At the door to his office, he looked back. "Did she say why she was calling? "

"No, Father."

He continued on, and she heard him pick up the phone. Suppressing her curiosity as to why the famous consort of the maverick priest had called, Sister Jessica went back to her own office. It was lunchtime. She wrote out a quick note saying she'd be back in forty minutes and put it on her desk, where he'd be bound to see it if he looked for her, and left for the cafeteria.

Returning, she found Ignatius at work. In the two years she had been with him, she had learned to sense when he wanted to be alone. The few letters she had for him to review and sign could wait until tomorrow. She quietly settled down to work. The afternoon flew. All of a sudden, it was early evening and time for evening prayers. She found Ignatius still at his desk.

"Was there anything you wanted before I leave, Father?"

It took a moment for him to realize she was there. He

glanced up. She was looking as fresh and schoolgirlish as when she'd come to work in the morning, and he knew that she had to be dying of curiosity as to why Francesca Berenson had called, but was too discreet to ask. He felt acutely uncomfortable in not telling her.

"Nothing, Sister. Thank you."

"In the morning then, Father. Good night."

"Good night, Sister."

He watched her leave with the brisk, sure step of youth, and his heart wrenched. Was he not guilty of deceiving her as well as himself, thus adding to the burden of guilt he already carried? All day his mind had been tormented over his meeting with Allegra and her suggestion that as a priest he had been living a lie; that he could be creating, by day, a life filled with endless nights of horror. Half of him berated himself for ever having revealed so much to her. At the same time, he bitterly reproached himself for fearing the truth, whatever it might be, when he ought to be praying for God's help in revealing it.

Now there was the call from Francesca that perhaps portended some sort of a breakthrough where Father Zacharias was concerned, and which he should have welcomed.

Instead, it had only served to make his unease worse. There had been such desperation in her voice, such an urgent need to see him immediately, that he sensed something very important had happened; something that Pope Gregory, sick as he was, would want to know of immediately. He'd agreed to meet her at any time.

Since she was flying in from Baltimore, she'd said she wouldn't be able to get to him until past ten o'clock that night, and he'd given her directions to his apartment rather than to his office, where the lights on at such a late hour would almost certainly cause someone to investigate. With the unfortunate photos of himself and Jessica uppermost in mind, he certainly did not want the further speculation or gossip that his meeting Francesca at such a late hour would create. It was risky, he realized, to have her come to the diocese headquarters. But meeting her away from it would have been out of the question. Where could they possibly have gone where both he and she would not be recognized?

He forced himself back to work clearing up neglected diocese matters and stayed at it several hours, trying all the while to defend his concentration against the dark, unanswered questions about his life Allegra had raised.

It was past nine o'clock when he finally gave up work and retreated to his apartment. He made himself a tasteless microwave dinner in the apartment's functional kitchenette and then settled into one of the easy chairs to wait, trying not to think of anything at all.

The old cuckoo clock heralded ten, and he sat up with a start, realizing he'd fallen asleep. Where was his visitor? He made some coffee and waited impatiently until almost eleven. He'd given her precise directions. Was she lost? Or had she decided perhaps not to come after all? Then he heard the crunch of gravel under tires. A car was approaching on the private drive that led to his apartment from the chancery's main entrance. It had to be her.

He drew drapes across the windows to ensure privacy and went into the foyer. He heard a motor being shut off, a car door closing, then nothing. He visualized her hesitating, perhaps making up her mind whether at the very last moment to come or to flee. In her request to see him, he'd heard indecision as well as desperation, as though afraid that when they met he would summarily reject whatever she wanted to see him about. Certainly she would be as nervous as he. Finally, there was the determined, light click of a woman's heels on the flagstone walk leading to the door. Then the soft chime of the front door bell. His first feeling on seeing her was one of surprise. She had about her a fragility, a waif-like quality he hadn't noticed in New Orleans. Her almond-shaped eyes were haunted and darkly shadowed, her face drawn and pale, and her expression hesitant, almost frightened. Her voice, at first, bordered on tremulous. "Eminence, thank you so much for seeing me. I know it's a terrible imposition."

Momentarily off guard, he reassured her and led her to the study. She had a pale cashmere cardigan over her shoulders and wore a simple, scoop-necked cotton dress that made her look younger than he knew she was. She shivered when she sat on the couch, but he guessed it had to be from nerves. In the soft lamplight, she seemed even more vulnerable than she had when she first came in.

Whatever it is, he thought, *she's had a very bad time of it.* He asked if she'd like coffee and brought it from the kitchenette on a tray and served them both. Then, taking the chair opposite the couch where she'd sat, he prepared himself to focus entirely on her, on whatever her problem turned out to be, and to shut out the constant anxiety of being discovered.

Looking at her as she gratefully took a first sip of coffee, he became acutely aware of her femininity. Without speaking one word, her aura filled the little room. Because of it, he felt the kind of awkwardness he always suffered when finding himself alone with an attractive woman; an embarrassment, almost, as though she would worry that in spite of his being a priest he might make some unwanted gesture toward her.

"Now, tell me what this is all about."

"I'm not quite sure how to begin."

"Try the beginning."

She returned his smile. "Of course." She nervously straightened the hem of her dress and got her shoulder bag from next to her on the couch and began to rummage in it.

In the few moments that she did, he was suddenly struck by conflicting emotions. She'd pulled one leg up underneath her, and he remembered the president's daughter the night he'd been awarded the medal. It struck him that she and Francesca were in some ways very much alike. At the same time, he had the acutely uncomfortable feeling that he was sexually attracted to her.

But it was a feeling quite unlike his fleeting fantasy about the president's daughter or nearly falling under the spell of Merrill Christie. His awkwardness had fled, replaced by a strange anger. He felt that he wanted to reach out and pull her to him, not gently, but with a need to reassure himself through roughness. He had to struggle

to keep his eyes on her face and not allow them to wander down over the soft swell of her bosom to the gentle
length of her thigh. He remembered that he'd had the
same feeling in New Orleans, but realized he had so suppressed it that it had only surfaced at this moment. And
with gathering unease, he also realized it was the same
feeling he always had in the reoccurring and nebulous
dream in which his desire for some untouchable, faceless
woman always turned to rage and wanting to possess by
force.

"It's this," she said. She extracted an envelope from
her bag and held it out to him. "I received it yesterday."

Ignatius glanced at the envelope and saw it was from
the Vatican. Mancini? A letter direct from the Pope? No,
the writing on the address was too crude. It was almost
childlike. And there were misspellings.

"This has to do with John?"

"Yes."

He met her direct look for a moment. In her eyes,
there was a plea. But something else, too. A challenge, and
almost a glint of triumph, as though she were about to
present something that he would have to agree was worth
her coming; a sort of confidence on her part that he
would be a co-conspirator against whatever it was.
Resentment began to rise in him for that confidence; for
her being there so dangerously; for her intrusion with a
problem at a time that was so agonizing for him. She was
with the priest who had humiliated him with the truth,
the very truth that he could not publicly acknowledge
without risking his own hard-won standing in the

Church; by the priest's courage and strength that had made him secretly feel weak and foolish. It was bitter now to have to help him.

Trying to hide his feelings, he took the letter from the envelope, unfolded it, and read it carefully. Mancini, of course. But who was the informer? The letter intimated he was an insider. Yes, he would have to have had access to what were either secret conversations or secret memoranda. Bypassing Pope Gregory, especially where John Zacharias was concerned, was not something you did publicly.

He looked hard at the writing again. Like the address on the envelope, it was almost childlike, the letters awkwardly formed, the sentences rigidly declarative.

And then he thought he knew. Yes, he'd seen the same writing once when meeting with Mancini in his private suite. His secretary had been away someplace on an errand and the valet had scrawled a phone message. What was the man's name? Demetrius? Yes, of course. Demetrius.

An image of the cadaverous monk flashed through his mind. And indeed, why not? If the man's thoughts and religiosity were anything like his appearance, everything about Mancini had to be offensive to him. Unquestionably, Demetrius had pried in Mancini's private file. Certainly, also, he never would have written if the conspiracy he warned of was not real.

He looked up at Francesca. Perhaps it was the challenge he'd seen in her eyes, her sureness, that made him delay telling her immediately that he'd do all he could. "Are you sure I'm the right person to talk to about this?"

"I think you're the only person."

"Why is that?"

"When we met in New Orleans, I knew you were someone I could trust. I don't know why. I just did. And someone who had the authority to help us if you choose to. If you can't, I don't know who can."

Challenge had been replaced by an uncertainty and fear that his delay had caused. He folded the letter slowly, again making her wait and hating himself for it, trying not to think of John Zacharias. She'd asked for help. Could he, somehow? Did he dare ask the intervention of Pope Gregory when the man was so close to dying? And if not, then what?

The resentment in him swelled up again against her. "What makes you believe this isn't just some crackpot? There are plenty of them in the Vatican. Look at the writing."

"I—I don't know. I just didn't. Do you?"

He had to force the admission, "No. I think it's genuine," while feeling himself flush hot with shame.

She sensed his reluctance and took it to be refusal. Panic rose in her voice. "It will kill John. No, I don't mean outwardly. Outwardly he'll go right on. But inside. Inside he'll feel like a betrayer and betrayed. Both. Please understand. Please. He doesn't want to pull down the Church, just change it to be in Christ's image."

Tears welled in her eyes. She bowed her head, all her veneer suddenly gone. "Oh, God, help us, please." Ignatius put the letter back in its envelope and handed it to her. The love in her voice for the priest was like a twisting knife. He wanted to throw her down and force himself on her, to make Zacharias pay through her for all the pain he suffered.

A sound rose in his head like the wind before a summer storm. The room looked small and far away and Francesca's voice far distant. Everything became dark and confused. He felt himself falling, falling into his nebulous dream, and Francesca became the faceless woman.

Then in the darkness, he began to hear the sound of a bell. It rang endlessly, endlessly. And slowly it was light again. He became aware of where he was and of Francesca, seated on his couch and staring, frightened, at the telephone, and then expectantly at him.

He got control of himself, and reached for the receiver.

"Hello?"

"Eminence?"

"Yes."

"It is Father Tissot. Jean-Henri." The French accent was strong. "I called because I knew you would want to be told right away. Eminence—God has taken His Holiness from us. About an hour ago. While he slept." The voice broke with grief. "He is gone from us. He is gone."

CHAPTER

·28·

Some years before, Debbie Billus, a one-time waitress, bar maid, and carnival worker who was living a squandered life of alcoholism in one of the seedier quarters of New Orleans, was brought back to religion and given a fresh start by Sister Andrea, who used her influence to get her a job at the diocese as a night watchman.

A large woman with broad hips, a thick neck, and a heavy face, her tired-blonde hair always tightly permed, Debbie had neither imagination nor intellect. She did her job well, however, and with proud diligence. During her shift from midnight to eight, she routinely visited some dozen stations within the diocese buildings or on its grounds. At each, she carefully registered her passing by turning her watchman's key in the station's metal time box.

Nothing escaped Debbie's eye. She wore a uniform and carried a licensed .38 revolver. In the five years that she had faithfully and proudly gone her lonely nighttime rounds, she had twice prevented thefts in progress. She had also caught the beginnings of a potentially disastrous flood caused by defective plumbing. On another occasion, she had herself quelled a chancery fire before it got out of control.

At 12:15 A.M., on her first round, and as she passed Ignatius's apartment on her way to the cathedral station, she wondered why lights were on. At this hour, the apartment was always dark. She was thinking that perhaps His Eminence could not sleep, or was ill, when the front door of the apartment opened and Francesca appeared. Closing the door behind her, she walked swiftly to her car, started it, and drove off.

In the half hour after the phone call from Jean-Henri Tissot, both she and Ignatius suffered crushing emotions. They had sat in silence. Ignatius, his own misery for the moment forgotten, felt an almost unbearable loss. For her part, Francesca realized that with Pope Gregory gone, John Zacharias would now be even more at the mercy of Mancini. With absolute power until a new pope was elected, he would no longer need to resort to devious methods to excommunicate anyone he chose. If elected pope himself, which in all likelihood he would be, John's fate would be even more certainly sealed.

Ignatius broke the silence. "I have to go to Rome immediately." He spoke almost matter of factly.

"Of course."

Francesca pulled her cardigan around her slim shoulders, collected her shoulder bag, and rose. The news in one stroke had eliminated any further talk about the threat to John. It would be almost an offense to linger a moment longer.

"I'll do whatever I can," Ignatius said. In his grief, all his resentment and anger were gone. He felt only sadness and concern.

"Thank you, Eminence. Perhaps if we should meet again, you shall be pope."

He managed a smile. "I'm sure that would never be God's will. Please give John my respectful regards."

Francesca, a woman wise to men, had sensed his feelings about her, about John: the jealousy, the anger at her because of it. She also sensed that in his heart there was true belief in the reforms John demanded. But for reasons she didn't understand, that belief came up against what she was sure the Church had come to be for him. She thought that the world of the Church might be a refuge of some sort, a place of safety for some reason. Feeling the burden of the dilemma she'd put him in and caring deeply for his grief over the pope's death, she impulsively kissed his cheek before she slipped out the door, closing it firmly behind her.

Debbie had not immediately recognized Francesca. Her only surprise was seeing a woman, one she did not know as an employee of the diocese, emerge from the apartment at such a late hour. Never dreaming of anything untoward, thinking perhaps it was some Church commit-tee woman from town who'd come to dinner, or even a relative, she went on her rounds, circling the end of the chancery building and taking a shortcut across the silent lawns to the cathedral and the first of the time boxes there.

Reaching the paved driveway that led to the parking area before the cathedral entrance, she was surprised again, this time by the approach of a slow-moving car. At first blinded by its headlights, she quickly recognized it when it came abreast of her and stopped. It was the same car she'd seen the woman drive away in from the cardinal's apartment.

Francesca rolled down her window and called out. When Debbie came over, she said, "I'm sorry to bother you, but I drove in here by mistake and stupidly can't find my way out again."

You're lying, Debbie thought. *You weren't here by mistake.* For the briefest instant as the car came up, her flashlight had swept the driver's seat, and in that instant she recognized Francesca. She pointed with her flashlight to the exit road leading away from the parking lot. "You need to go out that way, miss. Then straight ahead, You'll see a sign directing you to the exit."

"Thank you so much. Good night."

Francesca drove off, leaving Debbie speechless and her mind in instant turmoil. It was that woman, she was certain of it. Hadn't she seen her enough on television and in all the photos of her in the tabloid papers? One of them in the *Globe* had shown her sunning stark naked with a man in some Mediterranean resort. And the accompanying article told all about the wild life she had once led.

Debbie could think of nothing else the rest of the night and was bursting to share whom she'd seen with anyone who would listen. That "anyone" turned out to be Sister Andrea, whom she chanced on just as she was coming off duty at eight. News of the pope's death was now on all radio and television stations, and the Mother Superior was on her way to the cathedral to say a special prayer for his soul.

The briefest of greetings, and then before the nun could continue on her way, "Sister Andrea, you won't believe who I saw last night."

"Tell me." Sister Andrea was only being polite. From experience, she knew, with the exception of fires, floods, or intruders, that most of what Debbie Billus had to report was of little or no interest.

"It was just about twelve-thirty, I guess. Yes, because I was on my way to the cathedral and I always check in there at twelve-forty. And that woman—she was here! Sister, I couldn't believe my eyes."

"Debbie, what are you talking about? What woman?"

"That woman. You know. I can't remember her name. The one who was a classy hooker, got two thousand a night, I read, or ten for a weekend, and travels around with that crazy priest, Father Zacharias."

"She was here?" Sister Andrea was barely able to hide astonishment. "Are you sure?"

"Oh, yes. She was with His Eminence in his apartment. I was just turning up the cathedral path when she came out and drove off."

"The Berenson woman? Debbie, that's impossible. The priest is in Baltimore."

"But it was her, Sister. I know it was. She couldn't find her way out and stopped to ask me. I was as close to her as I am to you now. All the pictures I've seen of her, and her on television, I know her face as well as I know yours."

Sister Andrea had always known Debbie to be accurate in her reports. Looking now at the excitement in her heavy face, she had the almost electric feeling that Debbie was right, and for a moment she could hardly think. What on earth was the woman doing here? And in His Eminence's apartment in the middle of the night? Surely that meant His Eminence meant to keep such a visit secret. Intuitively, she knew that for the moment it should stay that way.

"Who else have you told this to, Debbie?"

"No one yet. I'm just now coming off duty."

"Well, you're not to. You're not to speak of this to anyone. Understand?"

"But..."

"No buts, Debbie."

"Yes, Sister."

"It could be a serious matter and we will keep it between us, just you and me, until I decide if anything should be done about it."

"Yes, Sister."

Sister Andrea turned back into the brick building and went directly to the little room off the front hall that she called her office. The pope's death for the moment forgotten, she closed the door and sat heavily in an armchair in front of her desk. Alone, she gave in to the shock she had managed to hide from Debbie. She felt as though a vise was fixed around her head. There were sharp pains in her temples and she could feel her heart thudding fast, and there was a kind of numbness in her entire body at the same time. It was as though she had just witnessed a terrible road accident and seen someone killed right in front of her. That dreadful, evil, fallen creature. Coming at night to prey on innocence.

A dark thought began to form in the back of the Mother Superior's mind. At first she suppressed it, then slowly allowed herself to think on it clearly. Priest or no, His Eminence was a man and that woman was known to be an arch-seductress. Her mind flicked to the embarrassing photos of him and Sister Jessica. Was His Eminence so innocent after all? Had there perhaps been more in the pictures than his trying to comfort the girl over her mother's death? Had not the assistant to Cardinal Mancini called because the Vatican harbored the same suspicion? Had some sort of liaison perhaps formed in New Orleans between His Eminence and that woman?

A kernel of vindictive anger, always lurking deep in Sister Andrea's heart, suddenly grew and became more forceful: the bitterness at having to give way to the younger nun when she herself was far better qualified to assist His Eminence, the lost prestige of being the workplace business intimate of a cardinal, the daily contact with exciting events in the Church and with the famous, all handed to the pretty younger woman, when she herself had sacrificed so much and was so much better suited through her experience for the job.

Sister Andrea's eye fell on her open desk calendar. She flipped back a few pages and stared down at Julio Benetto's telephone number.

CHAPTER

29

For Benetto, luck played a hand. The call came through when Mancini was absent from his suite, conferring on the papal death with Cardinal Carezza and others. Having expected any report from Sister Andrea at best to yield a rumor, he was barely able to contain his own feelings and remain calm. Out of the blue, he had unexpectedly been presented with possible opportunity heretofore only dreamed of, and the moment he heard who the caller was, he taped the call.

"Are you absolutely certain of this, Sister?"

"Yes."

Benetto thought rapidly. A report coming from an obscure nun, even one revealing such a scandal, might not have credibility against a highly respected and popular cardinal. The astonishing news would need authority that no one could question. Above all, it would need secrecy. It would also do him no good, he realized, if he could not somehow delay Mancini's receiving the report through regular channels before he himself was in sole possession of it. And that "somehow" meant stopping it from reaching Rome until Mancini, along with himself, was isolated in the conclave. There, he was certain that official confirmation of the nun's report, added to hers and along with the tape of her telephone call to him, would be all he needed.

He gave Sister Andrea specific instructions to send in a detailed account of the incident by registered mail to her provincial in Chicago.

"Do not fax it, Sister. Complete secrecy in this matter is absolutely essential and faxes are not often secure. Furthermore, you are to discuss this matter with no one, do you understand? No one."

"I understand, Father. I have already solicited secrecy from the night watch who reported it."

"Good. And send a copy of your report by email to me personally. "

"Yes, Father."

Benetto closed the call with his appreciation of her informing him so promptly and leaving her with the impression that higher-ups in the Vatican would see she was suitably rewarded.

He then called the papal nuncio. Because of the pope's death, there was heavy traffic on the lines to the United States, and while waiting for the call to go through, he thought of the advantages to him of the conclave.

Isolated from the world, the leading contenders for the papacy, along with their supporters, would become like gamblers at the roulette table. They would lose perspective, feel a pressure to win they had never felt before, be ready to take risks they'd never dreamed they would take.

At some point, he was certain, the voting would be nearly deadlocked. That would be the point when he could play his hand either way. Revelation of the scandal for the price he demanded would break any impasse and put Mancini on the papal throne.

Or, if it seemed the American might turn tables by declaring support for the heretic priest, he could ask his price from him for withholding the information. If the American did become pope, the Congregation would take no action against him. A pope was virtually inviolable, especially from his own court.

His call finally went through to Washington. Using his position as Mancini's secretary, he got to the nuncio himself and taped this call as well. Risking Mancini's wrath should the call backfire and Mancini discover him overstepping the boundaries of his rank, he explained to the nuncio what he had discovered.

"His Eminence is overwhelmingly occupied at the moment, Excellency, with the demise of our beloved Holy Father. I hesitate to burden him further, even for a matter that could perhaps be of importance."

To his relief, the nuncio understood and expressed immediate interest at what this information could mean. He thanked him for his initiative in calling and said that he would ask for a report of the incident from the provincial of the Little Sisters of Saint Agnes of Tours and would take steps to verify the presence of the woman at the diocese.

"She would have rented a car at the airport. We'll get the mileage and the times she took it out and brought it back. That, and a check on her flight times, will make an open and shut case of it."

"Thank you, Excellency."

"You do understand though, Father Benetto, the need for absolute secrecy in this matter. We cannot have a scandal involving another cardinal right now. You must speak of this to no one."

Benetto smiled. "Of course, Excellency. I already have ensured secrecy where the reporting nun is concerned."

"Good. Also, Father, this may take a little time, even a week or so. We are simply overwhelmed here with all the extra duties incumbent on the death of His Holiness: the endless acceptance of condolences, not just by the Americans, but also by the many foreign dignitaries in Washington. Although I shall review the provincial's report and verify it as quickly as possible, it unfortunately cannot right now be my first priority."

Benetto tried to keep the delight out of his voice. Such delay fell right into his hands.

"Of course, Excellency. I'm sure His Lordship, Cardinal Mancini, will be most sympathetic. And Excellency, when you forward the report to the Congregation for the Doctrine of the Faith, may I take the liberty to suggest that it would be appreciated by His Eminence, I am sure, if you sent a copy to him at his personal office here, rather than through the secretariat. His Lordship would not want to seem to be usurping the congregation's authority, or have it put about through possible maliciously false gossip at the secretariat that he was involved in some sort of plot against Cardinal Heriot."

Benetto was not surprised at the assurance that this would be done. The nuncio owed his appointment to Mancini.

Benetto added things up. The conclave would be held in two weeks' time. It would take several days for Sister Andrea's report to reach the provincial, and several more days for the provincial's report to arrive on the desk of the nuncio. More time would pass before the nuncio acted on it, perhaps as much as a week. Transmission of the report to Mancini might not even get to him before the conclave started.

But if it did, either by diplomatic pouch or email, he could almost certainly intercept it. Mancini, suddenly overwhelmed by work, had ordered him to monitor his email as well as regular post.

As for a report to the Congregation for the Doctrine of the Faith, one that normally would only take a few days to come to light from some insignificant bureaucratic desk, might now take several weeks because of the pope's death.

Thoroughly satisfied that everything would now work according to his calculations, Benetto put in a third call. This time it was to Luciano, to arrange for dinner and celebration. That done, he busied himself arranging for distribution of Mancini's schedule for the following day to the various parties who would need to know it in order to adjust their own schedules accordingly.

CHAPTER

❖30❖

For those isolated in the ensuing papal conclave, it seemed impossible that Pope Gregory had been dead only two weeks. His death and funeral were already a fading memory. The only reality became the daily voting in the Sistine and the discreet nightly lobbying amongst the assembled College of Cardinals before each member retreated to his cell.

The fifth day of voting had brought little change in numbers. Black smoke had once more issued from the chimney into the sky over the Vatican. Rather than being diminished in numbers by those discouraged by the endless waiting, the crowd in the great square before the Basilica of St. Peter had almost doubled. Among some elderly veterans of several conclaves who waited in the warming spring nights, whispers began to be heard of a deadlock. They were not far from the truth. Mancini had gained a minor number of votes, Ignatius had lost several. Ngordo had lost ten. In desperation, some European cardinals had switched to Berssi. The tally at the end of the accessit was Mancini forty-two, Ignatius thirty-six, Berssi thirty-two, and Ngordo ten. Both leading contenders were a long way from a two-thirds-plus-one majority.

For his part, Ignatius continued to ignore both the electioneering and the results. High under the roof of the papal palace, he sat surrounded by silence and the shadows of night. He had tried to dismiss Allegra's socratic questions about his dreams and the honesty of his vocation; tried to sweep away her intimation that, in what she called "this life," the person he was betraying was God; tried not even to think that he had become a priest not because of true faith and desire to dedicate his entire being to Father and Son, but because he had hoped that devotion to God's Church and good works would rid him of his dreams; tried to ignore her suggestion that he was thus using God, not worshipping Him.

Everything she'd said hovered in his mind like a dark, insistent reality, impossible to ignore and more and more difficult to deny. The cold fear he'd begun to feel when with Allegra had become part of his every waking hour. Briefly, he'd tried to convince himself that his self-sacrificing years as a worker priest had been out of true love for God, while a small voice of truth within him agreed with Allegra that those years were a bribe.

His mind wandered and turned to those who had peopled his dreams: the innocents, men and women alike, each so real in his memory, who had trusted him and loved him, and to whom he had so often brought hideous death.

Staring out at the night, he could hear their voices, now as familiar to him as any in his daytime life, but as though echoing across some unbridgeable chasm from the dark, unreachable past. Hearing them, he heard their plaintive cries, the sounds of death and their dying. And he heard the hollow, mocking laughter of those for whom he had broken faith. And saw in the swimming sea of dream faces that marched behind his eyes the rage, the scorn, and the contempt for him that he had endlessly engendered, when so seldom, if ever, the love.

The night had begun to ebb into inky, predawn darkness before Ignatius left the window.

He closed his diary, lit the candles on the *prie-dieu*. Kneeling before the crucifix, he prayed—but not for himself, or his own salvation, or for God's forgiveness for all his wickedness.

He prayed, instead, and for the first time ever, for God's mercy and love for the souls of all his phantoms: people of ages past to whom he had done such grievous harm and caused such misery.

He prayed, too, that his hurtful desire for Francesca as revenge on John Zacharias had not caused her pain, and prayed for peace and God's mercy for John Zacharias himself if he should be unjustly excommunicated.

The attic room was silent. The flickering flames of the candles cast the shadow of the crucifix between them giant-like over the bare, whitewashed wall above the iron bed.

Ignatius's lips moved silently in devotion:

"*Fiat voluntas tua, Domine. Benedic anima mea Domino, et omnia quae intra me Sunt, nomini Sancto Ejus*—Thy will be done, O Lord. Bless the Lord, O my soul, and all that is within me bless His holy name."

The only sound was the distant whisper of Rome, stirring like a great sleeping beast as it prepared to greet the oncoming dawn. Suddenly, he began to hear voices, the murmur of conversation, so that there seemed to be people around him when there was no one. Startled, he stood up.

The attic room that had been warm had become cold and—in the candlelight—larger. The furniture appeared far away, and night air came through windows that were apertures without glass in its walls of whitewashed stone.

One voice seemed to be speaking to him directly: "You will act and act quickly."

Looking for the voice, he saw a long table with the remains on it of a Passover seder, and, beside himself, there were twelve men there. Eleven were seated, talking amongst each other. The twelfth, who had just taken him away from the others and had spoken to him, was Christ, and he was filled with dread.

Jesus spoke again and said, "When you have left tonight, you will go to the High Priest, Caiaphas, and then you will lead the temple guards to the Garden of Gethsemane on the Mount of Olives. You will find me there with the others, at the mouth of a cave."

"Master, no. I cannot and will not." In the candlelight, he looked around again. The others seemed not to hear.

Christ laid a gentle hand on his shoulder. "Betrayal is the ultimate sin of sins, and it has been prophesied that I shall be betrayed. And this I have also said to be the will of our Father and my mission. It will be done so that against such evil God's ultimate good may be seen more clearly, and thus all mankind may learn and benefit. You are the one I trust to have the courage and the will to do this, for Peter three times this day will deny me."

He didn't speak. During the seder, Christ had said that he would give a sop to the one among His disciples who would betray him. Now, as he watched, Jesus quickly dipped a piece of unleavened bread into some soup and held it to his lips.

"Take this, and leave," he commanded.

Things became confused then, his vision sometimes fragmenting into disconnected incidents: his obedience to Christ in taking the sop, then finding himself downstairs in the silent, darkened street without remembering how he got there.

A woman stood in the doorway, her thin cloak pulled around her, for the Jerusalem night was raw. It was Magdalene, waiting for Jesus.

"Where do you go, Judas? Where are the others?" He stared at her, at the rain of her hair falling around her sculpted face, at her gentle eyes, at her soft lips, blue from the cold. He imagined her body beneath her cloak and thin tunic, her breasts and thighs and seat of love, all that she had given to so many before Jesus, to whom she had given her soul. Raging desire for her suddenly numbed him. But it wasn't love. It was anger. Seizing her, throwing her down and himself between her legs, he would revenge himself on Jesus, who was ever right and superior.

Revenge for all the humility and inadequacy Jesus had made him feel.

And yet he didn't move. For his desire for Magdalene suddenly melted away as fast as it had arisen. Had he not already wrought revenge on Jesus when he had taken the sop from his Lord with protests that were lies? Jesus would die thinking him faithful, and never knowing he had seized his chance and willingly carried out His wish to be betrayed. When he didn't answer, she said, "Our Lord prophesied that tonight He would be betrayed. Will it be you?"

When again he remained silent, she knew. She shivered, and there was terrible pain in her eyes.

"You have always festered, Judas, at the path Jesus has taken to free us from the Romans. The path of love, understanding, and tolerance. Now you will be free to oppose them as you wish. Or perhaps not oppose them at all and simply rage on in your own private hell."

A small Roman patrol of helmeted legionnaires came by on the trot, their bodies bulky and protected from the cold by thick cloaks thrown over their iron and leather cuirasses, the scabbards of their *gladii*, the short, deadly, thrusting swords they lived by, rhythmically slapping their muscled thighs.

On seeing him and Mary, one shouted, "Still up, Jew? Your Passover's over! Get on home to your own woman and stop thinking to get between the legs of this one."

No respectable Jewish woman would be out on the streets Passover night, only Greek or Egyptian prostitutes who filled Jerusalem to pleasure the Roman legionnaires.

And another cried, "Better still, warm her up for us until we come back."

Laughing, they disappeared around a corner. The Magdalene said, "Go now, Judas, and do as you have been bidden."

He turned scornfully and left her for the great temple, as silent and empty as the surrounding late-night streets. But there were temple guards whom the Romans allowed, the cream of Jewish youth, for the Romans didn't interfere with their religion, even though they mocked it. There was the guard captain, one named Jonathan, and then endless dark steps and corridors lightened by the torches they carried. And, finally, there was the High Priest Caiaphas, still at his seder with his entourage of scribes and lesser priests. In their eyes, there was the scorn and the contempt all men feel toward any who betray.

A bag of silver was thrown at his feet. He stooped to pick it up; a kick sent him sprawling. There were derisive shouts of laughter; he was pulled upright and, clutching the bag, he found a leather leash-noose tight around his neck. Like a dog, he was led out through the temple's massive golden gates to where a young Roman centurion and his company waited, torchlight glinting from their helmets and battle shields.

And all for one man, who calmly awaited their arrival with no idea of resisting.

The noose yanked hard. He was pulled to the centurion, who spoke only one word. "Where?"

When he answered, he could barely hear his own voice.

"Speak up, dog!" The temple guard captain snapped his head up and slapped his face hard. "Answer the centurion."

He repeated Jesus's position on the Mount of Olives. The Centurion laughed and gave orders to his sergeant, a grizzled veteran lame from a leg wound in some far-off campaign. Torches were doused, and they moved off into the dark. The temple guards went first. It would be their arrest; the Romans were along only as a backup in case there was a trap and backup force proved necessary.

He stumbled over a tree root. The flat of a guard's sword cracked across his back. "Stay on your feet, you dirty little bastard, or it's the scourge for you too, if your blaspheming prophet is lucky enough to get away with only that."

They descended slowly into the Kidron Valley. There was no moon. They climbed down vineyard walls in the pitch darkness, weaving their way among the almond and olive trees. Roman soldiers and temple guardsmen alike cursed their bad luck at having drawn duty tonight. When they passed through the cemetery where Jehoshaphat was believed to be buried, the captain stood on a tomb and counted his men to make sure no one had ducked out.

There was grumbling when they crossed the Kidron brook. The water was filled with the fetid slush of blood and entrails from the thousands of animals sacrificed during the day at the temple. One of the Romans fell to his knees, vomiting. The grizzled sergeant kicked him to his feet. At the other side of the brook, they turned south and then started up a hill into an olive grove.

Fifty meters up the steep slope, there was a sudden

flare of torches from scouts sent ahead. The centurion laughed. "They've got him."

Dragged into the lights, and held fast, the noose twisting until it choked, he saw Jesus standing before all his other disciples, who blinked, bewildered and frightened at the sudden light and mass of armed men.

"All right, which one?"

The captain shoved him forward, and he went to Jesus, who smiled gently. "Courage, Judas. It is God's will."

He saw that Jesus did not know that this was what he had wanted, that his chance was finally there. But suddenly, his courage nearly fled at what he had to do. Knowledge of vengeance, long hoped for, was almost not enough. Then he overcame the weakness and clutched Jesus to him, and kissed his cheek.

At once, the captain shouted out, "That's the one. Yeshu Hannosri?"

"I am he."

Orders were barked. Guards surged forward. A knife suddenly flashed. A guard cursed and held his bloodied ear. One of the disciples had struck him. Swords rattled from scabbards, but Christ stepped in front of the man. "He meant no harm," he said. "He is only frightened. If you have come to arrest me, then do so and let them go free. They have done nothing."

Even as he spoke, his disciples melted away into the darkness. Nobody tried to stop them.

The Roman centurion appeared and snapped at his sergeant, "Strip his cloth away."

"Sir?"

"Strip him. If by chance he's not a Jew, he's ours."

The sergeant understood. If a gentile, Roman law would prevail. He unsheathed his sword and flicked the point of it into the shoulder knot that held Jesus's rough tunic to his body. The tunic fell, and He stood naked.

"Torch!"

The centurion roughly seized the prisoner and held the torch down. "There you are, Sergeant. He's a Jew all right. Maybe we should cut off the rest of it, eh?" He laughed and turned to the captain. "Yours."

The captain pushed a flushed face close to Jesus. "Blasphemer! Think you're God, do you?"

When Jesus said nothing, a storm of fury overcame the man. "Answer me, false prophet." He spat in Jesus's face and clubbed the butt of his sword hilt into Jesus's loins.

Jesus doubled over, and the guards around him laughed and were rough. They twisted His arms high behind His back and lashed His wrists with thongs. One struck Him across the back of His neck, knocking Him to the ground. And the captain, seized with ever-greater fury, launched a volley of kicks into His naked prostrate body to make Him rise. When He did, they noosed a leather thong around His neck, and another around one ankle, and dragged Him away into the darkness like a captured animal.

The centurion said to his sergeant, "There goes one who before they're finished will be glad to see a cross." He snapped an order to have the men fall in, and the Romans marched away.

Fragmented words and visions once more, and mockery from the few remaining guards. "Be off now, you wretched dog. You've got your silver. Count yourself lucky you've still got eyes in your head and a tongue in your mouth."

The leash removed. Kicks. Raucous laughter. Torches moving away to become dancing far-off lights. Then cold darkness and the stumbling walk through the night, every step an agony.

As Jesus was dragged away to make His sacrifice, as the full meaning of what he, Judas, had done struck home, the angry rage and jealousy that burned within him turned to ice. He had committed the ultimate sin, and suddenly there was the awful bitterness of regret. His master, who had loved and trusted him, was no longer there to vilify. And no longer, also, to lead. He was alone now with his guilt, his anger and triumph fled.

There was the temple, finally, and Caiaphas's entourage of priests with their mocking scorn as he took the silver that now burned his hand and flung it at their feet.

But it was too late. He saw Christ condemned by Pilate, scourged, crowned with thorns, and crucified.

It was left only to destroy himself, too. Flight from all of it. From Jesus. From himself. Flight to the desert.

High on the great, towering rock that was Masada, the hermit seer pointed his deadly claw directly at his heart. "Fallen angel. You shall live on and on, one tortured life after another, betrayal after betrayal. Your sin and guilt shall be with you forever."

The voice echoing after him as he sought escape in

death. And the rocks at the foot of Masada's sheer cliffs rushing up to smash him into darkness.

⎯⎯⎯ ◆ ⎯⎯⎯

In that darkness, in its ultimate eternal silence, a bell suddenly rang. There was light again. The attic room reappeared. It was day. In the Vatican buildings below, there were sounds of awakening. It was the eight o'clock bell to signal the cardinals to rise.

An old-fashioned washstand with a pitcher of cold water had been provided for him in his room, and, at the foot of the stairs, there was a bathroom with a shower he would share with two others. He went down and when he returned, a second bell rang. By the time he had dressed, and precisely at nine, there was a third. It was followed by the junior master calling out, "*In Capellam, Domini*—To chapel, my lords."

The sixth day of conclave voting had begun.

CHAPTER

❖31❖

For Ignatius, time had assumed another dimension. He was like one walking in sleep. His voting, as everything else he did that morning, was mechanical.

When Ngordo approached him to yet again plead for a decision on Zacharias, he hardly heard him or bothered with the implications of whatever answer he gave. The conclave was a distant affair. Reality lay elsewhere. It lay in the cold, bare room of the Jerusalem Passover seder; in the brutal torchlight in the Garden of Gethsemane; it lay in the gentle, reproachful smile of the Magdalene as he raged inwardly at her; in the mocking laughter of the temple priests; and in the scathing fury of the Masada seer condemning him to live and betray for all eternity.

"What shall I tell them, Ignatius? They look for an answer, whatever it may be. If you do not wish to speak yourself, you perhaps have only to let me spread word that you endorse Zacharias."

He had no answer. Despairing, the Nobel Laureate went away, determined at least to persuade those few still voting for him to cast their votes instead for Ignatius. If he could stave off, even if just for a day, the trickle of votes already swinging to Mancini from becoming a victorious flood, Ignatius might suddenly abandon his retreat. No one could read the future. Few liked the icy secretary of state. Most of those voting for him were only doing so to stay in his favor should it suddenly appear that he would be the winner.

The morning vote had been Mancini forty-four, Ignatius thirty-four, Berssi thirty-three, and Ngordo, nine. When the conclave reconvened in the Sistine in the afternoon, it was to give Mancini forty-four votes, Ignatius thirty-eight, Berssi thirty-six, and himself, Ngordo, two. The African's sacrificial strategy had worked.

The increased votes for Berssi meant some were still holding back from Mancini. Ngordo saw this as a good sign. The cardinals were not yet quite ready to rush to the secretary of state.

Mancini knew it, too. While the election seemed virtually in his hands, the reality was that it wasn't. The thought that his hated rival could possibly at the last moment come out of hiding and endorse the priest had brought his tormented nerves to the breaking point. For if such a dreaded thing should happen, white smoke would almost certainly quickly rise from the Sistine, and with it not only his dream of the papacy but also his powerfully privileged position as secretary of state.

That evening, almost the moment the cardinals had filed out of the Sistine Chapel, the secretary of state moved in ceaseless desperation among them, deprecating Ignatius himself as much as protocol allowed, insinuating reliable knowledge of his mental instability, as surely witnessed by his current self-imposed isolation, and promoting himself equally hard. He garnered a few more votes, but Ngordo, working with similar effort, did the same for Ignatius.

The status quo remained roughly the same, and Mancini slept little that night in the small but ornate waiting room just off the Royal Hall that was his cell. Vainly he sought some way, as he had so often, to reveal the confession he had heard so many years before, knowing dully, however, that even if he could, there was a chance he would not be believed and perhaps even be discredited himself for breaching the confessional's sanctity.

Thus, in the morning, with murderous hatred for Ignatius consuming all his thoughts, he made no effort to conceal his irritation when just after the first bell, Benetto, bringing his morning coffee, lingered to demand a word with him.

"I have no time right now, Benetto."

"Excellency, you would be wise to make time. It is a matter of the greatest importance, I assure you."

The effrontery took Mancini aback. He was used to obsequiousness in the secretary.

"Go ahead," he said icily.

The young priest's limpid eyes narrowed. His sibilant voice took on an unaccustomed steely tone. "I have information, your lordship," he said, "that will decidedly turn the election in your favor. Before I let you know what it is, however, I want to know what you will do for me in return." In the deathly silence that followed, he favored Mancini with a faint and unpleasant smile and added, almost as a punctuation mark, "When you are pope."

CHAPTER

32

When the first bell rang that morning, announcing the sixth day of the conclave, Ignatius awoke and dressed mechanically. He was at prayer waiting for the call to chapel when there was an insistent knocking at his door, still barred by the ceremonial crossed rods.

"Ignatius! My lord!"

The voice was familiar. Ignatius rose from the *prie-dieu* and admitted a somber Ngordo. The African said good morning then silently handed him a single-page memorandum.

"Last night I found additional votes that would have made you a very real challenge to Mancini. This morning I received this. Copies are even now being distributed to every member of the Sacred College."

He waited, and Ignatius reluctantly glanced over the memorandum. Sister Andrea's report had been formalized first by the Chicago-based provincial of the Little Sisters of St. Agnes of Tours, then by the papal nuncio in Washington. It stated briefly that a security officer had seen the notorious prostitute Francesca Berenson, currently the paramour of Father John Zacharias, exit Ignatius's apartment at twelve-thirty at night and drive away in a car parked there for most of the evening.

Gethsemane and all its dread betrayal receded for the moment.

Ignatius heard Ngordo say, "Agreed, this absolutely slanderous charge has no foundation. Lord knows what evil mind has descended to putting it about. I can't imagine who would believe it. There are some, however, who might decide that such a charge, no matter how baseless, could taint your papacy, if God wills such, and I fear Mancini's slim majority can no longer be considered at risk." Ignatius found himself reading the report a second time. He didn't respond. Ngordo was right. It would almost certainly give the papacy to Mancini. It had to be a personal triumph for Sister Andrea, who surely had seized a chance for revenge at his hiring Sister Jessica to fill the position she had so coveted. He could only wonder at the hypocrisy of her smile and pleasant demeanor, while all the time hiding a viper's resentment.

Ngordo had begun to pace the little attic room. "Your path, I am certain, should be to attack rather than to defend. You must lash out first and turn this smear into a boomerang. Can it truly be possible that this conclave could elect as pope the kind of mind that would stoop to achieve that sacred office through tactics so totally unworthy of our Lord and His love for us?"

Ignatius hardly heard him. He was filled with profound sadness at this embarrassment, not just for friends like Ngordo, but for all his staff, the colony of nuns and priests at the diocese, the many lay workers, too, who under Sister Andrea's poisoned influence would now have to suffer the profound disillusionment of seeing him as yet another member of the Church involved in a sex scandal. And he especially felt for Sister Jessica. What terrible damage would this do to her?

The watchman—Debbie Billus late at night, wasn't it?—seeing Francesca was fortuitous, surely. But he doubted Sister Andrea would have acted without encouragement. He was certain she had been asked to spy on him ever since the unfortunate photographs of himself and Jessica, and of course there could have been no other instigator except for Mancini or one of his hangers on.

He tried to think further and couldn't. He didn't have the heart to tell Ngordo that the report was true, and that all his efforts to garner votes on his behalf had been useless. Numbly, he handed it back to him. He said only, "This will be answered in chapel."

The nine o'clock bell rang before Ngordo could reply. The junior master of ceremony's voice rang out, "*In Capellam, Domini*—To chapel, my lords." Ignatius, with Ngordo following, abruptly descended the steep stair from the attic room.

In the solemn procession to the Pauline Chapel, he felt the eyes of many on him. He saw smiles and sideways looks and heard whispers and the occasional suppressed laugh. Looking about at the white hair and ample girths of his colleagues, he could only think, more than ever, that most lived in a world of their own, heedless of life with all its rainbow of passions that they had chosen to reject, while so often arbitrarily dictating the course it took with others.

He thought, too, that with the ever-increasing scandals among the priesthood at all levels, who among them was to cast the first stone? Who among them was a closet homosexual who had perhaps indeed indulged himself with young boys? Who among them had secretly kept a mistress, perhaps to sire a child who would never know his father? And who among them had spent, as hush money for their sins, or perhaps the sins of others, hundreds of thousands of dollars, even millions, in church contributions slated to benefit the poor, the infirm, and the elderly?

Proceeding to the Sistine after mass, and as the bishop sacristan once more intoned the Oremus, he could find no equation of any kind between most of his fellow cardinals and the truth in the profoundly religious metaphor of the chapel.

Far overhead there were Michelangelo's great ceiling frescoes of God separating light from darkness, creating the earth and sun and moon and planets; the creation, then, of man and woman; the tragedy of Noah; and the panorama of life from the celebration of naked youth to the stern patriarchal figures of the prophets.

And below, in the great Renaissance artist's giant *Last Judgment* that covered the chapel's entire north wall above the altar, all of mankind stood on the threshold of eternity. There, one could see the inferno and the damned, and, at the River Styx, Charon, hell's ferryman. Above them were the angels waking and lifting up the dead to Christ, seated in divine judgment amidst a violent turmoil of saints, apostles, and ordinary men. And finally, higher still, all the earthly passions were represented and the fideistic means for all resurrection.

Looking at the venerable face and figure of St. Peter in attendance on Christ, Ignatius remembered the elderly priest who had approached him in St. Peter's Square. And it was as though suddenly the old man, as though an angel, was there in the Sistine Chapel with him, his words the clarion bell of an angel:

God only bestows His blessing on those who follow our Lord in true faith, but there is still time. May He have mercy on you and light your way.

This time, hearing the warning again, Ignatius finally accepted what it was within him that waited to be confessed. He realized that almost from the beginning he had lost the truth as much as any of those of his colleagues he so disdained.

He saw in them now, as though in a mirror, the vanity and deceit of his own soul. He had once again betrayed Christ, in life as well as in his dreams. His professed loyalty to the Church, like that of his peers, had long been at the expense of true fidelity to the Savior. His becoming a priest had indeed been a lie. His vow to serve God had been not truly to serve Him, but to seek relief from the hell of his nightmares.

And in denying John Zacharias, he had cravenly compounded the lie, because in denying the priest he had denied all in which he himself believed in order to support his false and selfish bribe-offering to God through deceitful loyalty to His Church.

The persuasive pageantry of the papal funeral and the conclave fell away, and with it all indecision. Let others, in their ambition and self-serving, lie and play politics with Christ. Let others pervert His Word into worldliness according to their needs and in His Name amass power and wealth beyond imagination. Let others use His message to control men's hearts and achieve their personal goals.

He would not. Dream or reality, he was indeed Judas. But he would betray no longer. And he would seek, through true faith, to rectify the evil he had done.

Lost in awe of what he suddenly understood, beginning to fill with exultant joy, he became aware that Cardinal Saluzzo was speaking directly to him.

The hatchet man.

Saluzzo was holding up a copy of the report Ngordo had brought to him.

"My lord, Cardinal Heriot. This scurrilous missile of hate has indeed shocked all of us. The base accusation is that this fallen woman, a notorious prostitute who consorts with the heretic, spent the night in your company. And therefore, it insinuates that being only mortal, you are no longer in a state of grace. Slander such as this is undeserved by a man of such eminent reputation. Nor deserved, through you, by all of your esteemed colleagues in the Sacred College."

It took little thought to know what would come next. Content that irreparable damage had now successfully been done, Saluzzo would smugly ask for, and expect, a worthless denial that would seem to all a lie. That would be the time, Ignatius knew, to follow Ngordo's advice and attack. In a few words, he could vilify the report as false and whomever had engineered it beneath contempt. All would know he referred to Mancini, and there would be those among the wavering who would see such vicious behavior in a Mancini papacy as perhaps irrevocably perverting every level of the Church.

But there would not be enough of them, and when the smoke rose from the chapel at day's end, it would promise a new pope who would disdain all hope for Christ in the future.

"My lord," Saluzzo went on. "We ask for the record only that you speak out and put to rest any possibility of ugly rumor."

Then, silence—with Saluzzo barely able to keep triumph from his eyes. And Mancini's eyes merciless behind his rimless glasses, his face like gray stone. Others— Carezza, Berssi, Bagnis, Agnelli, heads thrust forward, hands clasped piously over their scarlet waistbands. Vultures, waiting.

Ignatius's eyes swept the room.

"My Lord?" That was Agnelli. Impatient. "God only bestows His blessing on those who follow our Lord in true Faith, but there is still time. May He have mercy on you and light your way."

Ignatius said calmly, "I cannot put the ugly rumors to rest."

A second. Two. Were his words understood? The cardinals stirred. There were murmured expressions of incomprehension.

Mancini rose, his smile ingratiating. "My lord, Cardinal Heriot. I believe you perhaps did not understand my lord Cardinal Saluzzo." A light and calculatedly self-deprecating laugh. "He asked only that you deny any possible impropriety between˙ yourself and the heretic's paramour."

Ignatius smiled back. "My lord, I choose not to dignify what you unquestionably consider impropriety with either denial or defense. I have this to say, however. This lady whom you call a prostitute, but who is perhaps more worthy of being called a saint, is the disciple of a man who in every word and deed exemplifies our Lord, and further, is one whom you would do well to follow."

In the dead, astonished silence that followed, a sudden rustle of clothing. The aged Cardinal Carezza jerked up out of his chair as though pulled by marionette strings, his usually parchment-white face livid, his thin mouth a slash. One withered, trembling hand extended from his croccia to point at Ignatius as though at the devil himself. In a piercing shriek, he accused with one terrible word: "Judas!"

Ignatius's eyes again swept the sea of faces that stared back at him. It was as though the entire college was frozen into complete immobility. There was no movement, no sound.

It was again time for the truth.

"Judas? Yes," he said calmly. "I am indeed he, and I have betrayed our Lord in this life just as He was betrayed in another. And just as many of you, yourselves, betray Him daily. But I shall betray Him no longer. Whether you choose me to lead you or not, I shall undo the wrong I have done and speak out on behalf of him you call heretic, but who walks in the true image of Christ. I shall speak out either from the Vatican or from my diocese or as a common priest of the people on behalf of everything he believes in and has had the courage to say publicly. As he has done, I shall do as his disciple and speak out for a Church that sheds all false grace and all vanity and is truly faithful to our Lord."

———◆———

In the second round of voting that afternoon, Cardinal Ignatius Heriot received seventy votes, Cardinal Mancini forty-five, and Cardinal Berssi five.

CHAPTER

·33·

The following morning, the College of Cardinals filed dutifully into the Sistine Chapel. Once more and, in a silence that barely hid their choking bitterness, the traditionalists knew in their hearts that they faced defeat. All the previous evening, Mancini had desperately sought to rally votes, to ensure the loyalty of those who had previously professed it, to seek, if only a handful, votes from the independents, to try to dissuade some of the conservatives from a path he deemed as "anti-Christ." From the guarded reception he received, the weak promises to "think about it," he knew he lobbied to no avail. Long after a junior cardinal had announced "*In cellam, Domini*—To your cells, my lords," and long after many others slept, he lay awake, his mind tortured by dreams destroyed.

Among the cardinals, seated on their canopied thrones, the silence continued, each cardinal struggling not to reveal his emotion as the wooden balls were drawn from the leather sack to determine who would act as scrutators that day. Dutifully, each cardinal filled in his ballot and one by one approached the altar, bent a knee, again swore his ballot bore the name of him whom he thought ought to be elected, and delivered his choice onto a paten, thence into one of the golden urns. And the silence of all became even more deathly still, the silence of the condemned, as the senior scrutator unfolded the ballots one by one and announced the name of the man voted for, and each cardinal quickly took up his pen to note the count on his own tally sheet.

"The most Reverend Lord Cardinal Mancini, thirty; the most Reverend Lord Cardinal Berssi, one; the most Reverend Lord Cardinal Heriot, seventy-eight."

Another ballot counted. And another. And then: "The most Reverend Lord Cardinal Berssi, three; the most Reverend Lord Cardinal Mancini, thirty-four; the most Reverend Lord Cardinal Heriot, eighty."

Many heads now were bowed, some in anticipatory reverence, some in defeat. The last three ballots had to be counted. But it was the next counted that to all assembled was the final one. "My most Reverend Lord Cardinal Heriot, eighty-one."

Ignatius alone had not kept tally. His thoughts were on the Mount of Olives, the torches of Roman soldiers, on the figure of his Lord, kicked and beaten and led away into the darkness like a dangerous, captured animal.

Looking up at Michelangelo's *The Last Judgment*, he thanked God once again for the revelation of his sin, prayed for forgiveness, and repeated once more his determination, if God so wished, to rectify the ill he had done by the lie he had lived.

Suddenly, he heard the voice of the scrutator and his own name, and then the silence that followed was broken. Coming to his senses, he became aware of another voice, that of the archdeacon. "Reverend Lord, the Sacred College has elected thee to be the Successor of St. Peter. Wilt thou accept pontifically?"

He felt the presence of Ngordo next to him and, turning, looked down into the Laureate's dark and smiling face, transformed by love, and felt his heart leap in grateful response for all his loyal friendship.

The archdeacon was saying, "Is it *Nolo* or *Volo*, my Lord? Will you reply No or Yes?"

The rest was a blur. His affirmative, "*Volo,*" the abrupt rustle of cloth as the canopies above all the thrones came down, the Sistine suddenly filled with kneeling men, and all eyes on him. The ballots were tossed into the ancient iron stove along with a chemical and a plume of white smoke rose above the Sistine Chapel, to curl gently around the great dome of St. Peter's before it disappeared into the sky over Rome.

There was the ceremony, then, of consecration, his acceptance of the pontifical ring, his being garmented in white with the ancient shawl of the *pallia* placed gently around his shoulders, and his determination, in honor of his predecessor, to take the name of Gregory XIX.

Accompanied by an entourage of ranking cardinals, some loyal, some silent in their still-bitter opposition, preceded by a shattered and white-faced Mancini, he came to the high balcony above the façade of the great Basilica.

There, obliged to acknowledge his own defeat, Mancini stepped to the microphone of a public address system and, spreading his arms in a traditional gesture, announced in a hollow voice, tremulous with emotion, "*Annuntio vobis gaudium magnum—Habemus Papem.* I bring you glorious news—we have a pope."

A sound like waves on the shore, then, a great roar that rose from the waiting faithful who jammed St. Peter's Square. Ignatius stepped forward to intone the *Urbi* and *Orbi*, and the world saw for the first time the quiet, slender figure of the man who for many years to come, it would reverently call pope.

———◆———

Ignatius's first act as pontiff was one that threw into consternation not only those of the curia who had for so long been loyal to Mancini, but many among the loyal conservatives, equally unused to such an unconventional demonstration of iron will by a pope so newly consecrated.

"We will go to the Church of The Holy Mother in Rome and celebrate the early morning mass that is always held there."

"But Holiness, that is a small church in a very poor, working-class neighborhood. It would not be safe."

Ignatius smiled. "I know it well. It will give our security force an idea of what they will be faced with while I am pope."

"Holiness, protocol…"

All arguments fell on deaf ears.

Ignatius ordered complete anonymity. Dressed in a plain black cassock of an ordinary priest with no sign of any rank, he was driven to the little church in an ordinary car borrowed from a Vatican clerical worker, his security force keeping a discreet distance away. It was the same humble church where he had attended mass on his first trip to Rome, and only a few yards from the inexpensive little *pensione* where he had stayed.

It took a moment for the young worker priest officiating there to accept that he was to assist this stranger in the mass. When he was finally persuaded who his visitor was, his shock was undisguised.

"We humbly beg you, my son," Ignatius said, taking the astonished priest's hands in his, "to grant us this wish. We will be forever in your debt if you comply. We feel it important not just to us personally, but to the faithful everywhere to know that the one whom God has chosen to be their leader began his reign with an act of humility and gratitude that will henceforth be the mark of this papacy."

To his joy, the young man rose to the occasion and assisted him throughout the mass. The congregation was poor, some perhaps even criminal, Ignatius thought, and to him their coming to the altar to receive the host gave the Eucharist a particularly special meaning. He felt himself once again the worker priest he had been in the cane fields of the South and reborn with a joy he had never known as his spirit reconsecrated in his faith.

Mass over, and in the vestry of the little church, he embraced the young man with heartfelt thanks and gave him his blessing, and as a memento of the occasion they had shared, a little gold cross he had always worn on a chain around his neck.

Returning to the Vatican, he directed his driver to go via St. Peter's Square. At the head of the Via della Conciliazione where it enters the square, he ordered him to stop. There, to the further consternation of his entourage of security forces and officialdom who were prepared to surround him in a phalanx, he firmly once more evoked his papal authority.

Ordering them not to follow him any farther, he descended from his anonymous car and proceeded across the vast square on foot and alone.

It was a beautiful spring morning. Still early, the great square was relatively empty of people. Those who had been camped out waiting for the papal announcement had been cleared away by Rome police, and there were only sweepers piling the detritus of the week-long wait for a papal announcement into trucks and hosing down the square's greatly worn paving stones.

Ignatius walked slowly, taking in the massive columns and statuary erected by Bernini centuries before, the towering dome of St. Peter's that seemed to fill the heavens above him, the jumble of medieval and Renaissance architecture that made up the Apostolic Palace.

He paused a moment, remembering his first vision of it all, and then proceeded slowly to the Portone di Bronzo and his future.

EPILOGUE

At the Vatican. XIV August. Anno Domine MMX. In nomine Patris et Filii et Spiritus Sancti: *Amen.*

This day marks the end of my first three months as Gregory XIX, the name I took in reverence to my beloved predecessor, may God rest his eternal soul.

The day after God willed me to take charge of His Church, and as my first papal gesture to give thanks to our Lord, I celebrated mass at an obscure church in a working-class quarter of Rome. I dressed as an ordinary priest and was fortunately not recognized by the congregation, although I was sure no one would ever conceive of a papal presence without fanfare so immediately after elevation to such an honorable office.

Throughout the mass, my resolve to restore the Church in Christ's image strengthened. I felt our Savior Himself calling me to do so, and although I knew the task would be Herculean, I returned to the Vatican confident that with God's help I would prevail.

During my first week, I accepted the resignation of His Eminence, Cardinal Agosto Mancini, as secretary of state. He requested and I have granted him retirement from Church activities. In his place I have assigned His Eminence Cardinal William Ngordo.

After discussions with our nuncio in Washington, I have ordered Cardinal Mancini's personal secretary, a Father Julio Benetto, to a small parish in southern Sicily so that he may learn the true meaning of priesthood. At his own request, I have sent Cardinal Mancini's valet, Brother Demetrius, back to the monastery from whence he originated and have ordered the Vatican Bank to provide all sums of money necessary to relieve the extreme poverty of that place so that the good Brother may successfully complete the mission on which he came here some years ago.

I have asked the bank, also, to provide full pensions, as well as medical assistance whenever necessary, to both Father Tissot and Brother Bertolino, and this past week I requested Father John Zacharias and his consort to act as roving ambassadors of the Church throughout the world and to continue to bring, to all who gather to listen, Christ's true message of love. To my joy, Father John has accepted and I have elevated him to Monsignor.

For my own valet, I have requested the assistance of the young Franciscan who served me so well during the conclave. He impressed me greatly with his honesty and devotion.

At the moment, I am being assisted by two secretaries sent over from the governatorio. They are able, but I have found myself more and more feeling a deep, personal loss in the absence from my life of dear Sister Jessica. Today I dictated a letter to the Governor General of her order in Rome requesting her transfer here, and I have sent a sum of my own personal money to her to assure a better home and life for her siblings. I am sure the presence of a young woman in the papal palace in a tailored skirt and blouse will profoundly shock the existing curia, who can only think of women as humbly submissive and in black habits. So be it.

Buried here and there amidst the hoary walls of the Vatican I have already discovered some quite remarkable clergy whose voices have been stilled for far too long. I look forward to their help and participation during my administration, especially during the synod of bishops that I shall convoke next year to renew all aspects of Church dogma and to help move it forward during the new century along all the lines my predecessor wished to see, and in agreement with much of what Father John has been advocating.

There is a long winter ahead with much to do. I have already begun to replace many of the entrenched old prelates in the current curia with younger and more worldly people, priests and nuns both, from outside the Vatican as well as from within. Most are aware, as am I, that if I am successful in initiating all the reforms I want to see, mine as well as much of what Father John has been asking, that I may well be the last pope as we know the papacy today, one of infallibility and seated in the papal chair for life.

But complete success will take time. I shall plan a week's rest in the spring, perhaps during the end of May. And perhaps I shall shock many of the remaining old guard here even more than I already have by inviting my Washington friends to join me at Castel Gandolfo, the papal retreat on Lake Como, and to swim in the lake's beautiful water. I will be curious to hear what they have to say about my nights being completely dreamless since my invocation as Pope. So much for my dear novelist friend's atheism. I shall make her eat her words.

Benedic anima mea Domino et omnia quae intra me sunt nomini sancto ejus—*Bless the Lord, O my soul and all that is within me, bless His holy name.*

ABOUT THE AUTHOR

David Osborn has been a stone cutter in a French quarry, a television director, a farmer, and saw extensive combat in World War II as a Marine Corps pilot. While expatriated in Europe during the Stalinist era, he clandestinely worked with the Czech resistance to help a number of people escape to the West. The author of a score of successful motion pictures and television plays, his nine previous novels include *Open Season, The French Decision, Love and Treason, Heads,* and *Murder on Martha's Vineyard* and have been translated into more than fifteen languages. He currently lives with his former ballerina wife and their two children in Connecticut.